RYA

TI ess

s expert.

n.

A made up *The First Lea ombat and Confiscation Team, ar* . . .

Stripped of rank and honours in a Vietnam court-martial, they had been thrown in Leavenworth prison – and forgotten. Now they planned to make the army remember them – by robbing it of $600,000 . . .

William D. Blankenship

The Leavenworth Irregulars

CORGI BOOKS
A DIVISION OF TRANSWORLD PUBLISHERS LTD

THE LEAVENWORTH IRREGULARS

A CORGI BOOK 0 552 10202 4

Originally published in Great Britain by
Arthur Barker Ltd. (Subsidiary of Weidenfeld Ltd.)

PRINTING HISTORY
Arthur Barker edition published 1974
Corgi edition published 1976

Corgi Books are published by Transworld Publishers Ltd.,
Century House, 61–63 Uxbridge Road,
Ealing, London, W.5.
Made and printed in Great Britain by
Hunt Barnard Printing Ltd., Aylesbury, Bucks.

For Larry Curran, Jim Holmes,
Andre Kleinbardt and Dan McCaughna

The Leavenworth Irregulars

FRIDAY JUNE 30

That morning they stole a car from the parking garage of the Muehlebach Hotel. Ryan drove. Hazlitt sat next to him and Terrio squatted in the rear. When the armored truck left the Federal Reserve Bank an hour later they were behind it, knowing just where the driver would make his turns and how long the trip would take.

The armored truck stopped in front of the Kansas City Union Station fifteen minutes later. They parked across the street and watched the uniformed driver climb out and go inside the station. That was the routine. He returned within three minutes pushing a small cart. He looked around carefully before signaling an all-clear to his partner in the passenger seat. His partner talked to the people in back over an intercom and the rear door opened.

Four heavily armed men in plain clothes climbed out. Federal marshals. Two of them carried shotguns and the other two bristled with automatic weapons. Pistols bulged under their arms as well. They spread themselves around nicely while the driver and his partner loaded six heavy gray mailbags onto the cart.

"Two new marshals," Ryan observed.

"I'll bet that one old boy caught pneumonia," Hazlitt said. "Summer pneumonia, by God. He was coughing stuff up last month. Dang near made me sick."

Terrio grunted. He was a mild hypochondriac who didn't like to hear talk about sickness.

"There they go," Ryan said. The two uniformed guards pushed the cart into the station, with the marshals escorting them. The marshals did a good job of not bunching up. Their eyes covered all points of the compass. They were very professional.

"Sheeit," Hazlitt said. "We'd never take that money here. Not without a lot of shooting."

Terrio put his fingers in his ears. "And Hazlitt just can't *stand* the sound of shooting," he trilled in a falsetto voice.

Ryan and Hazlitt laughed, more surprised than amused by Terrio's joke. Terrio had been a very brooding cellmate in Leavenworth and had not loosened up much since their release almost a year ago. This was the first joke they had heard him crack in five years. Ryan thought Terrio must feel very confident about the job, and that gave him added confidence. Terrio was the only professional criminal of the three. If the job felt good to him, it must be good.

"Let's catch a train," Ryan said. "Watch your fingers."

Ryan wore gloves because he was driving, but Hazlitt and Terrio had simply been careful about not touching things. They used the backs of their hands to lever open the doors, dragging their duffel bags out with them. They pushed the doors closed with their legs and abandoned the car.

They all wore army uniforms. Class A summer. Khaki with army green belts and caps. Plain black GI shoes. They were not in the army, though they had all been soldiers once. Not too many years ago. Each had honestly earned the decorations on his chest and the stripes on his arm. They had lost their stripes at their respective courts martial but they had sewn them back on for this job.

After a moment they followed the men and the six bags of money into the cavernous silence of Union Station, staying about fifty yards behind.

"This is gonna be a cinch," Hazlitt chirped. "I can feel it." Terrio grunted again, returning to his more normal pessimism. Ryan walked between them with the duffel bag balanced heavily on his right shoulder. He had very wide shoulders, triangulating down to a narrow waist. He was a tall man, fair without being blond, and he walked with a smooth deliberation that lacked grace only because of his head. Massive and blocklike, it moved with the sudden reflex motions of certain predatory animals.

"A cinch," Hazlitt repeated.

"Nothing's a cinch," Terrio said sourly. "From the moment you're born nothing goes right. Why should this be different?"

For Dan Ryan, listening to Hazlitt and Terrio was like being trapped between stereo speakers, one adjusted for bass and the other for treble. Paul Terrio was an Italian from the North Side of Chicago, squat and chunky like a middleweight fighter on the verge of going to seed. He was dark, with a perpetual shadow of a beard and sagging, downturned black eyebrows that darkened him even more. He walked with short stamping steps, as if killing ants as he went. LeRoy Hazlitt was an opposite. Long legs that ambled along. Tall, with yellow hair the texture of coarse straw, and a pimply red face. An eternal optimist, he could not see the bad side of anything. He'd even been reasonably happy in prison. Once in Leavenworth he'd stood up against a claque of junkies who were trying to enlist a new kid into their ranks. They ganged Hazlitt down and broke out every tooth in his mouth before Ryan and Terrio could reach him and pound the junkies into a whimpering retreat. When Ryan visited him in the hospital, the first remark out of Hazlitt's swollen mouth was, "They say them false teeth are easier to take care of than your own."

At the luggage room in the station one of

the marshals signed a piece of paper and took charge of the cart. The armed guards returned to their truck as the marshals wheeled the cart through the luggage room and out another door toward the platform where the Kansas City–to–Los Angeles train was waiting. Ryan knew exactly what would happen to the money now. He let the duffel bag fall off his shoulder onto one of the benches in the waiting room.

"I'll get the tickets."

Terrio and Hazlitt dropped their bags.

"Christ!" Terrio swore. "I'd forgotten how heavy these damned things can be."

"Mine's not too bad," Hazlitt said.

Ryan went to the counter and paid for three one-way tickets to Fort Riley, Kansas. Then the three of them drank coffee from the machine in the waiting room. Terrio complained about the coffee. Hazlitt drank two cups. They looked like three ordinary GIs on leave or on their way to new assignments, which was exactly how they wanted to look.

They had dug out their old uniforms for the job. Ryan wore the stripes of a sergeant first class, with infantry brass on his collars. The blue and white patch on his right shoulder indicated he had served in combat with the Third Infantry Division, which was true. Terrio was a former mess sergeant in an artillery outfit, and wore the proper brass for that unit. Hazlitt had been a corporal in the First Cavalry Division. He talked basic army language, a rural Southern accent intermixed with military slang. Ryan was positive they would have no trouble passing for transient soldiers at Fort Riley. They even carried forged military orders in large gray official army envelopes stuffed in their duffel bags. Their impersonation would last at least two days before the military bureaucracy realized it had absorbed three men who were not what they appeared to be. That was more time than they needed. Everything had been planned. Logistics. Intelligence. Operations. A robbery that would be a military maneuver in a literal sense. Hazlitt had even invented a military designation for their three-man unit: "The First Leavenworth Combat and Confiscation Team, Irregular."

A garbled announcement blared over the old loudspeaker system. The door to track six opened and the few people who still ride trains got to their feet. The men picked up their duffel bags and walked down the tunnel.

The passenger train moved as slowly as Ryan had expected. Two hours later they were only a few miles west of Topeka. Hazlitt and Terrio dozed while Ryan watched the countryside, comparing the flat fields of wheat with his orchards in California. He decided that growing wheat wouldn't be as much fun as growing fruit. Today was June 30. He would have to be home soon for the plum harvest. He was eager to get back and see the growing and picking cycles completed so that next year he would be able to handle it himself. Julie had carried the whole responsibility during his four years in prison, but now he would be there to help her. Once this job was finished.

Julie Ryan sat on the back steps of their house outside Gilroy, California, on the northern edge of the Salinas Valley. The house stood in the middle of a 160-acre orchard, eighty acres in plums and the same in walnuts. Spread out around her were a dozen empty half-gallon ice-cream cartons. Wearing a pair of rubber gloves, she was carefully spooning small amounts of ammonium carbonate into the lids of the cartons. When each lid held approximately two ounces of the chemical, she used a wood block to spread it evenly around the lids.

A car rumbled up the gravel driveway. Julie smiled, recognizing the rattling tailpipe of Maria Ronda's elderly Ford. She picked up an ice pick and began perforating the bottom of each carton.

"Julie?" Maria called.

"In back," she answered.

Maria came bustling around the house with her usual quick steps, her hair held back by a red bandanna and her plump brown arms pumping energetically.

"Husk-fly time again," she chirped, talking in the jumble of ice-cream cartons and chemicals.

"You said it," Julie groaned. "I have a feeling they're going to be bad this year."

"That's what Luis says. We put out our traps yesterday. Let me help you." Maria plopped down and began fitting the filled lids onto the bottoms of the cartons as Julie perforated them. A hooked piece of sixteen-gauge wire was attached to each carton. The traps would be hung from the trees in random locations throughout the walnut orchard. For the next few weeks Julie would periodically count the number of walnut husk flies drawn to the traps by the chemical. When the number of flies caught in the traps began to climb rapidly, it would be time to spray the orchard.

Maria assembled the devices expertly. She and her husband, Luis, owned a nearby orchard planted in the same crops as the Ryan place. Maria glanced around as she worked. "Where's Dan today?"

Julie's hand stopped in mid-air. She gripped the ice pick tighter. Then began punching holes again. "Gone away."

"Oh?" Maria continued working. Julie would tell her about it if she wanted to. If not, that was all right, too.

Julie sighed. "He says he has a job to do, Maria. He won't tell me what kind of job. I begged him to stay. Once a month since April he's gone away for three or four days at a stretch. He's promised me this will be the last trip. He'll be home by the end of next week, he said, and he'll never leave like this again. But I don't know whether to believe him."

"You've been happy since he's been back," Maria ventured.

"Yes. And I thought Dan was happy, too."

"He's certainly taken to growing. Luis says Dan has picked up everything he could teach him."

"I know. I know." Julie stabbed the ice pick into the porch step and let it quiver there. "But I fought husk flies and brown rot and prune rust and black line and all the other problems by myself for four years. I expected Dan to pretty much take over when he got out." She shook her head, letting her amber hair fly in the sun. "Now I'm beginning to wonder if the whole long wait was worth it."

She felt Maria's hand on her arm. "Sure it was. Dan's a good man. A serious man. Still tight and troubled, but good. Luis was like that, too. You know he was. He went off on drunks half a dozen times after he got out. He just had to work the hate out of himself."

Maria's husband had also served time once. Almost a year, for cutting a man in a tavern fight in Salinas. Their husbands' prison sentences made a strong bond between Julie and Maria. They had often compared the problems together—dealing with curious neighbors, sublimating sexual desires with work, budgeting money, and learning to run four sections of land without a man.

"I suppose you're right," Julie said. "But I warned Dan. He can't leave me like this ever again."

"He won't then. That man loves you, Julie. And he needs you. Anybody can see that." She slapped Julie on the leg. "Let's put out these traps before the husk flies think they own your place."

They each picked up half a dozen traps by their wire hooks and walked out into the orchard. The ground was very wet. Dan had done a good deal of watering and irrigating before he left, but Julie would have to handle it this week by herself. Another sore point.

The traps were set in widespread parts of the orchard, slung from branches. Julie and Maria marked the trees where the traps were planted by wrapping bright red engineer's tape around the trunks.

They strolled through a section of the plum grove on their way back to the house. The new plums, which would dry out into prunes after harvesting, were already beginning to get their high purple color.

Julie loved the orchards, but she was prepared to leave them now. If Dan went away once more she would put the place on the market. It would sell quickly. She and Dan had been married only three months when they bought the orchards as an investment for the future, pooling their small savings to make the down payment. The trees had been scraggly, deficient in zinc and potassium. The former owner had acquired it as a tax loss and let it run into the ground. Dan was shipped to Southeast Asia shortly after they bought the place, and six months later came the incredible news that he'd been court-martialed and sent to prison.

Julie had been living in an apartment in Carmel, playing piano and singing at the Officers Club at Fort Ord near Monterey. When the club decided it didn't need an entertainer whose husband was in Leavenworth, she moved out to the orchard and began putting it in shape. She met Luis and Maria and they helped her. When money ran short she found jobs at other night spots in Carmel, which was not too far over the hills to the west. Julie was popular enough to find jobs fairly easily. Her popularity came partly from an aloofness that stimulated the competitive appetites of men and partly because she wasn't beautiful enough to anger women. Instead of beauty she had bearing, a splendidly fluid way of moving and speaking. Plus green eyes that were frank almost to the point of militancy, a smile that presented itself only when she was genuinely happy and relaxed, and a generous, lithe body.

But she hadn't smiled much since Dan went away again, the fourth mysterious trip since he had come home from Leavenworth nine months ago. Maria saw this and tried to turn Julie's attention away from Dan's absence by asking, "How many tons do you think you'll harvest this year?"

"A hundred and eighty. Maybe two hundred."

"That's not bad."

"What are you and Luis expecting?"

Maria hesitated, but knew Julie wouldn't appreciate a lie. "Two hundred and fifty tons, Luis says."

"Two hundred and fifty. You'll make a good profit this year. At four hundred dollars a ton we'll just about break even."

"Maybe your walnuts will do better," Maria suggested.

"They'll have to."

They stopped in a clear, sunny spot. Maria reached up and took a piece of fruit from the tree.

She pulled a small pressure gauge from the pocket of her Levis and used it to measure the firmness of the fruit.

"You're going to have a late harvest," she predicted.

"If I'm here," Julie answered.

"Fort Riley!" the conductor called. He stopped and touched Ryan's shoulder. "Your stop, soldiers."

"Thanks," Ryan said. He looked out the

window. The train had come out of the vastness of central Kansas into Fort Riley. Riley is an open post, which means that both soldiers and civilians may come and go freely through it. Highway 24 runs directly through the post. Its openness was one reason Ryan had picked Fort Riley for this job. But the prime reason was that the Seventh Infantry Division was stationed at Riley, commanded by Major General Arthur Hanson.

Terrio and Hazlitt still dozed. They could sleep anywhere. He gave each of them a shake. "Terrio. Hazlitt. Time to move." They called each other by last names. Always had. Ryan supposed it had something to do with retaining a piece of privacy in a cramped prison cell.

Hazlitt shook himself. "God*dam*, but I had a sexy dream."

"My back is killing me," Terrio groaned, stretching.

The train began a long, shuddering stop. When it finally pulled to a halt at the Fort Riley station, they hoisted their duffel bags again and went out to the platform between the cars. The conductor opened the door. Ryan swung down to the ground. Terrio and Hazlitt followed. They found themselves looking at a ring of military policemen. At least a dozen MPs were thrown around the tiny Fort Riley station in a semicircle. Ryan wasn't surprised to see the MPs armed with "grease guns," .45-caliber submachine guns with tube-shaped barrel receivers and collapsible frame stocks. Grease guns are an outdated weapon, but the army clings to its old equipment and traditions.

Ryan was counting on that trait to make the job a success.

"Don't worry, troopers. We ain't after you." A thickset MP lieutenant came up to them. "You looked a little surprised to see all these weapons pointed your way," he said, chuckling. "We're picking up the payroll. You troopers got here just in time for the pay line."

"Yes, sir," Hazlitt said. The three of them saluted. "For a minute there I thought I was back in 'Nam. On the wrong side."

The lieutenant chuckled again and returned the salute loosely. "Transferring in?"

"That's right, sir," Terrio answered. "Can you tell us where the replacement center is?"

"Straight up the hill. I'd give you men a lift but we got this little detail here."

"Thank you, sir, anyway," Ryan said.

"Sure. See you men again." The lieutenant moved down the train toward the baggage car. The four marshals had come out of the car. They were passing papers back and forth with another officer, Captain Trencham, the post controller and paymaster. Ryan had learned quite a bit about Captain Trencham in the past four months. He was a small, angry man. He hated any deviation from routine. He was bitter about being a company grade officer, believing he should have been promoted to field grade years ago. At the moment he was arguing with one of the marshals concerning the papers he was about to sign.

As they walked past the marshals Captain Trencham was saying, "Regulations clearly state that form DOD 5581 must be signed in triplicate by the paymaster as well as yourself. I will not violate that regulation."

"Just sign the papers," the marshal said. "I don't know why there's only two copies and I don't give a damn."

The six gray bags were being loaded into the lieutenant's jeep by two MPs with grease guns slung across their backs. They contained the payroll for a large part of the Seventh Infantry Division as well as the Fifth Army contingent on the post. Because the army is the last big organization in the country that continues to pay many of its people in cash instead of checks, there would be somewhere around $600,000 in those bags. Ryan, Hazlitt, and Terrio walked on up the hill without appearing to pay any attention to the money. As they reached the top of the hill the MPs came cruising past, five jeeps loaded with armed men. The lieutenant's jeep was in the center of the line. Ryan knew where the money went from here: the paymaster's office at division headquarters. Tomorrow would be payday throughout the United States Army. Each company commander at Fort Riley would report to the paymaster's office, accompanied by two armed guards selected from his own unit. Each commander would collect the payroll for his company and return to his barracks. The entire company would fall out, and the captain would pay off his men according to records provided by the paymaster. Except that tomorrow morning would be different. Because tonight they would steal that payroll right out of division headquarters.

"Where's that replacement center?" Terrio puffed. "This thing's gonna break my ass." Terrio's duffel bag was unusually heavy because it held safecracking tools and plastic explosives.

"It's only a little ways now," Hazlitt said. "I'll carry that mother for you."

"I got it," Terrio growled. "I just wanta know I don't have to carry it out to the boondocks."

They had reached the upper parade ground, which was surrounded on all four sides by graceful old buildings constructed of solid blocks carved from the limestone ridges the other side of the Kansas River. This was the main post, where the support services for the division were housed. Division headquarters. Replacement center. Stockade. PX. Service club. Post chapel. NCO Club. Hospital. Gymnasium. Officers Club. Post Library. Theater. Bachelor officers' quarters. The combat troops were in regimental barracks in three camps around the main post. Camp Funston, Custer Hill, and Camp Forsyth. The main post looked very much like a small city, with service wives shopping for groceries at the PX while their men went about their work.

They reached the replacement center, a two-story barracks with a wide veranda running around all four sides on both floors. They found the company clerk's office and dropped their bags outside the door.

"Reporting in," Ryan said.

A buck sergeant in fatigues was typing with two fingers. He didn't look up. A Specialist Third Class took care of them. "You got orders? Gimme two copies."

They took the official envelopes out of their duffel bags and gave SP/3 their orders. The army orders were ridiculously easy to forge. They were simply typed up and mimeographed. They bear only a man's name, rank, serial number, the unit he's reporting to and being detached from, the date he leaves, and the date he's ordered to report to his new assignment.

The SP/3 glanced at the orders and looked at Terrio suspiciously. "You're reporting in a day early, Martelli." Martelli was the name on Terrio's orders.

"I had a fight with my wife," Terrio said.

The SP/3 grinned. "Who won?"

"I'm here a day early, ain't I?"

They had decided that the dates should vary slightly on their orders to avoid making them look too much like the three-man team they were. The names on the orders were phony, of course. Terrio carried orders to report to the Food Service School at Fort Riley for assignment as an instructor. Ryan was supposedly reporting in as a new platoon sergeant with the 33rd Battle Group, Second Infantry. Hazlitt was supposed to be going to the 21st Armored Battalion as a tank commander.

The SP/3 didn't question their orders. He simply skimmed them to see where the men were going. The next morning he would send the orders to their new units and within a couple of days the receiving units would clear them to report for duty. In this case, however, the Food Service School, the 33rd Battle

Group, and 21st Armored Battalion would discover they were not expecting these particular replacements. They would send the orders back to the replacement center for clarification. By that time, however, the replacements would have disappeared.

"Pick up your bedding in the supply room," the SP/3 said. "It's in the basement. Grab yourselves some bunks upstairs in the noncom wing. Chow at sixteen thirty."

"Thanks," Hazlitt said.

They went upstairs. It looked like every army barracks they had ever seen. There were two rows of bunks with steel lockers behind them. Empty lard cans painted red and filled with sand dangled from the posts that ran down the center of the squad room. They were used as butt cans. Only a few noncoms were lying on their bunks, and they paid no attention to the newcomers. A replacement company is a strange place. No one knows anyone else. Everyone is waiting for orders and no one has anything much to do. At least the noncommissioned officers don't. The enlisted men are hustled onto KP or other details. No one makes friends in a replacement company because no one is there long enough. A convenient place to hide.

"Let's grab those bunks," Ryan said. They went down the squad room to three vacant bunks with mattresses rolled up and bare of bedding.

"This is dang near perfect," Hazlitt said. Terrio grunted his agreement. The other bunks near them were vacant. They slid their duffel bags into lockers, took the padlocks off the bags and used them to secure the lockers, then went downstairs.

A fat Specialist Fourth Class greeted them. "Three new ones!" he boomed. "You boys gonna like Riley."

"We're drawing bedding," Ryan told him.

"Sure thing," the SP/4 laughed. "Here ya go." He went to one bin and pulled out six sheets, to another for three blankets, and to a third for three mattress covers. Hazlitt noticed a pile of pillow slips on the counter and took three.

"Not those!" the SP/4 warned. "No. You don't want those, Corporal."

"Why not?" Hazlitt asked. "They're clean, aren't they?"

"Them are for niggers," the supply man said solemnly. "Niggers been sleeping on them. I can tell by my nose, no matter how much they clean them over in the laundry. You boys can thank me for knowing the difference. And I got all clean bedding for us white men to use. I got it all divided up down here, don't you worry."

"We need pillows, too," Ryan said.

"Right here," the SP/4 said. "And you can take my word—"

"I know," Terrio broke in. "You got them divided up."

"Right," the SP/4 beamed.

Going back upstairs, Hazlitt said, "God-*dam* but this army just don't change much."

"That's what we're counting on," Ryan reminded him.

A young private first class was buffing the floors of their squad bay, making long sweeps with the buffer to bring out the highlights of the wood.

"Always cleaning," Terrio muttered. "Buffing. Spit-and-polishing. Used to drive me crazy."

"Hear now!" Hazlitt whispered as he bent to make up his bunk. "Don't you say that around Sergeant First Class Ryan. He's regular army. You know that."

Ryan grinned. "AR AY All the Waaay." He was once very regular army and proud of it. But he'd taken Hazlitt's riding for so long that he enjoyed it now.

"Let's find the day room," he said when they had finished with the bunks. "We'll recon the post after chow."

The day room was in the basement, too. Its comforts consisted of a pool table and two Ping Pong tables; a black and white TV that got one station from the nearest town, Junction City; some easy chairs with stuffing beginning to squeeze out; old magazines; and a couple of checkerboards. They shot two games of pool. Terrio and Ryan each lost five dollars to Hazlitt, who was raised with a pool cue in his hand in a small Texas town where the billiard parlor was the only place to go after ten P.M. When the mess hall opened they went upstairs for chow.

"Christ, what a rotten mess hall," Terrio said as they filed down the chow line. Ryan was forced to agree. The entrée was chicken, covered with about a half inch of crisply fried flour but almost raw underneath. The mashed potatoes had huge lumps with watery fluid between. The peas could have passed for ball bearings. As a former mess sergeant, Terrio's professional palate was offended. He threw down his knife and fork and just drank coffee. "Look at this crap! I'm too nervous about the job to eat, anyway."

"I'll take your tray," Hazlitt volunteered. "I dearly love my fried chicken." His chin was about six inches above his tray and he was eating like Henry VIII after a fast. Ryan and Terrio were used to it. They just didn't watch.

While Hazlitt was finishing Terrio's plate, one of the cooks, apparently the replacement center's mess sergeant, came out from behind the serving line and walked over to their table. "Which one of you is Sergeant Martelli?"

"I am," Terrio answered. "What's it to you?"

"Company clerk told me you're a cook. Thought we might talk a minute." He sat down in the empty chair at their table. He was dressed in white pants, T shirt, and a tall white chef's hat. A sweet odor floated around him. Vanilla extract, highly favored by mess sergeants as a substitute for whiskey because of its high alcohol content. He wore black boots bleached gray around the soles by the hot lemon-and-soap mixture used to clean floors in army kitchens.

"Tell you what, Sergeant Martelli," the cook grinned, showing his yellowed and pitted teeth. "I need a number two man in this here mess. It's good duty, sarge. Damned good. No one gets on your ass because no one's here long enough to care. Shit! The company commander takes his meals at the BOQ. Soft duty, I'll tell ya."

"I've got orders for the Food Service School," Terrio said. "I'm reporting in as an instructor."

"You don't want that duty," the mess sergeant scoffed. "That's hard work. Those instructors over there bust their balls every day. In this mess you'd have good hours and all the KPs you need. Some days I got eight KPs in here."

"But I've got orders," Terrio reminded him.

The cook leaned forward, revealing other aromas as powerful but not as sweet as the vanilla extract. "I got a pal over at division personnel who can fix that. He'll write up new orders and you'll be transferred from the Food Service School to the replacement center. What d'ya say, Sarge?"

Ryan knew what Terrio wanted to say. He was about to tell the cook he had the worst mess hall in the army. But Ryan didn't want any attention drawn to them, so he put in quickly, before Terrio could speak, "Sounds like a good deal, Martelli."

Terrio understood. He bit back his words and said, "Maybe so. I'll think about it. That's what I'll do. I'll let you know in the morning after breakfast."

The cook beamed. "Now you're talking. Come on. Let me show you around the kitchen. It's a damned fine kitchen, Sarge."

Terrio let himself be pulled to his feet and followed the cook behind the serving line. They disappeared into the kitchen.

"Terrio's ready to strangle that old rooster," Hazlitt laughed. "But I don't see why. I think the chow's pretty good here."

"You always think the chow's pretty good."

Hazlitt shrugged. "I reckon."

Terrio returned a minute later.

"What's the kitchen like?" Hazlitt wanted to know.

"A botulism factory," Terrio said. "Let's get the hell out of here."

They picked up their trays and piled them on the steel counter in front of the KP who was washing cups and trays, tossing their utensils into a bucket. As they left the mess hall the cook waved at Terrio. Terrio waved back and answered under his breath, "So long, you fucking poisoner."

Outside, Ryan said, "Hazlitt, you recon the motor pool where the MPs draw their jeeps. See what kind of guards are on duty tonight. They should still have recruits pulling that duty. Terrio, walk on over to the division headquarters and make sure everything is set up like it was when we came through last month. I'll sit over in the canteen at the PX where I can watch the six P.M. MP guard mount. Meet me there no later than seven. Hold it . . ." A lieutenant wearing fatigues and an artillery-man's red scarf around his neck approached them. They saluted as he passed and continued talking when he was out of earshot. "Don't talk to anyone unless you have to," Ryan said. They were passing the NCO Club as a brown army limousine rolled past them. A red plaque shaped like a flag stood out above the car's right front fender. Two silver stars gleamed on it.

"Hey, Ryan! It's your buddy General Hanson," Hazlitt said.

Ryan glimpsed Major General Arthur Hanson as the car shot by and they snapped off their salutes. They saw him touching the back of his neck. Haircuts were an obsession with General Hanson. A trademark. He had his hair trimmed twice a week—Tuesdays and Fridays—and expected his officers to do the same. Wherever he went the number of barbers tripled. He must have just come from the barber. His steel-gray hair was short but full and he sat in the rear of the chauffeured staff car with the air of a Caesar in his chariot. His summer uniform was crisply fresh and tailored to complement his linear figure. The small eyes set deeply into his thin face appeared to be staring at some unfortunate enemy on the horizon.

"So, that's your pigeon," Terrio said. Ryan had talked about Hanson many times, but neither Terrio nor Hazlitt had seen the man during the four months they'd spent setting up the job. They didn't blame Ryan for wanting his revenge, and if they could make some money out of disgracing the General, all the better.

"That's him," Ryan said.

"He'll be a mighty sick two-star tomorrow," Hazlitt chuckled.

"I hope so," Ryan said fervently.

Terrio and Hazlitt shut their mouths while Ryan worked off his anger. They knew just how much Ryan hated Hanson. Hanson had really screwed Ryan back in Vietnam, when he was just a brigadier general commanding a sector. The General had a reputation as an action man, an overreactor. If orders came down to increase the body count by ten percent he'd by God kill twenty percent more Viet Cong. If one village was identified as a communist stronghold, he'd burn it out along with two or three others in the vicinity just to make sure he didn't miss anyone.

So when orders came to crack down on GIs who were stealing army supplies and selling them on the black market, General Hanson moved fast and hard. Roadblocks were set up throughout his sector and MPs began searching every GI for contraband. One of those arrested was Sfc Daniel Ryan, who was carrying a package stuffed with bottles of iodine, APC tablets, bandages, and a miscellany of other medicines. He explained that he was taking the medicine to an orphanage south of Saigon that was low on medical supplies. He did so every month, gathering up only those supplies he found lost or abandoned in the field. No one would listen. Ryan was one of about twenty men found in Hanson's sector with small amounts of army property. All were court-martialed. All were found guilty. The Saigon government cooperated with General Hanson's command by refusing to allow the doctor from the orphanage to testify at Ryan's court-martial. Ryan discovered that the order came from General Hanson himself, who wanted convictions to show to his headquarters.

Later there were questions about why

General Hanson had not been able to turn up the big black market dealers in his sector. A few people even whispered that the General himself had a tie-in with some of those big operators and that he had warned them about the roadblocks and searches. But by the time the rumors began, Ryan had already been dishonorably discharged and shipped back to the States to begin his sentence.

Ryan stopped. "We'll separate here. I'll see you at the PX canteen at seven o'clock. Don't get into any trouble. Salute any officer who comes within fifty feet of you. And dammit, Hazlitt, try to get some military snap into your walk. You look like a hound dog sniffing his way home."

Hazlitt chuckled and strutted off in an imitation of Patton inspecting his troops. He turned and called back, "How's this, Big Sarge?"

"Beautiful," Ryan said. It was hopeless. Hazlitt had a farmboy walk and always would. They could only pray that no one would pay attention to him.

"The big clown," Terrio muttered.

"Don't worry," Ryan said. "He can handle himself, and no one's going to stop him anyway. This post is as loose as goose shit."

"Yeah," Terrio said, sounding unconvinced. "Well. I'm going to recon division headquarters. See you at seven."

General Hanson's chauffeured staff car took him around the upper parade ground, past the small house once occupied by Custer and now preserved as a monument to that fallen warrior, and down Highway 24 to the Officers Club. As he stepped from his car the General noticed a speck of green on his driver's belt buckle. He lifted his swagger stick and tapped the buckle with the .30-caliber bullet that formed the tip of the stick. "Do some work on that brass while I'm having dinner, Sergeant."

"Yes sir," the sergeant replied. He stepped a few paces ahead to open the front door of the club for Hanson.

Inside, another anxious subordinate hurried over to greet the General. "Your guest is waiting in the lounge, sir," Captain Frederick reported. As manager of the Officers Club, Captain Frederick was delighted to have the General make a practice of taking his meals at the club. He was encouraged by the trend away from eating with the troops among so many high-ranking officers. The captain considered General Hanson an outstanding officer and a fine gentleman. He savored the soft Virginia burr in the General's speech and admired his custom uniforms. He didn't at all mind tearing up the General's mess bill each month and balancing out the small loss in the shrinkage column of his books.

"This way, sir." Captain Frederick dipped his head self-effacingly as he led the General to the lounge. Brannigan was at the bar drinking scotch from a shot glass. He wasn't the only man in the club dressed in civilian clothes for dinner, but he was quite obviously the only civilian there. His bulky, rumpled figure was totally unmilitary. His seamed face showed not a trace of intimidation as the General approached. Without even rising, Brannigan stuck out a big hand and said, "Hi'ya, Arthur. Good to see you again."

The General shook hands warmly with Brannigan. It's been too long, Bob."

"Split a bottle of scotch with me?"

"Certainly. But why don't we move to my table? I think they're probably ready for us in the dining room."

The General waved vaguely in that direction and Captain Frederick materialized at his side. "Your table is ready, sir." Frederick was horrified by Brannigan's breezy informality, his unpressed clothes, and the lack of deference he showed the General. But he managed a very correct smile as he seated Brannigan and instructed their waiter to bring the General his usual dry Martini and Mr. Brannigan a scotch and water.

"Skip the water, son," Brannigan barked. "If I have to wash my hands, I'll go to the pisser."

"As you wish," Captain Frederick said stiffly. He had not been called "son" by anyone since long before receiving his commission fifteen years ago. And officers at his club did not refer to the latrine as "the pisser." He withdrew from the table.

"You're looking good, Arthur," Brannigan smiled. "A Stateside tour must be just what you needed."

"I like this post," Hanson admitted. "It's the home of the cavalry, you know. It has traditions. A past and a sense of history. If we have time after dinner I'll take you to the post museum and General Custer's home. The exhibits are very impressive."

Brannigan laughed harshly. "I'm not too interested in a memorial to a man who got his ass whipped, Arthur. My taste runs more to winners."

The General's face set into the straight, cold lines Brannigan had come to recognize over the years as anger.

"Sorry," he shrugged. "You got your traditions and I got mine."

The waiter brought their drinks and hovered nearby. It wouldn't be unusual for the General to frown, announce that his drink had not been mixed properly, and send it back. But this time the General sipped and smiled and the waiter went away.

"Did you fly up in your own plane?" he asked Brannigan.

"Sure did," Brannigan replied. Anxious to cancel out his earlier conversational mistake, he said, "I took your advice and used that field over near Junction City. It's a good little airport. Only took me two hours to get here from Tulsa, plus the twenty-minute cab ride from the field. I've got a new plane, you know. A Cessna Citation. Twin fanjets and it seats eight."

As always, General Hanson was repelled by Brannigan's appearance and manners. He reminded himself that Brannigan was, after all, only a civilian. And that a man doesn't become one of the biggest building contractors in the country by using impeccable manners. But Brannigan was a reliable man to deal with, quick to understand what was expected of him and ready to deliver on his promises. Sipping his Martini, General Hanson decided those qualities more than offset Brannigan's crudeness.

"It's too bad we couldn't arrange our meeting for next week," General Hanson said. "I'm having Fire Storm shipped into the post over the weekend. You'd be pleased to see how beautifully he's developed."

"Yeah," Brannigan mumbled, but he was glad Fire Storm wasn't on the post. The thoroughbred race horse had set him back twenty-five thousand dollars four years ago. Brannigan realized he had no reason to feel sour about the deal. The contract his company had received to build the service club, swimming pools, and new barracks at Hanson's former command area had netted his company a hell of a big profit. Still, Brannigan didn't particularly want to look at a race horse he'd bought for someone else. The most he'd do would make a little conversation about the nag.

"Have you been stabling Fire Storm at your home in Virginia?"

Brannigan had shrewdly picked a topic certain to enthuse the General, who smiled broadly for the first time since they had sat down together. "Yes. But I miss the riding, so that's why I decided to have Fire Storm shipped out here and hang the expense."

Since when did you pay a bill with your own money? Brannigan said to himself.

"They still ride to hounds in Virginia, you know. I try to get back for the season, but it's difficult. So many demands are made on a general officer these days, quite apart from his military duties."

Like scrounging for every loose buck in

the State of Kansas, Brannigan thought sourly.

"And then, of course, I missed so many hunts during my Vietnam tour that I've pretty much resigned myself to the loss."

If it were a cash loss you wouldn't take it so quietly.

Brannigan gradually became aware that he was becoming drunk. He very deliberately turned the empty shot glass upside down as the waiter came up to inquire about refills. Brannigan liked to drink, but he tried to avoid it while doing business. Besides, he had to fly the Cessna back to Tulsa tonight and he wanted to be cold sober before putting his hands on the controls. During a takeoff at Phoenix a year ago he had clipped a power pole with his wingtip after having a few too many drinks at the airport bar.

General Hanson continued to talk about Virginia and fox hunting and his home on a lush twenty acres outside Roanoke. Brannigan wondered what the General wanted this time. As for himself, he knew what he wanted—the contract to build new helicopter hangars, maintenance buildings, and runways at the airfield here at Fort Riley. The field was scheduled to become a major training center for helicopter pilots, with about ten million dollars already budgeted by Congress for construction. The job was not being put out on a low-bid basis. Instead, the Department of Defense procurement people were negotiating the prime contracts. Brannigan had already greased the right palms in Washington. He had only to take care of General Hanson and the job was his.

But what did Hanson want? Brannigan decided he wasn't drunk at all and signaled the waiter to hit him again. General Hanson seemed unaware of Brannigan's melancholy. He was talking about a hunting dog he'd owned as a boy. Brannigan passed the time trying to guess what Hanson's price would be. It wouldn't be money. That was too crass for the General. He was too smooth to take cash like the boys in Washington. An expensive race horse, sure. A thirty-foot sloop for helping out on that hospital contract; the boat was tied up at Virginia Beach now. But not cash. Nor would the General ever admit that the expensive gifts Brannigan gave him had anything to do with the contracts Brannigan's firm received. The contractor accurately saw that the General was trying to conceal the truth from himself as much as from the accountants at the General Services Administration. He needed to blur the edges of reality so that he could continue to see himself as a "military gentleman of the South."

Brannigan realized the General was staring at him. "What?"

"I said that your chance for landing the contract for the new helicopter facilities looks very good."

"Oh?" Brannigan saw that food had been placed in front of him. Hanson had ordered his own favorite dish, rack of lamb, for both of them. Brannigan didn't care what he ate. At last Hanson was getting to the point. "You've heard something?"

"Nothing *definite,*" Hanson said. "But I was on the phone to DOD procurement the other day and they said your preliminary drawings were very well thought out."

"Good . . . good." Brannigan forked at his salad. *Get on with it, you two-star phony.*

The General cleared his throat and chewed a piece of lamb exactly ten times, as he did each morsel of food that went into his mouth. He sipped at his glass of Pinot Noir. "I'm thinking of doing a little construction work myself."

"What kind of construction, Arthur?" *Let's have the bottom line.*

"I have a small piece of property up in the Dakotas. Beautiful spot, right on a lake. The pheasant hunting is marvelous up there, so I thought I'd build myself a hunting lodge. Just a small place."

"Two or three bedrooms?" Brannigan asked, very alert now.

"Three, I think." The General spoke as if he had just decided on that. Actually he had given the matter a great deal of thought. "A large living room. Two baths. Small dining room and kitchen. Detached garage."

"Roads?"

The General laughed and shook his head. "No, no. The road is already in. I'll just need a driveway from the road to the house. Matter of a couple hundred yards."

"Sounds like about two thousand square feet of house," Brannigan guessed.

"Yes. That would be just about right."

As he ate, Brannigan rapidly figured his construction costs. A good crew from his own shop, plus some local sub-contractors. He was sure he could find a way to bill the army for part of the materials. The place could probably be built for under thirty thousand that way.

He pushed the empty salad plate away and drank his Pinot Noir in one draught. The General winced at that but Brannigan didn't care. "Tell you what, Arthur. If you aren't already too far into this project, I might be able to help you out. I've built a few lodges like that and I think I might have a set of plans kicking around that you could use. I might even have some spare material left over from a job that I could throw in the pot, so to speak. Why don't you tell me exactly where your property is and I'll see what I can do."

The General managed to look surprised. "Why, that's very generous of you, Bob. Thanks. Say"—he put down his wine and patted the pockets of his uniform—"I believe I have the particulars with me." He pulled a folded piece of paper out of his tunic and passed it across the table.

When Brannigan unfolded it he found a Xeroxed copy of a grant deed and a surveyor's drawing of the property.

"Good enough," he said. He slipped the paper in his own pocket. The subject would never be mentioned again. Hanson would talk to his friends at DOD and the contract would come through. Brannigan would build the lodge and pay the bills through a dummy account. He would send the keys to the General in the mail. He lifted his knife and fork and cut into the lamb. Cash would have been so much simpler.

Ryan cut across the upper parade ground to the PX, which was bustling with a strange mixture of dependent civilians and servicemen. Because it was now past chow time, large numbers of teenagers were circulating around the main post. They were sons and daughters of the troops stationed at Riley, using the PX, barbershop, library, bowling alley, and movie theater. A good many of the troops were also in civilian clothes by this time, giving Fort Riley an even greater resemblance to a busy small town.

The new PX canteen had a glassed-in front where Ryan settled down at a table with a bottle of beer to look over the stockade across the road. A few chasers were still bringing prisoners back from work details. A prison chaser carries a shotgun and supervises two prisoners while they do jobs like policing up litter along the roads or mowing lawns. Ryan had pulled prison-chaser duty many times. The prisoners were invariably regular army troopers who had made some fairly serious mistake and were paying for it with two or three months in the stockade. They were seldom angry about it, and never antagonistic toward the prison chaser. They knew that six months from now they might be the chasers and you might be the prisoner. Ryan was never able to forgive himself later for slipping into that kind of reminiscence. If he'd been on his toes he might have avoided Moody. As it was, he suddenly felt a hand thumping his shoulder and heard a loud voice saying, "Dan Ryan! Good to see you, buddy."

He looked up into the smiling face of Master Sergeant Joe Moody.

"Big Joe! How the hell are you?" Ryan put his hand out and let Big Joe Moody crush it. "Sit down."

"I don't mind," Moody said. He was an enormous man, built for drinking beer and lifting tons of coal, which had been his principal occupations before joining the army at the age of nineteen some twenty years earlier. Moody plucked a napkin out of the holder on the table and wiped the chair before sitting down. He was wearing a two-hundred-dollar uniform made out of fine linen dyed army khaki. He owned ten such summer uniforms. And though his shoes were cut like plain black regulation GI issue, they were made in London of the softest leather.

"I'm surprised to see you here, Joe. This doesn't seem to be your kind of post."

Moody motioned to the civilian waiter, who hurried over to put a bottle of Heineken's in front of him. "Riley's not bad."

"Not if you can get Heineken's when you want it. I asked if they had anything better than this stuff, and the waiter acted like I'd ordered him to scrub a latrine."

Moody looked pleased. "Let me get you one. I keep some of my private stock here for when I come by." He raised his enormous arm and punched an index finger in Ryan's direction. The waiter hurried over to serve a Heineken to Ryan.

"Thanks."

"Anything for an old buddy." Moody

grinned. "We had some interesting times back at Fort Ord."

"We did," Ryan admitted. "What are you doing these days? The same thing?"

"Damn right," Moody said. "I'm running all the service clubs on the post."

"You mean there's no officer over you?"

"Sure. They got an officer adviser who's supposed to be in charge of all the clubs, but his backbone's about ninety percent water. Just the way I like it."

"Even so, isn't Fort Riley a little small for you?" Ryan was desperately trying to keep Moody's attention focused on himself. Otherwise Moody might start asking questions.

"My setup here is smaller than the one I had in Germany," Moody admitted. "But its bigger than the club at Fort Ord. The thing is, Danny boy, it's not how big your setup is. What counts is the kind of support you get from the brass."

Ryan examined Moody's expensive clothes. The dollar cigars sticking up out of his pocket. The diamond ring on his hand. He sipped the expensive imported beer. "You mean the support you get from General Hanson?"

Moody shrugged and tipped some of the beer into his glass. He was too careful a man to admit that the General was in on his action. Instead he said, "General Hanson is a fine officer. I'm proud to be serving under him."

"I get you," Ryan said. And he did. Moody was a famous and admired man throughout the army's noncommissioned officers corps. As a nineteen-year-old corporal in Korea he had won the Distinguished Service Cross and two silver stars for his soldiering. His specialty had been night fighting. He'd crawl out into no-man's land in those freezing winter nights and find two Chinese troopers sleeping together for warmth. He'd cut the throat of one of them and let the other find himself snuggled up to a dead man in the morning. Dispatches gave him a lot of the credit for breaking the morale of a tough Chinese regiment near Inchon. Some years later, when he made sergeant, he wangled a soft assignment managing an NCO club. He brought in good entertainers and started bingo nights and poker nights and the club made money, not only for the army but for Moody. Any entertainer who wanted to play Moody's clubs kicked back ten percent of his salary to Moody. He took five percent of the bingo and poker take. Liquor suppliers gave Moody presents. Loan-sharking was the next step.

It didn't always work that well, of course. Now and then Moody would run into an officer who would threaten to bust him if he didn't close down his sidelines. When that happened Moody would have himself transferred to another post where the commanding officer was likely to be more cooperative. Usually for a price. Some commanders wanted a piece of the action, others just wanted Moody to serve up a new girl every Thursday night. Moody was always happy to oblige. Ryan wondered what kind of a deal he had with General Hanson.

"So that's me, Ryan. Now what about you?" He peered at Ryan's stripes. "Still a sergeant first class? How come? Top soldier like you should have made master sergeant years ago."

"I made master," Ryan said, improvising wildly. "Down at Fort Hood. But I ran into a pencil jockey from the Point. We had a couple of go-rounds and I came out of it minus one stripe."

Moody shook his head. "Those bastards from the Point will ruin you every time. I got kicked off a post by one down South, so I know what you're talking about." He tilted the glass to his lips again, then suddenly lowered it. "Hey! Whatever happened to that broad you took away from me—what was her name?—Julie Walters. Yeah, old Julie. You ever see her?"

"Julie?" Ryan felt his stomach cramping.

Moody tossed half a bottle of beer down his throat with a flick of his hand. "Julie Walters. By God, you better remember her! You gave me one helluva beating out back of the Noncom Club at Fort Ord over that broad."

"Sure. I remember her now. Haven't seen her for about five years, though."

"'Zat right? Shit. I should have saved myself a stomping and waited till you dropped her. She was nice tail. Officer stuff."

"She was sweet all right. But she hated your guts, Big Joe."

Moody frowned, genuinely distressed. "I never understood that. I treated her good. She was a helluva popular entertainer in the lounge, and I only took five percent off her."

"But you wanted her to screw your CO."

"She told you that, huh." Moody looked

delighted, as if he had just won a citizenship award. "It's true. My CO wanted her as bad as I did. What happened to her after I shipped over to Germany?"

"I have no idea."

"Too bad. I'll bet she's still worth a toss."

"I'll bet she is," Ryan agreed.

Moody knocked back the rest of his beer in a single swallow. "So you're transferring in here. We'll be seeing each other then."

"No," Ryan said quickly. "I'm just in transit on my way to Dix. Stopped in to pick up my pay and see a few people."

"Oh. Well, stop by the club later and I'll slip you some Wild Turkey." He stood, a mountain on the move. "Good to see you, Dan."

When Joe Moody had gone, Ryan's stomach began to relax. He was somewhat surprised that Moody even remembered Julie. Moody always had a dozen women around him. He supposed it was the beating he'd given Moody that kept Julie in his mind. Funny he wasn't still sore about that. At the time he swore he'd get even.

Running into Moody could be bad. He might put things together later, seeing Ryan on the post the night the payroll gets lifted. Well, it's happened. At least he didn't see Terrio and Hazlitt.

The new guard mount was beginning to form up at the stockade. Ryan put Moody out of his mind and concentrated on that. Jeeps were pulling up to the stockade to unload MP's who were going off duty. They filed inside to the provost marshal's office to sign out with the duty sergeant. The new shift of MP's was falling in slowly on the long porchway at the front of the building.

Ryan began counting and stopped. Something wrong. Couldn't be that many on duty. He counted again. Fifty-six! Fifty-six goddam MPs! Four times in four months Ryan had sat in this same spot the night before payday, in civilian clothes just to be safe, and had never seen more than thirty MPs form up. Why fifty-six tonight? He had figured there would be five patrols of two MPs circulating around the post itself, with ten more patrols working the nearby towns for AWOLs and drunks. Tonight there would be almost twice that number. Why?

The lieutenant commanding the detail called "Ten-*hut!*" The MPs snapped to attention, clicking their boot heels in a rather ragged unison. Ryan would never have allowed that kind of sloppy soldiering. He watched the lieutenant move along the line with the sergeant of the guard at his elbow. As the officer stepped in front of an MP he would bring his .45 automatic out of its holster, pull back the slide, and present it to the officer for inspection. This particular officer gave each man and weapon a very brief inspection. Ryan was disgusted. He'd been taught that getting ready for guard duty was like going to dinner with your best woman. Your grooming should be immaculate. Your personal weapon should be sparkling clean and ready to use. No wonder these men couldn't even come to attention properly. If Ryan had been conducting the inspection, the sergeant of the guard would have a sprained wrist from writing gigs and half the men would be sent back to barracks to shape themselves up.

"Fall out!" the lieutenant called. The MPs milled around the porch for a few minutes while they slipped clips of ammo into their .45s, then gradually dispersed toward their jeeps. They sat in the jeeps awhile, filling out new trip tickets before rolling off to their assignments. So there would be at least ten MP patrols on the post tonight instead of five. Say five patrols on the main post instead of two. Ryan contemplated that and sipped his beer until Terrio showed up.

"Right on time," Ryan said.

"Let me get a beer," Terrio grumbled. "I been walking my heels off." He bought a Falstaff and came back to the table. "Everything's just like it was the last time you cased the main post. Only one guard in front of division headquarters. A skinhead."

"Good."

Skinheads were young recruits, easily spotted because of their extra-short haircuts and unfaded green fatigues. They pulled most of the guard duty at Riley in order to get experience. None of them carried loaded weapons, nor did they have any live ammo in their cartridge belts. High-security areas were guarded by special detachments.

"What about inside the building?" Ryan wanted to know.

"The same," Terrio answered, drinking noisily. "Duty officer in the communications center in the basement. He's got a runner with him, a Pfc who looks like he's just out of basic. Upstairs, two MPs in front of the paymaster's office. They're armed with grease guns. Oh, and I saw Captain Trencham go into the building. What if he's still there when we take the place?"

"We'll just handle him with the others. Do you think he'll be there long?"

"I don't know. I guess he's double-checking his pay records for tomorrow morning."

"Still pushing for his majority," Ryan grinned.

"Yeah." Terrio glanced around. "Everything okay here?"

"Not completely. The MP guard mount was almost double its usual size tonight. Twenty-eight patrols of two men each instead of fourteen."

Terrio did a double take. "Christ! Are they on to something?"

"I don't think so. The guard mount was too routine. No special instructions."

"Shit!"

Ryan could see Terrio developing the worst conclusions. "Relax. There has to be a reason other than us."

"I hope so."

Hazlitt joined them a few minutes later, looking smug. "I got good news. Number one, they still have skinheads guarding the motor pool. Number two, this is free-beer night at the Crossroads Club. There'll be so damn much noise on the main post tonight that we could blow that paymaster's safe all the way to Kansas City without anybody hearing it."

"That explains the extra MPs," Ryan said. He told Hazlitt about the double shift that just came on duty.

"What's the Crossroads Club?" Terrio demanded. He didn't like to be in the dark on details.

"That's the enlisted men's club," Hazlitt explained. "Once a month they have free-beer night. Every Pfc and skinhead on post will be there, swilling down pitchers of beer." Hazlitt became nostalgic. "Damn. By midnight there'll be two hundred troopers too drunk to make it back to barracks. They'll fall down somewheres, and along about one A.M. the MPs will come along and pick them up and haul their asses back to barracks. Happened to me a-plenty. I recollect one free-beer night I walked out of the Crossroads Club too pissed to see where I was going. Somebody pointed me at my barracks. Well, the club's down there near the railroad tracks and I started to walk across the tracks. Trouble is I was too pissed to see or hear the damn train coming. Heard someone yell at me to watch out, but I walked right into the side of that train. My sleeve hooked onto something, and I was picked up and tossed about a hundred feet in the air. Right over the Crossroads Club! Those that saw it happen thought I was a goner. I landed like a mortar round twenty yards the other side of the club. Never broke a bone. Too drunk. But I ached like a whore's ass the next day."

Terrio shook his head. "You're crazy, Hazlitt. I don't see how you've lived this long."

"I got magic power in my pecker," Hazlitt claimed.

"You got shit for brains," Terrio countered.

"Knock it off." Ryan looked at his watch.

"We've got three more hours before we move. Let's go back to the replacement center and sack in for a while. We'll go ahead on schedule at ten thirty, figuring the MP detail will be busy with the drunks down at the club." Ryan knew he had to tell them about Moody. "One more problem. While you were gone I bumped into a man who knows me. He could connect me with the job later."

Terrio and Hazlitt looked concerned but not alarmed.

"If you want to abort the job I'll understand. The FBI will be on this one fast. They could tie me to you if Moody puts things together and tells them about me. Though the chances are he won't make the connection. What do you say?"

"I already got the money spent in my head," Hazlitt said.

Terrio made a chopping motion with his right hand. "I never back away from anything. You know that, Ryan."

They finished their beers and walked slowly back across the parade ground to the replacement center. The offices of the company clerk and commanding officer were closed. The mess hall was deserted. A tiny office under the stairway was occupied by a lone corporal who was charge-of-quarters for the evening. About all he had to do as CQ was check in any replacements who turned up during the night and wake the cooks and KPs in time to fix breakfast.

"Nice and quiet," Hazlitt said.

They went upstairs and lay down in their bunks, waiting for lights out. There were only three other noncoms in their squad bay. Two of them turned in early. The other smoked one cigarette after another while he read a newspaper. Lights went out at ten P.M. The one noncom who was still awake stripped to his shorts and slipped into his bunk. Ryan, Hazlitt, and Terrio stayed on their bunks, lying on their backs with their arms behind their heads as they had done on endless nights in Leavenworth.

Moody's office at the NCO Club was located just off the lobby. From the big swivel chair behind his desk he could watch the action in the bar. Not that there was much action the night before payday. Most of the troops were too broke. Tomorrow night would be busy, when everyone had a full month's pay. But those who did want to see Moody knew when he would be available. Every night from ten to eleven Moody held court at his desk. John, the bartender, had automatically placed a half-filled tumbler of Wild Turkey and two cigars on the desk five minutes before Moody was due.

As he unwrapped the first cigar, Moody waved across the dark expanse of polished hardwood floor at John. John put aside his towel and poked his finger at a trooper who was nursing a shot of twenty-five-cent bar whiskey. The man was dressed in medic whites. He walked quickly through the bar to Moody's office.

"Joe. How are you?"

"Good, Marty. You keeping them healthy at the infirmary?"

"Like always." SP/5 Marty Leachman, a medic at the Camp Forsyth infirmary, glanced behind him to make sure only John could see into the office from the bar. "I got something for you tonight."

"Let's have it."

Marty reached inside his white jacket and pulled out five unmarked plastic medicine bottles. He sat them on the desk one by one. Each bottle was filled to the top with red-and-white pills.

"Amphetamines," Marty said. "Five hundred of them. Very pure stuff."

Moody drew on his cigar and watched the gray ash redden. "I'm not really in the market for this, Marty. I told you before. I know some people in Chicago who'll take all the heroin you can bring out. But this is kid stuff."

"You can get a dollar a cap for these in any of the big cities around here," Marty protested. "Take it to Kansas City. Wichita. Anywhere around here."

"I don't peddle this shit myself. You know that."

"I know," Marty said. His head drooped.

"How'd you get them?" Moody asked.

"It took me two months," Marty said miserably. He was an emaciated little man who thought in terms of nickels and dimes. Moody had felt for some time that the medic might be turned into a profitable contact if he could be brought along properly.

"Tell me about it."

Marty sighed.

"Maybe I can take these off your hands after all," Moody coaxed.

The medic brightened. "Yeah? That's great. I was afraid I'd have to go all the way to K.C. to get rid of them. A guy could get mugged or sliced up by those speed freaks down there."

"Tell me about it," Moody repeated.

"It was pretty easy," Marty said with more enthusiasm. "The doctors make out the prescriptions, and when the pharmacy clerk fills them, he gives them back to me to administer. So on the way back to the patient, I hop into an unoccupied examining room and empty maybe a third of the grains from the capsules into a vial I keep in my pocket. The patient gets two-thirds of the dose he's supposed to have and no one knows the difference. Not even the doctors."

Moody nodded approvingly. "Sounds like a good system. Why wouldn't it work for harder narcotics? Heroin, for instance."

"We're just a little infirmary," Marty explained. "If a guy's so sick he needs that stuff he's a candidate for the hospital."

The cigar had gone out as Moody listened carefully to Marty's scam. He relit it and sipped the Wild Turkey again. "Sounds to me like you're in the wrong spot. You should be working at the hospital in some section where you could use the same gimmick with hard narcotics."

"Jesus, Joe. They keep a much tougher eye on the hard stuff."

"I understand that," Moody said smoothly. He motioned past Marty to John, indicating that he wanted a shot of Wild Turkey for his visitor. John came in immediately and put a glass in front of Marty, who smiled gratefully. He was appropriately flattered at being asked to work for Big Joe Moody, but shrewd enough to see how dangerous the work would be. He followed Moody's lead, sipping at the expensive bourbon. It was stronger than any he had ever tasted. Marty liked bourbon. He liked scotch. He liked the whores in Kansas City. And he knew that people who did business with Big Joe Moody did very good business indeed.

"I don't know how I could get myself transferred into a spot like that, Joe."

"Just find out what job you should have in the post hospital in order to chip off a little narcotics now and then. Say a tenth of a kilo a month. You wouldn't even have to short every patient to get that amount. Just somebody here and there. Patients who aren't so sick that the doctor would notice they aren't getting as good a reaction from the medication as they should."

Marty sat with his shoulders hunched. "That's good," he pondered. "Just a little now and then. That might be safe, if I were in the right spot." He made his decision and downed the rest of his drink. "I can find out what job I'll need, but how do I get myself transferred?"

"I'll arrange it," Moody guaranteed. "I have plenty of friends over at division personnel."

"Okay," Marty said. "I'll be back to you in a few days." He stared at the pills on Moody's desk. "You said you could handle these?"

"I don't really want them, Marty. But here's something to tide you over until we can transfer you into the hospital." Moody extracted a large roll of bills from his pocket and separated two one-hundred-dollar bills from it. He pushed them across to Marty, who snatched up the bills greedily.

"Thanks a lot, Joe. I appreciate this." He gathered up the amphetamines and slipped them into various pockets in his whites with a nervous laugh. "No use letting these go to waste."

"Of course not," Moody said drily.

When Marty had gone, Moody asked John to get hold of one of the jocks on the Fifth Army boxing team, a corporal named Bo Evans.

While he waited for Evans, Moody did a little more business. A liquor supplier came by to deliver twelve cases of booze and to give Moody his usual ten percent kickback. Although John handled most of the loan-shark business, he had to refer any loan for more than fifty dollars to Moody, and there was a sergeant from the 27th Infantry who needed a hundred to go on emergency leave to Arkansas, where his father was dying. Moody let him have the hundred at the usual interest rate—twenty-five percent per month. A first lieutenant from Camp Funston came into the NCO Club in civilian clothes and asked Moody what it would cost to arrange a transfer to a European command. Any outfit would do, as long as it was in Europe. Moody told him three hundred dollars and was surprised when the lieutenant paid him cash on the spot.

"It'll take about a month," Moody said.

"The faster the better," the lieutenant replied. "I have to get out of Kansas or I'll go crazy." When the lieutenant had returned to officer country, Moody phoned the division personnel officer at his apartment in Junction City. He gave him the name and serial number of the lieutenant who wanted the transfer and promised to mail a hundred and fifty dollars in cash to the personnel officer's home in a plain envelope—as usual.

By that time Corporal Bo Evans had slid nervously into the chair across the desk. Evans was dressed in a dirty gray sweat shirt and blue sweat pants. He probably had not worn a uniform for more than six months out of his ten years in the army. Evans was a jock. A professional army athlete. He boxed in the summer, played football in the fall and winter, ran track in the spring. He lived in a big, foul-smelling squad room on the second floor of the post gymnasium along with thirty or so other jocks who were also on permanent temporary duty as athletes. At the age of twenty-eight, Evans' sandy hair was thinning and his wind wasn't what it used to be. But he could still pick up ten yards punching over tackle or go four rounds in a ring and please the crowd. However, he could only function as a jock these days with a few belts of liquor in him, and he was spending more money on booze than he made as a corporal. That's why he owed money to Joe Moody and why he couldn't stop fidgeting as he sat across from the big man.

When Moody rang off on the division personnel officer, he asked Bo, "How much do you owe me right now?"

"A hundred and fifty," Bo answered. He frowned. "A hundred eighty-seven fifty with interest, I guess."

"I'll forget that tab if you'll do me a favor, Bo."

Bo Evans suddenly forgot how much he needed a drink. "Name it, Joe." He watched with only a mild agony as Moody drained his own glass.

"I want you to work a guy over."

"Sure," Bo agreed, elated. What could be easier? "Who do you want stomped?"

"His name is Dan Ryan. He's a sergeant first class. I owe him some bruises."

"He'll get them," Evans promised.

Moody looked skeptical. "Don't think I'm handing you an easy out, Bo. Ryan is tough. You'll need a couple more jocks from the boxing team to take him, believe me. I tried it once myself and he handed me my balls. That's why I'm turning him over to you and the other jocks. I've already taken my lumps from Ryan. This ain't something I want buzzed around. I'm only telling you so you'll take the job seriously."

Some of Bo's enthusiasm evaporated. Anyone who could take Big Joe Moody in a brawl must be half ape. "That's a little different, Joe. I'll do the job because you're canceling my debt. How do I get a couple of boxers to go into this with me?"

Moody produced his roll of bills for the second time in the evening and passed some of them over to Bo. "Here's fifty for you and another hundred to split with the men you'll need. Try to get that new heavyweight, Larson. And Pepper Moran."

"Oh, they'll do it for fifty bucks," Evans assured him. "Especially the night before payday."

"I don't want it done tonight. I just saw this guy a couple of hours ago and he might figure out I was behind it if you nailed him tonight." Moody unwrapped his second cigar and leaned across the desk. "Ryan is bunking at the replacement center. He's on his way to Dix; that means he'll be gone in a day or two so you'll have to work fast and smart."

He lit the cigar and drew deeply on it. "Do it tomorrow night. I want him busted up good, but not killed. Take his wallet to make it look like a simple payday robbery. There's a dozen robberies every payday on this post, muggings mostly. The provost marshal won't go too far with it. You guys can split whatever you take off him."

Evans nodded. "I'll go over to the replacement center in the morning and spot him. I can line up the other guys tonight."

"Okay." Moody leaned back. "Ryan's had this coming for a long time."

At ten thirty Ryan sat up and swung his legs off the cot. "Let's go," he whispered.

They got up and silently opened their lockers. Ryan folded down the sides of his duffel bag and took out a pair of gleaming black boots with white laces. He put them on. Next he slipped on an MP armband. He also took a Sam Browne belt out of the bag and fastened that around his waist and over his shoulder. A heavy army-issue .45 automatic went into the holster on the belt. Last, he donned a white MP cap and white gloves.

"How do I look?" Terrio asked in a low voice.

Ryan checked him. Terrio and Hazlitt were also in MP uniform. "Good," he said. "Here. Fix my brass."

Ryan took the infantry brass off his collars and let Terrio exchange the insignia for the crossed-pistols emblem of the military police.

"You guys look fine," Hazlitt grinned. "I'd just damn near give myself up to you."

From the locker Terrio pulled a bulky zipper bag containing his tools. "Put your other shoes and caps in this," he said. All three of them dumped their Class A shoes and army green caps in the bag.

When they were ready to go, Ryan reminded them to walk in step. They went downstairs past the CQ's cubbyhole. Outside, they headed for the MP motor pool about half a mile away. They walked in step, giving the impression of three MPs on a special detail. Terrio was in the center with the bag. The streets were dark and the traffic was light.

As they neared the motor pool they could hear the sounds of voices and music from the Crossroads Club, which stood a few hundred yards from the motor pool.

"Looka there." Hazlitt pointed across the road at the figure of a man lying on his back under a tree. "The old boy didn't quite make it to his bunk."

Before they reached the motor pool they

saw two more drunks passed out where they had fallen. There would be plenty to keep the MPs busy tonight.

At the entrance to the motor pool a single sentry was pacing under the yellow light at the top of the gate. When he saw three MPs coming at him out of the night, he did what he was supposed to do. He stopped, brought his M-16 to port arms, and called out, "Halt!"

The three MPs halted.

"Who goes there?"

"Military police detail," Ryan said crisply.

"Advance and be recognized."

Ryan moved ahead to the sentry. He was a boy of seventeen or eighteen. He looked quite pleased with the way he had handled the challenge.

"I'm drawing a jeep for a special detail," Ryan told him.

"Drawing a jeep?" The young recruit looked alarmed. Nothing in his seven weeks of infantry training had prepared him for this. "I don't know, Sergeant. I don't have any instructions about that."

"This is the MP motor pool, isn't it?"

"Yes."

"And I'm an MP."

"Yes. But the sergeant of the guard told me not to admit anyone without written orders from—"

"What's the fifth general order?" Ryan snapped.

"Sir—I mean Sergeant. The fifth general order is—that is, the fifth general . . ." A fear of total incompetence spread over the youngster's face. "I don't know, sergeant," he said in a small voice.

"Inspection *harms!*" Ryan barked.

The guard did a smart enough job of raising his weapon and sliding back the bolt. Ryan snatched it away from him. The guard's hands fell to his sides. He stared straight ahead. Ryan had meant to just make a show of inspecting the M-16, but he became engrossed in the job. Even in the dim light he could see flecks of carbon in the rifle's action. He held it up to the light and peered down the barrel, sticking his thumb in the chamber to reflect the little available light. Just as he suspected. In six months the barrel would be pitted, and five years from now the weapon would blow up in somebody's face. Sloth and carelessness. Ryan hated those faults. He could smell them here at Fort Riley. He had felt them spreading through the army before his court-martial. In a few years a once superb military machine had been turned into a cranky, dirty old bureaucracy. He was glad to be out of it. He handed the M-16 back to the guard.

"You've got a ton of carbon in there, soldier. Get it cleaned out as soon as you're back in barracks. Right now open that gate for me."

"Yes, Sergeant," the guard snapped, willing to do just about anything to get this tough MP off his back. He ran over to the gate and swung it open. Ryan walked through and stuck his head inside one of the jeeps. All the vehicles had their canvas sides and tops up because of Kansas' whimsical summer rains. The gas gauge registered only a quarter full. Jeep gauges are notoriously inaccurate, and

Ryan didn't want one that might run out of gas in the middle of the job. He walked to the next vehicle in line, recalling that in the old days every vehicle returned to a motor pool had to be refueled at that time. Everything was falling apart in this new army. The next jeep had an almost full tank. Ryan climbed in and flipped the starter. The motor turned over. He drove out of the motor pool and stopped outside to pick up Terrio and Hazlitt.

"That was easy," Terrio said. "Worked just like you figured."

"The whole job's going to work," Ryan said, really feeling it at last. "This army's all fucked up. It's no match for the three of us."

Ryan drove slowly through the main post toward division headquarters. They passed a few soldiers driving their own cars and saw two MPs hauling a drunk up out of the gutter and into their jeep.

The division headquarters was just across Highway 24, which divided the post in half. A big two-acre lawn spread out in front of the building, giving the headquarters an appropriately stately air. A circular driveway ran up to the building. Ryan drove up and pulled to a stop at the front door. They got out and stood facing another skinhead with an unloaded M-16.

"Halt! Who goes there?" The guard called.

"Military police detail," Ryan said again.

"Advance and be recognized," the trooper called, though he was barely ten feet away from them.

Ryan stepped forward a pace. "We have

some emergency shipment orders for the duty officer. He's supposed to TWIX them out right away."

The guard looked relieved to be faced with nothing more complicated. "All right." He shifted his M-16 from port arms to order arms and opened the front door with his free hand. "They told me the duty officer is located in the basement."

"We'll be a while."

"Sure," the guard said. "Say, are there a lot of guys down at the Crossroads Club?"

"You bet," Hazlitt answered. "The beer's flowing like water down there tonight."

"I know," the guard said sadly. "Sure wish I'd been on tomorrow's guard roster."

"You'll get your free beer next month," Terrio said.

They went inside and walked downstairs to the basement hallway.

"Ready?" Ryan asked.

Terrio and Hazlitt drew their .45s, as did Ryan. They walked down the hall past rows of empty offices. Light spread into the hallway from one office at the end of the hall. The sounds of country music came from a radio. Ryan stepped through the door and moved to the left. Hazlitt followed and Terrio hung toward the rear.

The two men in the office didn't even look up at first. The duty officer sat behind a scarred wooden desk, staring at a cigarette in his hand. He was a young lieutenant. Ryan could tell at a glance that he was a reserve officer, probably ROTC, putting in his two years after college. The officer belatedly sensed their presence and raised a round face. His eyes bulged. Ryan was already on top of him.

"What the hell are you doing, sergeant?" He half-rose in his chair. "No!" Ryan grabbed his shirt at the throat and hauled him the rest of the way up. "Sergeant!" Ryan wanted him out of reach of the phone, so he dragged him a few yards and pushed him into a chair.

"Shut up," Ryan told him.

Hazlitt pushed the Pfc into another chair next to the officer. He was a pink-cheeked boy not out of his teens.

"You'd better put those guns down," the duty officer warned. "I don't know what you men think you're up to, but you'll be in pretty big trouble if—"

"Shut up," Ryan repeated. He looked at their chests. The Pfc had a piece of white cloth tape over the left breast pocket of his fatigues stenciled with the name Manners. The lieutenant wore a black name plate on his shirt bearing the name Fox. Ryan ripped off Fox's name plate and threw it on the desk.

"Say—" the lieutenant began.

Terrio stepped past them, smashing a small transistor radio with the barrel of his .45. The country music stopped. Terrio hated country music.

"Be quiet," Ryan said. "I'll tell you this once. We're after the payroll upstairs. If you make a sound we'll kill you. We don't need to use these guns. We can do it silently. One sound and you're dead. Understand?"

"The payroll?" The duty officer cringed in his chair. "You'll never get away with this."

"That's all," Ryan said. "Not another word. Get in there."

Hazlitt had already opened the door to a closet. Ryan yanked the two soldiers to their feet and was pushing them in that direction. The Pfc's mouth hung open as he let himself be moved without a sound. Someone would have to explain this to him tomorrow.

Ryan was pushing them into the closet when the phone rang. He looked at Hazlitt, who went over and sat down at the desk. Hazlitt put down the .45 and picked up the phone, glancing at the name plate Ryan had tossed on the desk.

"Division headquarters. Lieutenant Fox." Hazlitt frowned as he listened. Then said, "Yes sir. Just a moment, sir." With his hand firmly covering the mouthpiece, he said, "A captain in the 23rd Infantry out on Custer Hill needs to reach one of his noncoms who lives off post. He can't find the man's address and phone number. He says it should be on file here."

Ryan dragged the duty officer out of the closet. "Where?"

Lieutenant Fox, looking really scared now, pointed to a large revolving card file on a table in the corner.

Hazlitt put down the phone and went over to it. He flipped through the cards and found the information the captain on Custer Hill wanted and went back to the phone. "Yes sir. Sergeant Mendoza's number is 553-4529. You're welcome, sir." He hung up and grinned at Ryan. "No problem."

Lieutenant Fox was tossed back into the

closet, and Ryan turned the key in the lock. "Stay with it," he told Hazlitt.

Terrio said, "Watch this a minute," and put the zipper bag down carefully. He and Ryan left Hazlitt watching the phone and went down the hallway to the stairwell leading upstairs. They climbed to the landing near the first floor. As they passed the main entrance they could see the guard outside continuing his pacing.

The first floor was a short flight of stairs above street level. Before mounting the steps they put the .45s back in their holsters.

"Ready?" Ryan asked.

Terrio cleared his throat.

They climbed loudly up the steps and marched down the hallway, which was well lighted compared to the basement. They stepped in unison, their arms swinging in regulation style. Halfway down the hall the two MPs in front of the paymaster's office straightened and stared at them. One of the MPs glanced at his watch. Too early for their relief. They looked at each other, puzzled but not apprehensive. They saw what appeared to be two MPs exactly like themselves. They accepted what they saw. But there was a procedure to be observed. Regulations. They crooked their grease guns in their arms and came to positions approximating attention.

"Halt," one of them said half-heartedly. "State your business."

"Inspection," Ryan answered.

"Inspection?" The MPs looked at each other again, then back at Ryan and Terrio. "What the hell are you inspecting?"

"Weapons inspection," Ryan said smoothly. "The provost marshal's got a bug up his ass about improper weapons procedure. He found a round in the chamber of some poor bastard's .45 tonight so we have to chase all over the goddam post inspecting weapons."

"Sheeit," one of the MPs said. "That's one colonel who's got his head screwed on back asswards."

"Sorry," Ryan said. He stepped forward a pace, Terrio following. "Just take a second."

A glimmer of suspicion flickered in the eyes of the MP who hadn't spoken, a black professional soldier with three rows of ribbons on his chest and a head the shape of an ice chest. "I never heard of no weapons inspection in the middle of guard detail. That don't make no goddam sense at all."

"Provost marshal's orders," Ryan said, making it one step closer.

The black MP started to bring his grease gun to a ready position. "We'd better check this—"

Ryan and Terrio jumped. Ryan hit the black MP squarely in the chest, sending the grease gun flying against the wall. Before the second MP could move, Terrio hit him twice with his right hand while his left hand closed around the man's weapon. They fought for no more than ten seconds, the black MP almost dragging his sidearm free of its holster before Ryan could nail him across the side of his head with the heavy force of his own .45. When it was over, Ryan and Terrio were standing above the two fallen men breathing like buffalos.

They snatched up the grease guns and spare .45s and threw them aside.

The door to the paymaster's office swung open, throwing another shaft of light into the hall.

"What's going on out here?" Captain Trencham's petulant voice called. "I'm trying to work. Can't you men stand guard duty without all that noise? I'll have—good heavens!" He emerged into the hall. Blinking. His little bookkeeper's chest palpitating like a sparrow's. "What's happened here?"

Terrio pulled him farther out. Trencham's eyes rolled wildly toward his office as he grasped the situation. "The payroll! You're after—" Terrio hit him in the stomach and he collapsed to the floor gasping for breath.

"Get the elevator," Ryan ordered. Terrio went another few steps down the hall and pushed the elevator button. They had walked these halls many times in the past four months, dressed in uniform and acting like ordinary soldiers going about their duties. They knew every office and every turn in the corridors. They knew the elevators and stairs. When the elevator door opened, Ryan grabbed one of the MPs by his feet and dragged him inside. Terrio did the same. Then he picked up the small body of Captain Trencham and hauled him into the elevator, too. They went down to the basement and stowed the three men in the closet with the duty officer and his runner.

By the time they finished that job, the black MP was conscious and feeling well enough to try to scramble to his feet. Terrio put his .45 in the MP's face. "One sound and I'll take your damned head off." The MP scowled and let himself be helped to his feet by the duty officer, who kept saying, "Don't try anything with these guys, sergeant. They'll take it out on all of us. Don't do anything. They'll make us all pay. Just hang loose, Sergeant. They won't get away with this." He was as submissive and frightened as the black MP was mad and dangerous.

"Listen to the officer," Ryan told him. "He's giving you a lawful order." Trencham and the other MP were still mostly unconscious, their heads rolling occasionally and their mouths making groaning and gagging noises. Ryan shut the door on them.

"Watch the black MP," Ryan told Hazlitt. "He's got more guts than the others."

"They won't go anywhere," Hazlitt promised. "Have you looked at the safe yet?"

"We're going up there now," Terrio said.

The dinner party had become a jolly affair, with the General surprisingly witty and relaxed. Earlier, a three-piece combo had set itself up on the bandstand after General Hanson had told Captain Frederick that he wouldn't mind a little after-dinner music and dancing. The combo, looking hungry for ideas, led off with "Stardust." The junior officers brought their ladies to the floor. Military gentility. Brannigan hated it.

They were halfway through dessert when General Hanson spilled his coffee. Captain Frederick, who had been monitoring the General's service as always, rushed over. The General stood and brushed him aside. The club manager was alarmed by the General's appearance. His narrow face, usually slightly red from his daily tennis game, was white—so white it made the steel gray of his hair look dark. So white that the veins in his straight, rather pointed nose could be seen from across the room. His tall figure quivered like a bow.

"Hello, Arthur."

General Hanson stared at an officer who had entered the dining room. He was, like Hanson, a major general. His appearance duplicated Hanson's down to the decorations on their uniforms. There was only one superficial difference between them: Hanson wore a class ring from the Virginia Military Institute, and this new man wore a West Point ring.

"Jack." General Hanson nodded curtly. "What are you doing here?"

"I was on my way to Fort Carson in an L-19. There's a storm over western Colorado and my pilot insisted we put down here at Fort Riley to wait it out. Believe me, I didn't want to visit your post any more than you care to have me here. I'll be gone as soon as the weather clears in the west. We'll just have a bite to eat, if the kitchen is still open. I realize it's a bit late for dinner."

"We'll open it," Hanson shot back. "The sooner you're fed and on your way, the better." He realized that Brannigan, Captain Frederick, and a few people at nearby tables were watching and managed a smile as he turned to Frederick. "This is General Cunningham, Captain. I'd be obliged if you would attend to him yourself. Put his dinner on my mess bill. And his aide's dinner, too, of course."

General Cunningham's aide, a captain, was standing behind him, obviously embarrassed at the scene his commander had created. He looked even more embarrassed when Cunningham answered, "We'd prefer to pay our own mess bill."

Hanson's chin trembled. "As you wish." He sat down and replaced the overturned coffee cup on its saucer, ignoring General Cunningham and his aide as they went past and took a table in an isolated corner.

Brannigan had observed the conflict with interest. He had never seen General Hanson's elaborate façade of manners crack before. Whatever this General Cunningham knew about Hanson was powerful stuff. Brannigan wished he had a piece of it himself.

"Kind of a salty fellow, that General Cunningham," Brannigan said in an exploratory way.

There was no answer from Hanson. A waiter brought a fresh cup of coffee and put it in front of him. The General simply continued to stare at the tablecloth. Brannigan could see that Hanson was still furious, holding his anger inside him. Presently General Hanson added a dollop of cream to his coffee and began stirring.

As Hanson stirred he thought of the last time he had seen General Cunningham. It was in Vietnam, a rainy day at Corps headquarters. The sounds the Vietnamese village chief had made came back to him. Nasal screams. The CIA man had stuffed a rag in his mouth. Asked him questions. Who is the Viet Cong political leader in your village? What position do you hold in the Viet Cong hierarchy? Where are the antipersonnel mines cached? Who has access to them? The man couldn't answer with his mouth gagged, of course, so Hanson had repeatedly offered him paper and pencil. Tell us and we'll stop, he had said in his limited Vietnamese.

But the man was stubborn. He hated all Americans. The CIA man said to tighten the wires. They had worked together before in Hanson's area. He had taught Hanson some of his trade. Hanson had discovered an enormous emotional relief in using the techniques. That wasn't the reason he participated, of course. It was the information that was vital. Troops were stepping on antipersonnel mines every day. He tightened the wires. The man's genitals bulged in unnatural shapes. More nasal screams. Suddenly the door opened. The military policeman guarding the door was swept aside by General Cunningham, who stared at the Vietnamese strapped to the chair. His voice rose, cursing. The CIA man stood back, physically as well as administratively detaching himself from the military. Hanson explained. This procedure was not against army regulations. It was part of the Phoenix program. Interrogation and elimination of subversive elements. The Congress of the United States had voted funds for the Phoenix program. It was necessary. A head-to-head shouting match erupted between them. Finally Cunningham had said something that Hanson never dreamed would be said to him.

"You are unfit to command!" Cunningham shouted.

Unfit to command!

General Hanson picked up his coffee. His hand shook. He steadied himself. Across the room Cunningham was looking over the menu and chatting with his aide. Unfit to command! The West Point ring on Cunningham's hand flashed as he turned the menu. That was it. The Point. If I had gone to West Point instead of the Virginia Military Institute, Cunningham would not have dared to speak those words. For perhaps the millionth time he silently cursed the memory of his father, who had insisted on VMI because it was so much closer to their home in Roanoke.

It was unbearable to have Cunningham here. Hanson's eyes searched the room. They fell on a major from the 27th Infantry who was dining with two of his company commanders.

"Excuse me for a minute, Bob."

Hanson got up and went over to the major's table. "Major Cutler, I want to speak to you for a moment."

The major, a youthful red-haired officer who had never lost his freckles, stumbled to his feet in surprise. He had served in the division for two years without speaking to Hanson. "Yes, sir."

"Step over here."

The General led the way to an alcove off the main dining room. "Major Cutler, today I saw a copy of the preparedness report you intend to submit for your battalion. It shocked me. You contend that your own battalion is undertrained and unprepared for combat duty. You know our mission requires us to be prepared for combat duty at all times. Just what is the meaning of that report?"

Rattled at this unexpected questioning by the division commander, Major Cutler nevertheless tried to explain his reasoning. "Sir," he began, "the problem is our training schedule. We just haven't been able to give the men the training they're supposed to have. For instance, they were scheduled for three days on the close combat range this month. Instead they spent those three days whitewashing rocks and lining them up along Highway 24 to beautify the post. Then, the one day they were supposed to spend on the grenade course was wasted on a parade. Another day was lost—"

"Major Cutler!" Hanson had almost forgotten Cunningham in his new rage. "The parade was held for Lieutenant General Morris DeCroix, deputy commander of the Fifth U.S. Army, who was inspecting our division. The post was beautified for his benefit, also. Hardly a waste. If you can't understand the simple need to present an image of readiness to your superiors, then you aren't much of a soldier."

But Major Cutler was a line officer who had seen in Vietnam what happens to unprepared troops. "Sir, with all due respect to yourself and General DeCroix, he could have inspected the men on the grenade range."

General Hanson lowered his voice, but its edge grew sharper. "Major, I will give you until twelve hundred hours tomorrow to withdraw and resubmit your preparedness report. Those reports are copied to Fifth Army Headquarters, and I won't have my own officers degrading my command. Is that clear?"

It took only a second for Major Cutler to decide on his answer. "Yes, sir." He breathed a long sigh of relief as General Hanson turned on his heel and stalked away.

When he returned to his table, the General was in improved spirits. He was still annoyed at having Cunningham on his post, but he felt better now that he had reasserted his feel of command by giving Major Cutler the chewing out he deserved.

"Shall we top off the evening with a brandy?" he asked Brannigan.

Ryan and Terrio had returned to the paymaster's office, Terrio lugging his tool bag. When they entered the office, Terrio took one look at the safe and said, "Jesus! It's a Bonnett!"

"What's the matter?" Ryan asked anxiously.

"The matter!" Terrio cried, making a harsh sound that could have been a laugh or a cry of exasperation. "Nothing's the matter. A Bonnett is an old safe line. They stopped making them almost forty years ago. This one must have been here since some time in the thirties. Only the military would still use one."

Terrio knelt and began taking things out of his tool bag. "A Bonnett," he repeated. "I broke in on one of these things. Opened it with nitro. I used too much and damn near blew my fucking head off."

The safe was a noxious green and half the size of the wall it was set into. The old-fashioned gold script lettering in one corner read:

A. C. Bonnett Company—Est. 1892—St. Louis, Mo.

"Is the alarm rigged the way you expected?" Ryan asked.

Terrio studied the infrared alarm system installed high on the wall above the safe. It looked like a camera, but its optical system was designed to sense infrared energy along a three-foot path across the front of the safe. No one could reach the safe or the alarm device without moving through that path. The infrared energy produced by a human body would trigger the system and ring an alarm at the provost marshal's office two miles away. "That's about where I expected it to be," Terrio said.

He had learned what type of alarm system protected the safe by going through army procurement bid announcements at the General Services Administration in Washington. Once Terrio pinpointed the device purchased for use at Fort Riley, he bought a couple of them and experimented with different ways to deactivate them. He had devised three alternate plans for going around the system.

"I'll try the wall first," Terrio decided. He cut through the wallboard gingerly, using a handsaw, at about the elevation he expected the power cable for the alarm system to be located. Once the hole was made, he reached down between the studs and searched for the cable with his hand. When he found it he lifted the cable up to where he could see it.

"Just like I told you," he gloated. "They've got the cable protected by a flexible plastic hose." He showed it to Ryan; the power line for the alarm system could be seen through the plastic hose. Cutting the line would also cause an alarm at the provost marshal's.

"Let's see if we can move that eye." Terrio fitted a pipe wrench tightly to the hose and began twisting it slowly and steadily. Ryan watched the camera-like box mounted on the wall. It began moving slowly. Terrio was twisting the cable housing in a way that was gradually altering the direction the device faced. A few seconds later he had twisted the alarm system's cable one hundred and eighty degrees, so that the box itself was now pointed at the ceiling instead of the floor. "There." Terrio looked satisfied. "That kind of alarm picks up changes in infrared activity but not sound or movement. We could blast the safe clear across the parade ground now and the infrared system wouldn't even blink."

He began pushing at a big table near the safe. "Help me get this stuff out of the way." Ryan helped him manhandle the table across the room, then grabbed a corner of Captain Trencham's desk and dragged it away, too, Terrio liked plenty of space to work in. Ryan trusted Terrio implicitly to open this safe though he'd never seen him open one before. He knew Terrio was an expert safe man because Terrio had told him he was, just as he knew Hazlitt to be an expert with firearms only because he had listened for four years to Hazlitt talk about what he could do with guns. In the old days in the army Ryan would never have let a man do a job until he had proven in rigorous training that he could do it. Ryan was sometimes surprised at himself for trusting these two men so absolutely. He wasn't the kind who made close friends. Growing up in an orphanage had taught him to stay aloof, uncommitted. The experience of losing men in combat had strengthened his determination to keep a strong shield erected around himself. Julie, Terrio, and Hazlitt were the only people who had ever broken through that shield.

"I need more light," Terrio said. He was on his knees with an electric drill, boring a hole just under the immense round combination lock in the center of the safe. Ryan grabbed a lamp from one of the tables and set it on a chair in front of the safe.

"Better," Terrio said without stopping his drilling. The drill made relatively little noise for a high-speed tool. Terrio had muffled the sound by wrapping acoustic wall insulation around the motor area of the drill.

Feeling useless, Ryan said, "I'll see how Hazlitt is doing. How long do you think this will take?" They'd planned on thirty minutes to open the safe.

"Another ten minutes," Terrio estimated. He laughed, a sound Ryan had never heard. "Maybe less."

Ryan went downstairs to the duty office. Snatches of muffled conversation came from the closet, but Hazlitt looked relaxed. No one could hear Terrio's drill or the small sound their prisoners were making. The walls and doors of the old building were unusually thick and well constructed.

"Everything all right here?" he asked Hazlitt.

"Perfect. I had one more call. From a bar

over in Junction City. They were bitching about a soldier who got drunk and passed out in their john. He locked the door and no one can get in. I told them I'd send some MP's around."

"Nice work."

"How's it going up there?"

"Fine. The safe is even older than we figured it would be."

"Hey now! I guess that'd make even old Terrio happy."

"Yeah. I heard him laugh."

Hazlitt looked awed. "Jesus! Terrio laughed? Wish I'd been there to hear *that.*"

"I'm going back upstairs."

"How long will you be?"

"Ten more minutes on the safe. Then five minutes down the hall. We're on schedule."

He left Hazlitt and checked the guard in front of the building through one of the windows. The sentry was walking his post by the book. Weapon on shoulder. Walk twenty paces. About face. Walk twenty paces. About face. Walk twenty paces. About face. He was concentrating so hard on procedure that he wouldn't notice if someone lifted the headquarters building off its foundation. The army. Tied to tradition. Unable to function. Hamstrung by its web of rules and regulations. *To hell with them,* Ryan thought. *I'll be my own army.*

In the paymaster's office Terrio was almost finished. There were four large holes drilled around the dial of the combination lock. They were packed with putty-colored plastic explosive. Terrio was running fuses from each of the holes to a longer, single fuse that connected them all together.

"You won't be able to hear this outside," he promised. "Turn over that table."

Ryan turned the table on its side and slid down on his haunches behind it. A second later Terrio closed the office door and came behind the table with him. He slid down with his back against the wall. His white gloves were gray with dirt and perspiration. He had the zipper bag with him and he took a twelve-volt battery out of it. The gloves made it a little difficult to attach one of the two wire leads to the terminal on the battery. He did it slowly. Then he glanced up, his black eyebrows arching and his usually dark face bright with expectancy, and said, "Here we go, Ryan."

When he touched the second wire lead to the other terminal, the plastic explosives went *BAMMM* with about the same sound as a sledge hammer hitting a concrete wall. Although it wasn't really loud, the blast cracked Ryan's ears. He threw his hands up to the sides of his head and swallowed hard.

Terrio gaped. "Christ! I shoulda told you to open your mouth."

"Never mind," Ryan said, gulping again. They got out from behind the table. A pall of smoke hung in the room.

Terrio laughed again. "Look at that bastard."

The combination lock hung from the safe by a few shards of steel. In its place was a jagged hole about ten inches in diameter. They went over to the safe and Ryan was about to try to tug it open when Terrio stopped him.

"Let me do it. I ain't peeled one of these babies in a long time."

"Go ahead," Ryan smiled.

Terrio pushed down the handle with both his hands and pulled. The door made a creaking sound in one corner. It had been knocked crooked on its hinges. Terrio put his foot against the wall and pulled harder, grunting as the door slowly moved. It scraped the floor, gouging wood. Ryan tensed to help him, but decided not to. Terrio was getting too much pleasure out of his work.

"Okay!" Terrio shouted when the door was open far enough for one man to squeeze through. He levered himself inside the safe, and Ryan heard his muffled voice say, "It's here. I've got it." The edge of one of the gray mailbags popped through the narrow opening. Ryan grabbed it and dragged it out, tossing it on the floor in the center of the room. Terrio pushed the others out one at a time, until all six bags were piled in the center of the floor. Then he let Ryan help him out of the safe.

"Payday," Terrio grinned.

"It's been a long time between paydays," Ryan said. "This should make up for the ones we missed. Let's move them." Ryan got his hands around the straps of three of the bags and lifted them as high as his waist. Together they must have weighed fifty pounds.

When Terrio began dragging his three pouches out the door, Ryan stopped him. "No. Carry those. You're leaving drag marks. They'd see where we took them."

A gray line of dust trailed the path where Terrio had been dragging the mail bags. He cursed. "You're right. I could have blown the whole deal right here." He lifted the bags and together they staggered down the hallway with their load, stopping in front of the darkened office of the division personnel section.

"Put them down easy," Ryan warned. Terrio didn't have to be told twice. He set the money down as if it were a week-old baby with a bad cough.

"I'll get my tools," Terrio said. He left Ryan at the door and went back to the paymaster's office, returning in a second with the zipper bag. He took a strip of plastic out of the bag and went at the door latch. The latch popped and the door opened.

"Get the shades," Ryan said.

Terrio crossed to the window and drew them. They were old-fashioned World War II–style blackout shades. No one would be able to tell from outside that the lights were on in this room.

"I'll do the tags while you open the cage," Ryan said.

Terrio nodded and crossed to a corner of the office that had been partitioned off from floor to ceiling with heavy-gauge steel mesh. The mesh made a cage about twenty feet square. A door was built into the cage, which was filled with close to fifty bulky duffel bags. Terrio sank to his knees again in front of the door to the cage, going to work on the lock with a slender steel pick.

While Terrio performed his specialty, Ryan looked for the shipping tags. The personnel office was large enough to hold thirty desks where clerks kept track of the ten thousand men in the Seventh Infantry Division. One of the clerks, an SP/5 named Dobbs, was in charge of clearing short-timers for their discharges. Every day thirty to fifty soldiers were mustered out in this room, and SP/5 Dobbs handled their paperwork. Ryan knew his routine pretty well, not only from spending three days hanging around the personnel office but from watching thousands of men get mustered out during his ten years in the army. One service Dobbs performed for men being discharged was to ship their belongings home at government expense. Any man who wanted to take advantage of this service brought his packed duffel bag with him on the morning of his discharge. SP/5 Dobbs would have the man fill in his name and home mailing address on a shipping tag, then Dobbs himself would attach it to the man's duffel bag.

Ryan found the tags in Dobbs' desk and filled out two of them, putting a different false name and address on each tag. Both addresses were in Kansas City, furnished apartments they'd rented for the month. When he had filled out the tags, Ryan opened Terrio's tool bag and pulled out two green duffel bags folded tightly together. He shook them out. Loaded three payroll bags into each duffel bag. Locked them with padlocks.

"I've got it," Terrio said. He stood up and pushed open the door to the cage. "Ready?"

"Almost," Ryan answered. He found the seals in Dobbs' desk and rummaged for the pliers Dobbs used to close the seals. The seals themselves were small, round pieces of lead attached to eight-inch lengths of wire. Ryan slipped the wire through the lock at the top of the duffel bag, doubled it back, and slid the end of the wire through a tiny hole in the piece of lead. Then he squeezed the lead with the pliers until it mashed into the free end of the wire, sealing the lock. The pliers had the official emblem of the United States Army built into them. The emblem was reproduced on both sides of the seal, insuring that no one would be tampering with the lock.

"Ready," Ryan said. He took one of the bags and Terrio took the other. They stowed them in the mesh cage with the other duffel bags that had been collected from troops mustered out that day. First thing the next morning the division mail center would pick up the bags and take them to the railroad station. They would be shipped out on the first train coming through the post.

Terrio closed the door and relocked it. They turned off the lights, raised the blackout shades, and relocked the door to the personnel section.

"See you babies in K.C.," Terrio said, gathering up his tool bag.

They picked up Hazlitt at the duty officer's desk. He was on the phone again.

"Yes, sir. Right, sir. I'll have it waiting for you at five hundred hours, sir." He put the phone down and winked at his partners. "Some bird colonel expects me to lay on a helicopter to take him to Fort Leonard Wood at five A.M. He's gonna be mighty disappointed."

"We're through," Ryan said.

"You got it all?" Hazlitt's lips were dry and he licked them hungrily.

"Every dollar," Terrio answered.

Hazlitt laughed and picked up his .45. "I'm sure glad I didn't have to use this thing." He holstered the .45 and they left the office.

The same guard was still on duty outside. He again brought his weapon to port arms. Ryan nodded to him as they got into the MP jeep. They drove off into the night.

"Get out of that MP gear," Ryan said when they reached a dark stretch of road. Hazlitt and Terrio began taking off their white gloves and hats, MP armbands and brass, and the heavy black boots with the white laces.

"I'm sure glad to be shut of this stuff," Hazlitt said. "I wasn't born to be no MP."

"Sure you were," Terrio argued. "You're a natural-born fink, Hazlitt."

"Sheeit."

They retrieved their black shoes and army green caps from Terrio's bag, along with Ryan's. The road led down to Marshal Army Air Field. It went over the Kansas River at a particularly deep spot. Ryan stopped the jeep on the bridge and took off his own boots and MP gear. He dropped the gear in the zipper bag along with his partners' stuff and put on his own black shoes and cap. They looked just as they had when they stepped down from the train at the Fort Riley station that afternoon, like three GIs with widely varied backgrounds.

As soon as Terrio had zipped up the bag, Ryan took it and walked over to the rail. Leaning out, he dropped the zipper bag. In the moonlight he saw it hit the water and sink immediately. The drill and other tools were heavy enough to take it right to the bottom, where it would mire and rot in several feet of mud.

Five minutes later they abandoned the MP jeep and were strolling casually back to the replacement center.

"Nice night," Ryan observed.

"Too hot," Terrio disagreed. "This goddam state's only good for wheat and catfish."

"What do you know about catfish?" Hazlitt scoffed. "You ever laid up on a river bank at dawn waiting for one to nip? Ever felt your line plunge and seen that ugly old bastard whipping around down there? The hell you have!"

An MP jeep shot past them on the road, headed toward division headquarters. The MP next to the driver was hanging on with both hands.

"I think somebody got out of a closet," Ryan said.

"That black MP," Hazlitt guessed. "I caught him trying to bust the lock on the closet while you two were cracking the safe."

"You don't 'crack' a safe," Terrio said contemptuously. "Nobody's used that word in thirty years. You can 'open' it or 'peel' it or 'shoot' it. You don't 'crack' it."

"Okay," Hazlitt said agreeably. "I got to admit I was wrong. All those years I thought you were bullshitting us about how good you are with a safe."

"Ahh. You wouldn't know a safe if you saw one. You'd think it was a giant pussy."

"And I could open one of those fast enough," Hazlitt bragged. "Or shoot it or peel it."

"Like hell!"

"Keep it down," Ryan whispered. They were going up the steps of the replacement center, and Ryan didn't want the CQ disturbed.

There was not much danger of that. The CQ was sitting in his cubbyhole with his feet propped up on a radiator and a stack of comic books at his elbow, making giggling noises over Daffy Duck. They went past him quietly.

The few other noncoms in their wing were still asleep. They undressed silently and got into their bunks. They had lain there only a few minutes when a rash of sirens broke out. Ambulances and more military police heading for division headquarters.

"Jesus, I'm tired," Hazlitt said.

Within two minutes he and Terrio were asleep. Ryan remained awake for about half an hour. That was how it had always been in prison. Terrio and Hazlitt always went to sleep immediately, leaving Ryan to his own thoughts about Julie and California. Tonight, though, Ryan was thinking about Major General Arthur Hanson and the damage the robbery would do to his career. No general officer who lost his division's payroll would ever get another good assignment. Ryan speculated about what would come next. First Hanson would be transferred to a new assignment, a desk job in some backwater like Fort Sam Houston. He would cease to be invited to take part in seminars at the Command and General Staff School. His driver would be a corporal instead of a sergeant. His new quarters would be cramped, and he wouldn't have his own cook and housekeeper; he'd have to hire someone to come in. He'd be forced into retirement in about a year, but probably not at the rank of major general. Hanson had gone from colonel to brigadier general to major general in six short years, but his permanent rank was still colonel. The two stars had not yet been confirmed as permanent rank because general officer promotions had been made so fast in the Vietnam years that the Department of the Army had not been able to carry all the new generals on the Table of Organization as permanent ranks.

Now Hanson's stars would never be confirmed. And he would probably not get the sixty percent disability usually extended to retiring generals to fatten their retirement checks by exempting much of their income from taxation.

Soon Ryan was sleeping, too. And sleeping well.

SATURDAY
JULY 1

The driver of Colonel William Martin's jeep broke all the post speed laws getting from division headquarters to the post commander's residence half a mile away. Martin was out of the jeep and running up the walkway before it came to a complete stop. He took the steps up to the front porch in one leap and hit the doorbell impatiently.

There was a light at the rear of the house. Martin assumed that General Hanson must still be awake because he knew the General was alone in his quarters. Hanson's wife was spending the impossible Kansas summer at their Virginia home.

He was mistaken about the General's being awake. The light was still on because General Hanson had found it difficult to go to sleep in the dark for several years now, another reason Mrs. Hanson took extended vacations away from her husband. The General came slowly awake to the persistent sound of the doorbell, his head aching slightly from the drinks with Brannigan and his stomach still heavy with rack of lamb.

"I'm coming," he mumbled, slipping into a robe. He glanced at his watch as he shuffled to the front door. Almost one A.M. He'd have the hide off someone if this was unnecessary.

The ashen face of his provost marshal, Colonal William Martin, brought him more fully awake. "What is it, Colonel?"

"There's been a robbery, sir. Three armed men forced their way into division headquarters and broke into the paymaster's safe. They took the payroll, sir. The whole damned payroll!"

"My payroll?" The statement was utterly incredible. "They took my division's payroll?" When Colonel Martin failed to deny this absurdity, the implications began to penetrate the General's throbbing head. "You mean to say three men gained entry to my division headquarters . . . overpowered your military police guard . . . broke into that huge safe without the duty officer's hearing a thing . . . *and took this division's payroll!*"

"Sir, the duty officer was jumped, too. These men were dressed as MPs. That's how—"

"I don't *care* how they were dressed. Have you caught them yet?"

"No, sir. Not yet. But we . . ."

General Hanson turned on his heel and stalked away, leaving Colonel Martin talking to empty space. He fidgeted for a couple of minutes until the General came rushing out of his bedroom hastily tucking in his uniform shirt tail. His face appeared to be pulsating in alternate shades of red and purple. They climbed into Martin's jeep and the driver went through gears he didn't know he had, heading back to division headquarters.

Martin continued his explanations as they drove. "As I was saying, sir, we haven't caught them. Yet. But I've notified the Kansas State Police, and every highway for a hundred miles around is roadblocked. Every air strip in central Kansas is being watched, too. They can't get away."

"They shouldn't have gotten *in* to begin with, Colonel! I hold you directly responsible for this entire mess. What kind of idiots did you put on the payroll guard, anyway?"

"They're two of my best men, sir," Martin said quietly.

Neither spoke again until they reached division headquarters, which was now fully lit and swarming with both military and civilian police. General Hanson hurried to the paymaster's office on the first floor. Although the sight of devastation was nothing new to him, he was shocked and frightened by the ugly mess of the safe and the black flash marks on the walls. Nothing in his years of soldiering had quite prepared him for this. He was used to dishing out devastation, not taking it. He had great experience in seizing the property of others, but his own headquarters had never been breached and looted before. He knew how to deploy an army but had no idea how to find three faceless men.

His feeling of impotence fed his fury. "Who was the duty officer tonight?"

"Lieutenant Fox. He's with G-3."

"Prepare court-martial papers on Lieutenant Fox."

"On what charges?" Colonel Martin demanded. He had known the old man would blow his stack, but he couldn't let him start lining up scapegoats this early in the game.

"Dereliction of duty."

Martin started to protest that Lieutenant Fox, as duty officer, was not even armed, but General Hanson snapped another question at him. "And who was the MP in charge of the guard detail?"

"Sergeant Robinson. He put up a helluva fight. He's at the infirmary right now with—"

"I want a special court-martial for both Fox and Robinson. Same charge for both of them."

"That will never hold up," Martin said stubbornly. He was afraid of the General, but he knew that if he didn't fight him on this he wouldn't be able to continue as provost marshal. The MPs under his command would make his job impossible. They were as clannish as civilian police.

General Hanson was watching him coldly. "Just have the papers drawn up and put those men on detention. I'll see that the charges stick."

"Sir. I must say respectfully that I'll be forced to go to the inspector general if the responsibility for this robbery is placed solely on Lieutenant Fox and Sergeant Robinson."

It was a desperate gamble on Martin's part. He doubted that he'd have the guts to go to the IG if push came to shove. If he did, he couldn't be sure the IG would take his side. And even if the IG did agree that Fox and Robinson didn't deserve to be singled out, winning a point through the IG's office has ruined plenty of army careers.

But Colonel Martin's words had their effect. General Hanson had been about to leave the paymaster's office, partly because of the stench of smoke lingering in the air and partly to avoid the infuriating sight of the empty safe. Instead he froze in his steps and smiled grimly at his provost marshal. "You wouldn't dare do that."

He knew his man pretty well. Colonel Martin was about to retract his threat and agree to take Fox and Robinson into custody when he recalled a recommendation he had submitted several months earlier to the adjutant general. "I may have to, sir. As you perhaps recall, my office recommended a beefed-up payroll guard some time ago. If that recommendation had been accepted, we might have prevented tonight's robbery. I'd be bound to report that to the IG, in my judgment."

Hanson stood rooted to his spot, his aristocratic features sharper and lacking the patina of Southern graciousness that he tried so hard to cultivate. The frequent rages usually seen only in his eyes were now evident in his entire bearing; his hands shook quite openly and his breath was coming in hard gasps. "Very well, Colonel. We'll drop the matter of responsibility for the moment. I repeat: for the moment. But you had better find those men and the money very fast."

He slapped the palm of his right hand against his thigh and walked out of the room. In the hallway a tall civilian with a farmer's stoop was listening patiently to the exterior guard who had admitted the three thieves into the building. He broke off his questioning to step in front of General Hanson.

"General? I'm Bob Huber. Kansas State Police."

The General looked at him with distaste. He didn't like to have civilians questioning his troops and poking through his headquarters. "State Police, you say. Have you found those three men yet? Have you any leads?"

Huber shook his head and ran a finger under his collar. "Sure haven't, General. But—"

"Why the hell not? What do you need to do the job, Mr. Huber? Just tell me and I'll give it to you." He threw his arm out. "I've got ten thousand men here. I can have every one of them turned out in two hours."

Huber chuckled softly. "General, you could give me forty thousand men and I couldn't do much more than I am now. I've got every highway and back road out of central Kansas covered. Every airport, too. And the Civil Air Patrol is looking for any unidentified helicopters that could have picked up those men. Nothing yet. The FBI's on its way here, too. There is something you can do, though."

"Name it." Hanson wanted action. Any kind of action that would show he was doing everything possible to erase this disgrace from his record.

"We have to consider the possibility that these three men really were soldiers," Huber said slowly. "Maybe soldiers from right here at Fort Riley. While we're out looking for professionals on the road, they could be in their barracks laughing at us." Huber chuckled again, amused by the look of amazement on Hanson's face. "Maybe I'm wrong. It's a long shot. But I'd like to see you organize a search. Look into every locker and the back of every truck and car on the post. And every supply room as well. Anywhere that money could be tucked away."

Colonel Martin had come up as Huber was making his suggestion. General Hanson turned to him. "That's a good idea, Bill. Get on it right away, will you?"

Martin was relieved by the General's sudden civility. He had never discovered whether the General's shifts from fury to Southern courtliness was genuine or calculated. And he was too eager to begin his search of the post to worry about it now.

"Right away, sir." He went downstairs to the duty officer's desk and began methodically phoning the officers he considered the most thorough and reliable on the post. They would lead the barracks search. It took him an hour to set up the search. His own MPs were already scouring the motor pools, warehouses, and other service buildings. If the money was still on the post, it would be found.

Joe Moody heard the news about the payroll robbery even before General Hanson did. He heard most things before they got to officer country. In this case a corporal going off duty at the stockade communications center brought him the news. The corporal slipped past John the bartender's baleful stare and dropped into Moody's visitor's chair.

"Did you hear about the robbery, Joe?" the corporal asked.

"What robbery?"

"Didn't you hear the sirens? Somebody just blew up the paymaster's safe at division headquarters and took the whole damn Fort Riley payroll."

"What? When did that happen?"

The corporal was delighted to bring hot news to a man as important as Joe Moody. He gave Moody the balance of what he knew as fast as he could. "They're looking for three guys dressed like MPs. They blew the safe an hour ago—probably on their way out of Kansas by now—about six hundred thousand in cash. They left the checks."

Moody stood up and went quickly through the bar and into the storeroom where the club supplies were kept. He checked to make sure no one was looking through the curtains separating the bar from the storeroom before jiggling one of the limestone blocks out of the wall. There was a space behind the block where Moody kept a green metal box. It contained two important assets: cash and a ledger book in which Moody's complicated dealings were recorded in a code of his own devising.

He took all the cash out of the box and counted it quickly. It came to slightly more than twenty thousand dollars. He put the bills back into the bulky manila envelope and stuffed the envelope inside his shirt. Then he replaced the green box and limestone block where they belonged.

Moody went back to the bar and called the corporal out of his office. "Give this guy whatever he wants to drink," he told John. "Then come in and see me."

When John had set up a couple of drinks for the corporal he joined Moody, who was on the phone calling in debts from soldiers who were overdue on their loans. He put the phone aside to tell John, "Someone's hit the division paymaster's office. They cleaned out the safe. The troops are going to bleed for money tomorrow."

"The corporal told me about it. Some job. How much you got on hand?"

"About twenty thousand. I hope to put together another five before morning. We should be able to loan out every cent between now and the time it takes them to bring a new payroll in here. We can make maybe ten thousand in interest this month. You'll have to help me handle the action tomorrow."

"Sure," John said. "I wonder who pulled that job?"

"I don't know," Moody grinned. "But they sure did me a favor."

The sun had not yet risen over the limestone ridges when the CQ stepped into the noncom wing to turn on the overhead lights and blow his whistle.

Terrio sat bolt upright. "Sweet Christ! Turn off those lights, you asshole!"

"Reveille!" the CQ shouted back, delighted to have drawn a reaction from someone. "Drop your cocks and grab your socks!"

Ryan rolled over. "Shut up, Terrio. You want that moron to get the idea you aren't used to reveille?"

Scratching himself under the arms, Terrio looked around blearily. "I forgot where I was." He picked up his pillow and threw it at Hazlitt. "Get up, you farmer. Reveille."

Hazlitt came awake with a series of groans and twitches. Terrio threw back Hazlitt's blankets and Ryan shook his shoulder. They went downstairs together in their shorts and shower sandals and waited in line for empty shower stalls. The water was hot and the chatter in the latrine loud. As he slowly came fully awake, Ryan began considering their plan for the day. If everything went perfectly they'd be out of Fort Riley by early afternoon. If not, the job they'd pulled would rate them a big welcome back at Leavenworth.

After showering they elbowed their way to three adjoining washbasins to shave.

"Thirty minutes to shit, shine and shave," Hazlitt chirped. "I don't by God know if I can do it that fast anymore. They gave us forty-five minutes back in the jar."

"Keep your voice down." Ryan warned. He always had to remind Hazlitt of that. It was annoying, but on the other hand Hazlitt's perpetual good cheer had made a lot of rotten mornings halfway bearable over the years.

Terrio cut himself shaving and swore for ten minutes. They barely had time to get back upstairs, make their bunks, dress in fatigues and combat boots, and fall out in front of the building for reveille. Noncoms assembled in the front rank, SP/3 and below in the rear. There were about fifty men present for reveille. Only eight, including Ryan, Hazlitt, and Terrio, were noncoms.

A graying, grizzled sergeant took reveille. "Good morning, gentlemens," he called before beginning to read off the name of every man currently waiting orders in the replacement company. Ryan, Terrio, and Hazlitt, each answered with a loud "Present!" when the phony names on their orders were called. One man didn't answer, a Pfc Hart.

"Hart!" the sergeant called. "Pfc Hart!" He glared around. "We got an AWOL here? Gentlemens, an AWOL don't look good on my morning report. Hart, you'd better speak up if you're here. If you're not, you'd better talk up anyway." Another glare. "Okay. Pfc Hart is AWOL."

After calling the roster the sergeant said, "I got a few announcements, gentlemens. First, someone's been leaving paper towels in the urinals every morning. The company commander's pissed off about that, gentlemens. And when he's pissed off, he don't approve no Class A passes. So whoever's stopping up the urinals with paper towels better get himself squared away.

"Next, there'll be a special inspection

right after chow this morning. All personnel will stand by their bunks. That includes permanent replacement company bodies as well as you transients."

Ryan exchanged glances with Terrio and Hazlitt. There was no question in their minds about the purpose of this particular inspection.

"Next," the sergeant continued loudly, "the company commander has noticed that some of you transients ain't stopping to salute the flag at recall every afternoon. Now I'll remind you gentlemens that in this man's army we have recall every day at seventeen thirty hours. That's when the flag's brought down, and you can all hear the bugle over the post loudspeaker system. You're supposed to stop whatever the hell you're doing, gentlemens, if you're out of doors, and salute the flag. We do that every day of the year. That's—" He paused as he pondered an important point. "That's three hundred and forty days a year!"

A few people snickered but the sergeant didn't notice. After one or two other announcements the formation fell out for chow.

"I could eat the bark off a gum tree," Hazlitt declared.

"That's what you're liable to get in this mess hall," Terrio warned. They ate quickly, Terrio avoiding the mess sergeant's eye. When they were leaving, though, the mess sergeant zeroed in on him. Terrio brushed him off by agreeing to sign on as his number two cook.

Then they went to their bunks and waited for inspection.

"Anybody know what this inspection is about?" one of the noncoms asked.

"Danged if I know," Hazlitt said. There were times when Ryan positively loved Hazlitt's air of country innocence.

A few minutes later an infantry captain burst into the barracks with a sergeant first class at his elbow.

"Ten-*hut!*" Terrio barked.

"At ease," the captain answered. He was a youngish officer, dressed in fatigues and carrying a clipboard. "I'm going to inspect your personal belongings and equipment. Open your lockers and stand by."

Everyone followed the captain's instructions. He inspected Hazlitt's locker first.

"Where you coming in from, soldier?"

"Scofield Barracks, sir."

"Dump the contents of that duffel bag on your bunk. The rest of you men do the same."

Hazlitt and the others obliged.

"Where were you last night, Corporal?"

"What time, sir?"

The captain had sagging blue pouches under his eyes. He'd obviously been making inspections since well before dawn.

"Say from twenty-two hundred to one hundred hours."

"Right here, sir. Sacking in."

"You didn't leave the barracks at all last night?"

"Yes, sir. I had a beer at the PX canteen a little earlier."

The captain grunted and went through the motions of inspecting Hazlitt's gear, though it was obvious there was no part of any army payroll there. He spent about three minutes with each man.

When Ryan was questioned he asked what this was all about.

"A robbery here on the post," the captain answered. He seemed to relax, letting some of his tension and fatigue drain off. "Someone took the division payroll last night. I'm afraid you men won't be paid today, if you take your pay in cash."

Ryan, Terrio, and Hazlitt made appropriately disgusted faces along with the others.

"Any idea who did it, sir?" Ryan asked.

"Hell no! That's why we're having a junk-on-the-bunk inspection, Sergeant. Between you and me we won't find the money at Riley. The men who robbed this post last night were pros. They're long gone."

Ryan couldn't resist one more question. "This must be a tough blow for the post commander, sir."

The captain almost stifled a quick smile, but not quite. "He's climbing the walls. Just climbing those GI walls."

When the captain was gone Hazlitt whispered to Ryan, "And you say I talk too damn much."

The rest of the morning dragged. They were waiting for the noon assembly. Traditionally, soldiers with no specific duty to pull begin their weekends after being dismissed from the noon formation on Saturday. Their plan was to hang around the replacement center all morning, collect passes at noon, change into the civilian clothes they had brought with them, and fade back into civilian life.

It didn't work out quite that way. About mid-morning the sergeant who took reveille came prowling. "You there, sarge," he called, motioning to Ryan. "I got a detail for you."

Ryan followed him downstairs where he found a half dozen lower ranks waiting.

"Take these here gentlemens over to the motor pool and draw a deuce-and-a-half. Run it down to division supply and draw twelve more bunks and mattresses. Here's the requisition."

There was nothing to do but carry out the detail. Ryan turned to the six men. "Fall in!" He formed them up in a rank of two's and marched them off. It felt strange to be leading a detail again. Even a grubby little detail like this one. He rather enjoyed it. The motor pool where the two-and-a-half-ton trucks were kept was about a mile away, out near Highway 24. As he marched his detail in that direction, he could hear a cacophony of auto horns. By the time they reached the motor pool, Ryan could see the long line of cars strung out on the highway.

The provost marshal had of course thrown up a roadblock after the robbery. Ryan had expected that. All cars leaving the post were being stopped and searched, causing an enormous traffic jam up and down the eight miles of highway running through Fort Riley. There were certainly other roadblocks throughout the surrounding counties. If they had tried to make a run with the money right after the robbery, they would have been nailed within hours. Allowing the army to ship the money out of Fort Riley while they holed up in the replacement center had been the right move.

The men in Ryan's detail were walking on each other's heels while they rubbernecked the traffic jam. "Eyes foward!" he barked. "Get in step there. You're marching like a bunch of goddam sailors."

At the motor pool he drew a deuce-and-a-half, put five of the men in the rear of the truck, and let a Pfc wheel the truck down to division supply to pick up the bunks and mattresses. They returned to the replacement center, off-loaded, and Ryan sent the driver back to the motor pool to return the truck.

He looked around for his partners and found Hazlitt supervising a detail of three Pfcs who were cleaning up the day room.

Hazlitt drew him aside. "Looks like we aren't getting out of here at noon."

"Why not?"

"One of the cooks took sick this morning. Probably from eating his own chow, Terrio says. Anyways, Terrio was grabbed and put to work in the kitchen. He won't be off duty till two o'clock at best. He has to supervise the cleanup after noon chow."

Ryan thought about it. "That's not so bad. There's such a traffic jam on Highway 24 that we wouldn't get off the post very fast even if we picked up passes at noon. They have to take off the roadblocks pretty soon or the whole post will be paralyzed. Everyone's going off duty at noon and half the post will head for town."

"Let's hope," Hazlitt said.

When the mess hall opened for chow, Ryan was one of the first in the dining room. He was curious to watch Terrio work and somewhat worried that he might have forgotten what he knew about cooking.

He was wrong. The chow was a hundred percent better than the day before. Salisbury steak and french fries were the entrée, and they were cooked just right. Ryan spotted Terrio bustling around the kitchen. The cook's white uniform he had drawn from the supply room was limp with sweat.

Standing over a KP who was working pots and pans at a big double sink, Terrio was yelling, "You gotta change the water more often. I told you that already. And get those hands down in there! Don't be scared of hot water. Your hands won't be red for more than a day or two."

The cook who had recruited Terrio was standing at the end of the serving line, his brow folded into a deep frown.

"Looks like good chow today," Ryan said to him.

"Yeah," the cook responded gloomily. "But he's turning my mess hall inside out." He sniffed noisily. "Claimed I don't know how to cook salisbury steak. Said I use too much grease for the french fries, too. A real smart ass." His eyes widened. "You know what? I don't think I'm going to fix it for that bastard Martelli to transfer over here after all. Let him work his balls off over to the Food Service School!"

"He'll be real sorry," Ryan murmured.

He found a rear table and sat down alone. Terrio's chow tasted fine. He really was a top cook and mess sergeant, as well as a first-class burglar. Terrio had always been a puzzle to him. The tight-mouthed, tough Italian would never tell him how a burglar from the North

Side of Chicago had come to join the army in the first place. Ryan guessed that he'd been on the run from someone, though the picture of Terrio running away from any kind of fight was hard to believe. He did know that once Terrio joined up he'd gone into cooking because he liked good food and figured that was the only way to get it in the army. Terrio said he had planned to serve his three-year hitch and go back to Chicago, and would have if he hadn't tangled with a chickenshit second lieutenant.

During one of the last Viet Cong offensives Terrio had set up a field kitchen at an advance fire base so the men would get at least one hot meal a day. He was up at the fire base when the enemy began dropping rockets on the position. Terrio was determined to serve his hot meal anyway, rockets or no rockets. But a green lieutenant commanding the fire base panicked and ordered Terrio to pack up his kitchen and get out. Then the officer climbed into the cab of the truck and went out with him, claiming later that Terrio was too scared to move and had to be taken out. When Terrio heard that story, he looked up the lieutenant and gave him a beating that put him in a rear-area hospital for five months. The result was a court-martial for Terrio and a forty-two-month sentence in the federal prison at Leavenworth.

"Man, am I hungry!" Hazlitt slid in next to Ryan with a tray piled to the point of overload. "That Terrio can cook, babe. Look at this chow!" He dug in with his usual gusto.

Ryan smiled but didn't watch. The food

was flying too fast and in too many directions. Where Terrio was a rather mysterious figure, Hazlitt was an open book. A disorderly, loud, and food-stained book. Hazlitt's problem was his good nature. As much as he knew about guns, he didn't really like to use them to shoot people. On one occasion in Vietnam Hazlitt's tank commander ordered him to blast a hut with his tank cannon and Hazlitt refused. He thought he had just seen a little girl of three or four scamper into the hut. Hazlitt's sergeant ordered him a second time to fire at the hut. Hazlitt refused again. His sergeant threatened him with court-martial and radioed another tank fifty yards to the left to do the job. Instinctively, Hazlitt swung his tank gun around and fired a ninety-millimeter shell at the muzzle of the other tank's cannon. It hit, smashing the tank's gun to pieces without injuring anyone inside. That's how Hazlitt had earned his five-year sentence in Leavenworth.

When he first met them Ryan thought they were the most screwed-up pair he'd ever seen. And they considered him the coldest piece of ice in the cooler. He asked to be put in another cell. The request was refused, and over the years Ryan had become grateful for that refusal. Terrio, despite his foul disposition, was a rock. Absolutely dependable. Hazlitt could brighten any day with his laugh. Gradually Ryan had emerged as their leader. Managing people and making the right decisions fast came naturally to him. Terrio and Hazlitt, along with Ryan's wife, Julie, were also the only ones who had ever discovered that Ryan used his quiet aloofness to hide a rather painful shyness acquired in the orphanage where he was raised.

Terrio popped out of the kitchen just then and began inspecting the trays the KPs had just washed and inserted in a rack at the front of the serving line. He ran his fingers over each tray, pulling out about one out of three and tossing them back into the tiny room where two KPs were operating the dishwashing machine. "Greasy!" he'd snap, throwing a tray. "Greasy . . . food particles . . . soap still on this one . . . grease . . . greasy . . . food . . . dirty . . . clean it again . . . food particles . . . grease . . . greasy . . ."

The cook who had originally begged Terrio to transfer to his mess hall stood on the serving line with a red face. Finally he walked over to Terrio and began talking to him rapidly but quietly. Their voices gradually grew louder. Ryan heard the cook saying, "Trying to run my mess hall for me. I been here two years and . . ."

"It's a goddam pest hole!" Terrio fumed. "You gotta make those KPs work. You gotta go easy on the grease and spend a little more time over the stove."

"Don't tell me how to cook!" the mess sergeant yelled, reaching for a heavy gravy ladle. Ryan jumped up from his table and headed for the serving line, but it was too late. The cook swung the ladle at Terrio's head. Terrio smiled and raised his arm to block the blow. The ladle bounced off his wrist—*thwang*—and Terrio winced. Then he grabbed the cook's white jacket. For a second Ryan hoped Terrio was only going to push the stupid bastard away. No such luck. He was making sure the cook couldn't back away or fall to the floor while he worked him over. Terrio hit the mess sergeant twice in the face with his right hand. The cook's head snapped like a gymnasium punching bag. Ryan had seen Terrio dish out that treatment before. By the second blow the cook's face resembled the bloody slabs of fresh meat that came into the kitchen. He slumped but was not allowed to slide to the floor. Terrio hit him two more times, picking spots over the cook's left eye and along the right side of his face that were still pink instead of red.

"Let him go!" Ryan said, finally reaching Terrio and grabbing his right arm.

"Sure." Terrio took his left hand away from the man's chest. The cook fell into the serving line, scattering pots of peas and knocking over long trays of salisbury steak. Lying there on the floor among the food the cook looked like some new kind of garnish for a huge chef's salad.

"Nice work," Ryan said in his ear. "Now how are we going to get you off this post?"

An expression of regret crossed Terrio's face for only a second, replaced immediately by a surly anger. "Nobody hits me."

An officer pushed through the crowd that had surged from their tables to watch the fight. "What's going on here?" He pointed to the mess sergeant on the floor. "Who did that?"

Terrio met his eyes. "I did. Sir."

The officer, a captain, was evidently the commander of the replacement company. Ryan looked at his decorations and saw immediately that he was too good a man to be shuffling replacements. He stepped forward and said, "I think I can explain this, sir."

"Well?" The captain looked him over.

"This man," Ryan continued, pointed at Terrio, "was pulled on duty this morning to replace another cook who went on sick call. Apparently the mess sergeant didn't like the fact that this new man put out a better line of chow than he does. He tried to slug this new cook with a gravy ladle. I saw it and I'm sure some of the other men did, too. And I can vouch for the fact that the chow is a hundred percent better than it was yesterday."

"That's the truth, sir," Hazlitt piped up in his most sincere voice.

"A lot better today," someone else put in.

". . . my guts out last night," another voice boomed.

". . . raw chicken again."

The captain's eyes flicked from man to man. Ryan could see him weighing decisions. The only thing the commander of a repple-depple has to do is shuffle paper and keep people from getting into trouble. Bringing charges against Terrio might put a black mark on his own record for not being able to run a quiet outfit like a replacement center without trouble. Maybe he'd never command another line outfit. Ryan saw the decision in his eyes before the officer spoke.

"You two," he said, picking two men at random, "get that mess sergeant off the floor and carry him to his bunk. You." He pointed at Terrio. "Clean all this up. Report to me at nine hundred hours on Monday morning for special duty. And feed the rest of the troops."

He turned on his heel and stalked off. Terrio flashed Ryan and Hazlitt one of his fierce frowns and shrugged his shoulders. "He asked for it."

"You're a danged menace," Hazlitt said cheerfully.

They went back to their tables and finished their meals. After chow Ryan and Hazlitt went upstairs to change to civilian clothes. Most of the replacements had already changed. There were a lot of people milling around the front of the PX, which Ryan could see from the second-floor veranda. They were broke and wouldn't be paid today because of the robbery. It would take two or three days for the Federal Reserve Bank to scrape up the cash and get it to Fort Riley.

After dressing, they gave their bunks and lockers a thorough wipedown. It wouldn't do to leave fingerprints around the barracks. Terrio joined them after his kitchen cleanup.

"Did you leave any fingerprints down in the mess hall?" Ryan asked.

"Nah." Terrio stripped off his clothes and tossed them into the locker. "I was careful. But I need a shower before we leave."

"Go on. Take your civvies with you and dress downstairs. I'll wipe down your area."

Ten minutes later they met Terrio on the first floor and collected weekend passes from the company clerk. It was standard procedure to give all noncoms a weekend pass from noon Saturday to reveille on Monday morning. No one would realize they had disappeared until then. The uniforms and other equipment they had brought in were abandoned in the locker upstairs. No fingerprints around and no identifying marks on the regulation GI clothing.

"See you guys in Kansas City," Hazlitt said outside. He turned and began walking to the Greyhound bus stop on Highway 24. Terrio went down to the station to wait for the three P.M. train. Ryan caught the local bus that goes through Fort Riley between Junction City to the west and Manhattan to the east. From Manhattan, Kansas, he would take a Trailways bus into Kansas City.

The local bus was stopped before it left Fort Riley and searched by two MPs. Each man's pass was examined and matched with his army ID card. Ryan carried a forged ID card that satisfied the harassed MPs. One soldier carrying a duffel bag full of laundry had to dump it out on the floor of the bus during the search. It wasn't until the bus finally left Fort Riley that Ryan began to relax. He also realized for the first time since the robbery that he was rich.

WEDNESDAY JULY 5

It took four days for Moody's loan-shark business to slack off. In those four days he loaned out twenty-two thousand dollars at his usual rates, twenty-five percent per month. A new payroll came in from Kansas City on the third under heavy guard. The payroll was immediately distributed to the company commanders. The troops were all paid by evening.

That night most of the money Moody had loaned out came back to him from men who now had their full month's pay. Even so, they had to give Moody the minimum twenty-five percent interest. So by Wednesday morning

Moody had stashed twenty-four thousand dollars back in the green box behind the limestone block, with another thirty-five hundred due by the next payday.

The month of July was shaping up very satisfactorily. He expected the take from liquor suppliers, bingo games, entertainers, and other sources to add another five thousand dollars to the fifty-five hundred in interest now due him. Even with a twenty-percent cut for John and ten percent for General Hanson, it would be the best month of the year so far.

John came into Moody's office and said, "You're wanted over to division headquarters. Conference Room A."

Moody looked up from the *Army Times*, which carried a long story on the Fort Riley robbery. "General Hanson wants to see me?"

"I don't know. It wasn't Hanson's aide on the phone; just some guy who said you're supposed to report to Conference Room A, division headquarters. I asked who was calling but he'd already hung up."

"I suppose the General had one of his flunkies call." Moody put aside the *Army Times*. "He doesn't like to have too much direct contact with me. I ain't exactly his type."

The previous month Moody's operations had taken in a gross of six thousand dollars. He'd netted half that after expenses. There were three other loan sharks on the post whose total business grossed less than Moody's, plus scores of little "five for tenners" who seldom had more than two or three hundred dollars out at a time.

General Hanson took his ten percent from

the three other big operators, as well as Moody. By Moody's estimate, the General raked in about a thousand a month from the four of them. Moody knew, too, that Hanson had his own little scams going. He was sure the General had been tied in with a black-market operation in Vietnam, for one thing. There were other unusual aspects to the General's background besides. His association with the Phoenix program, for instance. Moody hadn't believed those stories until he'd checked them out thoroughly.

"I'm going over to division headquarters then," Moody told John. He took a plain white envelope out of his desk and slipped six hundred dollars inside.

When he pulled up to DIV HQ and parked his jeep Moody saw that things had changed since the robbery. There were now two MPs guarding the entrance to the headquarters building. He found another on the second-floor landing as well as two armed men walking patrol in the hallways.

He looked into Conference Room A. General Hanson wasn't there, but a civilian in a business suit was shuffling through a stack of papers in an attaché case laid out on the long walnut table.

"Sorry," Moody said. "I thought I was supposed to meet someone here."

He started to back out but the civilian said, "Sergeant Moody? Come in."

Moody looked at the initial on the door and confirmed that this was Conference Room A. He went in hesitantly.

The civilian came around the table and

waved at one of the chairs. "Sit down, please."

Moody felt a rumble in his bowels. His instincts told him this man was trouble. He studied the man carefully as he acceded to the request—or was it an order?—that he be seated.

The civilian wore a gray off-the-rack suit that looked several years old. He was a short man whose rimless glasses tended to enlarge his eyes and make his face mouselike. There was a determination to his bureaucrat's seediness, though. Moody pegged him as the type of high-level government employee who cloaks his power in a kind of personal anonymity.

"John Saunders," he said, extending his hand.

"Master Sergeant Joseph Moody," he replied, shaking the little man's hand. It fitted into his own huge palm like the hand of a toy doll, but Saunders' grip was tight and aggressive.

Hanson came in accompanied by an aide, a captain whose name Moody could never recall. He seemed surprised to see Moody but he obviously expected Saunders.

"Mr. Saunders?"

"That's right." Saunders scurried across the room with birdlike hops. "Thank you for meeting with me on such short notice, General Hanson."

"Quite all right, Mr. Saunders. I'm anxious to learn what progress you've made."

"Let's sit down then," Saunders suggested. He waved the General into a chair with the same gesture he'd used with Moody. The General either failed to notice the proprietary attitude Saunders took toward the conference room, or decided not to notice it. Moody didn't see how the General could help noticing the way Saunders occupied the place at the head of the table. Whatever this meeting was about, Saunders was running it and wanted both of them to appreciate that.

The General, however, was preoccupied. He searched the room with a frown and turned to his aide. "Where's the coffee, Captain? I told you to have a pot of coffee here for the meeting."

"I'm sorry, sir," the aide apologized. "I did call the BOQ mess and order coffee. Rolls, too," he added hopefully, as if that extra thoughtfulness might partly atone for the missing pot of coffee.

"Well, where is it?" the General demanded, cracking his swagger stick down on the conference table.

The aide was beginning to sweat. "Perhaps they sent it to the wrong conference room. I'll look in the other rooms, sir." He hurried out.

General Hanson shrugged his beautifully tailored shoulders, making the twin stars on each shoulder wink in the filtered light from the windows. "I'm awfully sorry, Mr. Saunders."

Saunders had fidgeted through the missing coffee debate and now vigorously rejected the whole idea of coffee. "It doesn't matter, General. Really. Please have a seat."

Hanson sat down and regarded Moody. "I don't understand why Sergeant Moody has been asked to this meeting, Mr. Saunders. He certainly had nothing to do with the robbery. He would have been recognized by his size alone." Hanson laughed at the sheer absurdity of the idea.

"The robbery?" Saunders echoed. "I'm sorry, General. I'm not here about the robbery."

"I thought the Justice Department sent you down here," the General said. He leaned forward. "Aren't you the FBI agent who's been put in charge of this case? I was told a Mr. Saunders from the Justice Department wanted to interview me today."

"I'm not with the FBI," Saunders assured him. "Though I am an attorney with the Justice Department. I've come down here to serve you and Sergeant Moody with subpoenas to testify before the House Armed Services Committee in Washington in September."

"Subpoenas!" Hanson roared.

I knew it, Moody said to himself. This little man is grade-A trouble.

With a magician's "presto" flourish, Saunders produced two impressive packets of paper and pushed them across the table. One to General Hanson and the other to Moody.

"What am I supposed to testify about?" the General raged. "Am I to be crucified because a gang of thieves stole my division payroll?" He swept up the subpoena and opened it, studying the seven-point type with angry eyes. "What's this all about?"

Moody didn't touch his subpoena. He wouldn't give Saunders the satisfaction. Instead, he drew a cigar out of his breast pocket and slid off the wrapper with an elaborate charade of calm. Inside he was as upset as General Hanson. He had always known this might happen, but he had expected a warning. A phone call from a friend at the Department of the Army. An unsigned letter or telegram. The fact that not one of the high-ranking officers and important noncoms he'd done favors for had seen fit to warn him rankled more than the subpoena itself.

"The House Armed Services Committee is conducting an investigation into corruption in the military services," Saunders said. "I've been directing the investigation myself, General."

"Corruption!" General Hanson's right arm rose convulsively and for a moment Moody thought he was going to strike Saunders. So did Saunders. His jaw muscles flexed but he made no move away from Hanson. In fact, Saunders seemed to be welcoming a blow as *de facto* proof of guilt on the General's part. "I've served twenty-six years in the army without a single blemish on my record," Hanson raged on. "I don't need a bunch of politicians to remind me of my duties or badger me into retirement. Just what are your Committee's charges?"

"The Committee has no charges at the moment," Saunders answered promptly. "They have simply asked our department to gather information so they can ask you questions about—"

"What kind of questions?" Hanson waved his swagger stick. "Ask them now."

You're a fool, Moody thought. *Shut your mouth.* He could see that Hanson was starting to panic. The General had some dumb idea he could squelch the subpoena by answering questions put to him by Saunders.

"I couldn't do that," Saunders objected. "You have a right to legal counsel. I suggest you get yourself an attorney as soon as possible."

"I don't need an attorney," Hanson said with a laugh that, to Moody, had a touch of hysteria in it. "I've never done anything contrary to army regulations."

With a shrug, Saunders reached into his attaché case and drew out a blue folder. "I see no reason why I shouldn't give you an example of the kinds of questions you'll be asked next month." He consulted the blue folder, then looked at the General with the eyes of a practiced interrogator.

"Tell me, General, are you acquainted with a South Vietnamese national by the name of Trin Quon Lu?"

"No," Hanson replied vehemently. But both Moody and Saunders saw his mouth twitch a split second before he answered.

"Then you could not have had a business arrangement with this Trin Quon Lu during your recent tour of duty in Vietnam," Saunders continued.

"Of course not."

"You didn't accept a gift from this same man? A gift consisting of thirty shares of Xerox stock?"

"How could I?" the General said acidly. "I told you I've never heard of him."

"Then perhaps you can explain how those thirty shares of stock, originally issued to Mr.

Lu, came to be transferred to your brokerage account in Roanoke."

The General hesitated. He was clearly reaching for an answer. At last he said, "I occasionally buy or sell stock through a brokerage in Roanoke. Perhaps some shares bought for me through my broker were at one time owned by this man, Lu. I couldn't say. Perhaps Mr. Lu is in the stock and bond business himself."

Saunders allowed himself a smile. One a day, Moody guessed.

"Trin Quon Lu isn't in the brokerage business," Saunders said. "He's a black marketeer. Will you deny that you once issued an order exempting Mr. Lu's trucks from search on Highway 1 north of Saigon?"

"Of course I deny it! Why would I issue such an order?"

"That's one thing the congressmen will want to know. You see, General Hanson, we have a copy of that order."

He took one of the pieces of paper out of the blue folder and slid it across the table. Hanson snatched it up and looked at it suspiciously. The signature at the bottom resembled his. With a dawning horror he realized it was authentic. The incident recalled itself to him now. A blockhead of a captain had requested a written order to let Lu's trucks through his sector without being searched. Ordinarily he would never have committed such an order to writing. But the captain commanding that one insignificant roadblock had turned out to be one of those by-the-book types who insisted on it. The order was handwritten, scrawled across the back of a menu someone had produced at the roadside. It came back to Hanson now. His explanation had been that Lu was on an intelligence mission for the army. He had requested that the written order be destroyed after being complied with. For security reasons. How had Saunders gotten hold of it? Why had he submitted to that idiotic captain's request in the first place?

"This document is a forgery," Hanson said in a firm voice.

"Indeed?" Saunders reached across the table and plucked it from the General's hand. "In that case you won't want to soil your hands with it." He replaced it in the blue folder. "Another question then, General. Are you acquainted with a Robert Brannigan, president of the Empire Construction Company?"

"I've met him. Is that a crime?"

"Hardly. But have you ever taken gifts from him?"

"Not that I recall. He's bought me a drink now and then. Taken me to dinner. I've done the same for him."

"Did you intervene to help him win a contract to build the Forty-fourth Evacuation Hospital?"

"No!"

"Shortly after Brannigan's company received that contract did you accept a twenty-five-foot racing sloop from Brannigan?"

"No. I do own a racing sloop, but I paid for it myself."

"By cash or check?"

Hanson scowled. "I don't recall."

Saunders produced a photostat of a check. "You paid for it by check, General. For a ridiculously low sum. Five hundred dollars."

"Yes. I remember now."

Moody watched the General's hand tighten on his swagger stick. Saw the evasion in his eyes. You'll have to do better than that in the hearing room, he said to himself.

"Isn't five hundred dollars an awfully small sum for a twenty-five-foot racing sloop? An almost new craft at that?"

"It was in a terribly rundown condition," Hanson insisted. "The teak deck had badly rotted in spots. I had to replace most of it. And then the engine—the engine"—he stammered—"needed an overhaul. And the rigging was coming apart. . . ."

"That's not the information I have," Saunders interrupted. "The owner of the Southwind Marina in Virginia Beach says the boat was in perfect shape when you took title. I call your attention to the name of the payee on your check, General. The Thomas Plumbing and Heating Company. They were the previous owner of your sloop. Did you know that company is a wholly owned subsidiary of the Empire Construction Company?"

"No . . . I didn't know that."

"They didn't sell you a twenty-thousand-dollar sloop for five hundred dollars as a reward for your help in landing that hospital contract?"

"I told you. No."

"And what about the National Indemnity Corporation? Did you play any part in helping that company receive a contract to provide vending-machine services in the Fifth Army area?"

General Hanson opened his mouth, then shut it. He flashed Saunders the scowl he used to make field-grade officers cringe, but Saunders was a GS-17 and he hadn't cringed for anyone since he was a GS-9.

"And are you familiar with Aronaut Industries? They received a contract to provide dry-cleaning services at one of your former posts, Fort Hood, Texas. The president of that company has given us an affidavit stating that he provided a two-week cruise from Galveston through the Caribbean at his expense. He states that he did so in return for your help in securing that contract."

Again the General was silent. Unable to quell Saunders, he opted to ignore him.

Saunders shrugged and turned his attention to Moody. "Well, Sergeant. I assume from your silence that you aren't interested in answering any questions at this time."

Moody nodded slowly. His consistent refusal to take part in Saunders' meeting was grating on the little attorney. It pleased Moody to watch Saunders burn with the same frustration he had drawn from the General.

"Very well." Saunders stood and threw folders and documents into his briefcase. "I'll see you both in September. The date, time, and place are spelled out on the subpoenas. You won't be the only ones appearing, of course. I'm sure you'll find many good friends in the waiting room." He shoved the attaché case under his arm as if it were a football and straightened his glasses. "Until September then."

When he was gone General Hanson looked at Moody with an uncomprehending stare. "What does this mean, Sergeant?"

"It means," Moody answered with feeling, "that one of your brother officers or one of my brother NCOs got caught with his hand in the till and spilled everything he knows about how things work in the army to that smart little bastard Saunders. Saunders has been busy. It must have taken him and his staff a year to put all of it together."

"Why?" General Hanson demanded. "Why should he care? Why should he go after us like this?"

"Next year is an election year," Moody reminded him. "You know who the chairman of the House Armed Services Committee is, don't you?"

"Certainly. Congressman Ralph Barnes. But he's always been a friend of the army."

"That's right. But he wants his party's nomination for Vice President. This is his gimmick for getting his name before the public as a champion against corruption and wasteful spending. He'll nail us to the wall."

Hanson saw the logic immediately. He'd used similar ploys himself, conducting subtle campaigns to discredit particular senior officers in order to win a promotion or a better command. Now all the advantages of rank and position he had worked and politicked for seemed to mean nothing. Losing his payroll was bad enough; he realized he would never receive another promotion even if the thieves were captured and the money recovered. Going before the House Armed Services Committee would be even worse. They had so much information about him! He'd have to retire. And probably not as a major general. He'd be lucky to retire at a bird colonel's pay. He thought of his monthly expenses. The house at Roanoke, soaking up money. His horses. The cars His daughter's tuition at Bennington. His wife's vacations and "long weekends" in Bermuda and Acapulco. The bitch! Not a postcard all summer, but the canceled checks came in fast enough.

"I found it, sir!"

General Hanson's thoughts were pulled back to the conference room by his aide, who came panting in with a heavy tray stacked with cups, breakfast rolls, and a coffee urn.

"They delivered it to Conference Room C. I gave them hell about that, sir. I really did." The aide looked around for Saunders. "I wonder if Mr. Saunders takes his coffee black or with cream."

General Hanson's habit of command returned with a vengeance. He stood and tucked his swagger stick under his arm. "I've got a direct order for you, Captain. I'm ordering you to sit down and drink that entire pot of putried BOQ coffee and eat every one of those soggy breakfast rolls yourself. Then report to the Adjutant General. Tell him I want a different aide assigned to me and that I want you posted to the greenest basic training company on Custer Hill. I don't want to see your stupid face until you're at least a lieutenant colonel;

which means, Captain, that I *never* want to see it."

He executed a smart about-face and stalked out.

"What did I do?" the aide pleaded to Moody.

Despite his own gloom, Moody chuckled. "You found the coffee, sir."

Moody went to his jeep and drove back to the NCO Club. He walked in just as John was taking a long distance call for him. "Ben Lang at Fort Lewis," John told him.

He took the call in his office. "I know why you're calling, Ben. I got a subpoena, too."

"Who talked?" Master Sergeant Ben Lang's gravelly voice asked. "They know more about me than my wife does."

"I don't know who talked," Moody said. "But I don't think it was one of us. I think it was an officer. They've just got too damned much on the post commander here. Only an officer could have given them some of those leads."

Lang growled. "I always said never trust an officer."

"You always said that, Ben," Moody agreed.

"What do we do now?"

"Get a good lawyer, Ben."

Moody took his own advice. He put in a long-distance call to Charles Eliot Conrad, one of the best lawyers in Washington. Conrad took his call, and when Moody told him who he was Conrad laughed and said, "I thought I'd be hearing from some army people this week. I've been picking up rumors about a House investigation into military corruption."

"Wish I'd heard that rumor," Moody grumbled. "I've got three months' accrued leave coming. I'd have taken it and holed up somewhere."

"You've been subpoenaed to testify?"

"I have."

"Have you been doing something unmilitary, Sergeant?"

"Depends on your point of view, Mr. Conrad. Isn't that what you lawyers specialize in? Helping people find points of view that benefit your clients?"

"That's right, Sergeant." Charles Eliot Conrad's courtroom baritone lowered. "Do you want me to represent you?"

"Yes."

"Fine. I understand the hearings begin in mid-September. I'll want to see you here in Washington next month. Between now and then I'll find out exactly what kind of testimony the government expects to draw from you. When we meet we'll formulate a strategy to deal with the government's charges."

"Sounds good," Moody said. "Anything else?"

"My fee, of course. I'll need a fifteen-thousand-dollar retainer."

Moody knew that Charles Eliot Conrad was expensive. He was resigned to that. But he wanted to know just what he was buying. "How much of a defense do I get for my money, Counselor?"

"I'll help you prepare your testimony and represent you during the hearings. If the government decides to prosecute you following the hearings, or if the investigation concerning you continues beyond your initial appearance before the committee, I'll require additional fees."

"That pretty much lays it on the line."

Conrad's laugh, a familiar sound on television talk shows, was unembarrassed. "You'll find that my clients are seldom prosecuted and never convicted. That's why my fees are high."

"At those prices you should give written guarantees."

"Personally I'd be delighted to do just that. But the bar association is awfully stuffy."

"Okay," Moody said. "I'll mail you a check today."

"Good," Conrad said. "I'll get to work as soon as I receive it. Meanwhile, I'd suggest you put your financial records in a safe place. Don't discuss the investigation with anyone, especially the press. And don't communicate with any other army people who have been subpoenaed."

"Got it. Anything else?"

"Yes. When you come to Washington wear your best uniform and all your medals."

Moody felt better about his chances once he had talked to Conrad, but it was clear that life would never be the same after the hearings. He was sure he could avoid prison or court-martial, but everyone's eyes would be on him afterwards. It would be impossible to carry on his enterprises under that kind of public scrutiny.

He went to his green box and took out

fifteen thousand dollars. He gave the money to John and told him to get a cashier's check in his name and mail it to Conrad.

Afterwards Moody went over the coded accounts in his ledger. He used a simple book code of his own design, inspired by a short course in cryptography he had once dozed through at NCO School. It amused Moody to use the Uniform Code of Military Justice as the book on which his code was based. He totaled up his cash assets, including debts he knew he could collect within thirty days' time. That came to sixty-five thousand dollars, not including the fifteen thousand he had just given to John for the lawyer.

Moody sighed and went over the figures again. They came out the same. He supposed he would have to put out at least another fifteen thousand to Conrad before he was clear of this mess. That would leave him perhaps fifty thousand, plus the mobile home. Moody had a bunk somewhere at division headquarters that he had never slept in. His home was a forty-foot trailer parked in a mobile home park in Junction City. He had paid fifteen thousand for the trailer and almost as much to outfit it. It was furnished with a built-in bar and stereo system, furniture from Sloane's, a custom bathroom with marble and gold fittings, and an outsized closet to hold all his clothes. The master bedroom was filled completely by a specially built water bed that alone had set him back a thousand dollars. But he'd never find anyone to take the mobile home off his hands for what he had put into it. He knew he'd be lucky to get twenty thousand for it.

"Shit!"

It made him feel better to swear. All soldiers feel better when they swear. He swore again.

"Shit!"

"Joe?"

Moody looked up. Bo Evans stood there, wearing his customary foul-smelling sweat shirt and faded khaki pants.

"What is it, Bo? I'm busy right now."

"It's about that guy, Joe."

"What guy?"

"Dan Ryan. The one you wanted me to work over."

"Ryan. Yeah. How'd it go with him? I almost forgot about it."

It didn't work out, Joe."

"How do you mean?"

"Ryan wasn't at the replacement center."

"Sure he was. I saw him Friday night. He said he was just stopping over. The replacement center's the only place on the post where a transient can draw his pay."

"But he never did. Joe. He never signed in there."

"Huh." That was puzzling, but Moody had too many other things on his mind. "Didn't I give you some money for the job? I'll take that back."

Bo Evans had been hoping Moody would tell him to keep it for his trouble, so he returned the money with a slight resentment. Surely Moody would at least cancel his debt.

"What about the money I owed you, Joe? I figure I earned the canceled debt anyway."

"I don't," Moody said, staring at him coldly.

Evans tried to return the stare but couldn't. Moody's eyes seemed especially dark today. He cleared his throat. "Okay, Joe. But it wasn't my fault Ryan wasn't there. I did my part."

"You did nothing."

"I'm sorry you feel that way, Joe." Evans decided to make one more try at getting his tab canceled, banking on Moody's well-known passion for acquiring inside information. "I did find out something over at the replacement company, though. The feds are keeping a lid on it but the company clerk's a buddy of mine. Those three guys who stole the payroll bunked at the replacement center Friday night."

"What? How did they do that?"

"They checked into the company with phony orders Friday afternoon. Hit the paymaster's office that night. And drifted off the post Saturday afternoon with Class A passes. No one realized who they were until they were reported AWOL and the units they were supposed to join sent their orders back. No one ever heard of those guys. Phony names and serial numbers. Forged orders. The works. What a deal, huh?"

"Yeah. Those guys must have known the army pretty well." Moody forgot his own problems as he pondered the beauty and simplicity of the plan.

"Sure they did. Ex-GIs, that's what they were."

Moody thought about Ryan. He recalled the way Ryan had kept him talking about himself. He remembered Ryan's nervous laugh. That didn't make sense. Ryan had the nerves of a burglar. Maybe a real burglar?

"Any idea what those three looked like?"

Evans repeated the brief descriptions the company clerk had given him. One of the three could have been Ryan.

"That's good information, Bo. Thanks. I like to know what's going on at Riley, so I guess you did something for me after all. I will forget that little debt. And when John gets back tell him I said to set up a couple of drinks for you."

"Thanks, Joe." Bo Evans headed for the bar like a paper clip drawn to a magnet.

Moody leaned back. The more he thought about the idea of Dan Ryan stealing an army payroll the less likely it seemed. If ever there was a career soldier it was Dan Ryan. A sharp soldier. So how come he was still only a sergeant first class? That story about Ryan tangling with a West Pointer and losing a stripe was bullshit or he couldn't smell it anymore. And if he was passing through Riley, why hadn't he signed in at the replacement center? And wasn't Ryan paying a lot of attention to the MP guard mount Friday evening?

Well, it should be easy enough to check out Dan Ryan through the personnel section at the Pentagon. Moody was thinking about who to call in Washington when his phone rang. It was General Hanson.

"Sergeant, I believe you—ah—forgot

something when we met earlier today. You're rather late with—ah—your—ah . . ."

"Forgot something?" Moody felt the envelope containing the General's six hundred dollars bulging in his hip pocket. "That's right, I did. I'm sorry, sir. I'll send it over right away."

"Just give it to the orderly at my quarters, Sergeant. Discreetly, of course."

"Certainly, sir. In a plain sealed envelope."

"Very well, Thank you, Sergeant."

Moody put down the phone and stared at it in amazement. "You are one greedy son of a bitch, General."

THURSDAY JULY 6

"When do you figure?" Hazlitt asked.

"Today," Ryan answered. "Tomorrow at the latest."

They were sitting in one of the furnished apartments they had rented in Kansas City, waiting for the duffel bags to be delivered. Terrio was in the other apartment on the opposite side of the city. Hazlitt traveled back and forth between the two places delivering food. No one wanted to risk leaving the apartments uncovered during normal delivery hours. Between errands Hazlitt dropped in on porno movie houses.

Ryan unwrapped the cheeseburger Hazlitt had brought him and bit into it. "Not bad."

"You think so? Terrio didn't like his. He threw it at me."

"He's getting nervous just sitting around."

"So am I," Hazlitt declared. "If the feds figure out how we got that money out of Fort Riley, they'll be showing up on our doorsteps."

The phone rang and Hazlitt jumped a foot. Ryan answered it. Terrio said, "Mine came."

"When?" Ryan asked.

"Just now! A minute ago. Should I bring it over?"

"No," Ryan said firmly. "Stay there. If the delivery guy sees you in both places he might get curious. I'll call you when the second one arrives."

"Should I open mine and make sure the money's there?"

"No. Just hang loose."

Terrio swore and hung up.

Ryan pushed the cheeseburger aside and looked at his watch. Two o'clock. The other duffel bag should be arriving soon, depending on how many other stops the truck had to make around town.

A little before three o'clock the front-door bell rang.

"Go into the bedroom," Ryan told Hazlitt.

"I smell money," Hazlitt grinned, picking up the litter of their lunch and taking it with him.

Ryan answered the door. A Railway Express driver stood there with a clipboard in his hand and the duffel bag at his feet.

"John Wiley?"

"That's right."

"Delivery for you. Sign here."

Ryan's heart was pounding as he took the clipboard and signed a pink form, making his signature as illegible as possible.

"Feel good to be out of the service?" the driver asked while Ryan signed.

"Sure does."

The driver sighed. "I sometimes wish I'd stayed in for twenty."

He left and Ryan dragged the bag inside. Hazlitt rushed out of the bedroom and danced around the bag. "I'm a Texas millionaire," he chirped. "Lemme in the Petroleum Club, Mr. Getty and Mr. Hunt. I'm filthy rich!"

Ryan got on the phone to Terrio. "Ours just came. Hazlitt will pick you up. Remember to wipe down that apartment for prints. Someone might trace us there eventually."

Groaning, Hazlitt left to pick up Terrio. Ryan wanted to open the bag, but he knew Terrio wouldn't have opened his, so he forced himself to finish the cold cheeseburger.

When Terrio and Hazlitt arrived, they set both bags in the middle of the floor, and they all just grinned at each other.

"So *that's* what you look like with a smile on your face," Hazlitt said to Terrio.

"Yeah. Didn't you know, Hazlitt? It takes at least a half million to make me smile."

Ryan broke the seals on both bags and dumped the contents on the floor. The six gray mailbags looked as innocuous as they had last Friday when they first saw them at Union Station right there in Kansas City. Hazlitt used his pocket knife to cut the tops off the bags, and together they spilled the money out on the floor. It made a pile of green the size of a coffee table. Twenties. Tens. Fives. Singles. Nothing bigger than a twenty. All new bills in serialized sequence.

"We did it," Terrio sighed. "My uncle's gonna crap in his pants."

"Who?" Hazlitt asked, still gaping at the pile of bills.

"No one. Let's count it."

"Wait a minute," Ryan warned. Terrio was about to pick up one of the packages of twenty-dollar bills. "I don't think we should count it here."

"Why the hell not?" Hazlitt demanded.

"First of all, I don't want our fingerprints all over those bills. Second, if we take the packages apart they'll never be as compact again. Remember, we have to fit them into a couple of suitcases."

"Then how do we find out how much we stole?" Terrio complained.

"We'll let the German count it," Ryan said, but he knew his argument was weak. He wanted to count it himself. "Or, we can estimate how much is in each packet and count the packets."

"I want to get my *hands* on that money," Hazlitt said with feeling, twisting his fingers in the air.

"No. Ryan's right," Terrio agreed. "I don't want some FBI man to get hold of one of those bills six months from now and find my thumbprint on it. Let the German count it. We'll estimate what we've got, like Ryan says."

Hazlitt whined some more but finally agreed. The German would count it.

The German was Erwin Mann, a currency fence from Munich. While they were planning this job in Leavenworth they made a point of finding out who the big money fences were around the world. The number one currency mover was a Frenchman who worked out of Thailand. Number two was a Swiss who owned his own bank and used it to wash hot money, primarily for narcotics and arms dealers who did business strictly for cash. Number three was Erwin Mann. They selected him because this was a medium-sized deal, which was what Mann specialized in. Also, they reasoned that there would be less possibility of surveillance of the number three man in the business.

One week before the robbery they had mailed Erwin Mann two first-class plane tickets to New York. With it they sent a note saying simply, "Bring four hundred thousand dollars." There was also a confirmed reservation slip for a double room at the Bristol Hotel in New York in the envelope. The reservations were dated Thursday, July 6, and Friday, July 7.

There were several reasons why they believed Erwin Mann would show up with the money, despite the fact that he would have no idea who sent the tickets and hotel reservations. First, Mann would know he was dealing with knowledgeable people when he received the envelope at his very private estate in the Munich suburbs. Only a handful of people knew the address, one of them a prisoner in Leavenworth. The second ticket in the envelope, in the name of Heinrich Strasser, would also imply inside knowledge. Strasser was Mann's bodyguard and strong-arm man. Mann never traveled for business without him. Finally, when he received the tickets and reservations he would begin reading American newspapers. He couldn't miss the story of the payroll robbery; it had made the front section of every paper in the country. Mann would also know that military payrolls are made up of new bills, sequentially numbered, and that a bundle like that would have to be trickled into the world markets by an expert in order to avoid being traced. Mann would meet them in New York. Ryan was sure of that.

They caught a TWA flight to New York that afternoon. Ryan and Hazlitt sat together. Terrio sat alone. The money was stowed in the luggage compartment of the plane in two suitcases. Ryan held the stub for one and Terrio for the other. During the flight Hazlitt leaned over and whispered to Ryan, "Wouldn't it be just our luck if some goofball hijacked this plane?"

"You've been listening to Terrio again," Ryan said.

They picked up their luggage at the revolving turntable at Kennedy Airport and got out of the terminal with no trouble. They took a cab to the Bristol Hotel, where Ryan registered for them. He told the clerk they were salesmen who planned to hold a couple of long marketing sessions, and were the rooms he had requested ready?

They were. Four connecting rooms on the

ninth floor. Three of them were bedrooms and the fourth was a sitting room equipped for meetings with a large table and plenty of chairs. That was room 922.

"I appreciate your holding those particular rooms for us," Ryan said.

The desk man beamed. "Not at all, sir."

Room 922 connected with 924, which Ryan had reserved for Erwin Mann and Heinrich Strasser. When they were settled in their own rooms Ryan called the Hotel Bristol's outside number and asked the operator for Room 924.

They could hear Mann's phone ringing faintly through the wall to their left.

Mann answered. *"Ja?"* The voice was clipped and Teutonic. Ryan smiled and nodded to his partners.

"Is this Erwin Mann?"

"Who is calling?"

"The person who sent you the plane tickets and reservations for this hotel. I hope your room is comfortable."

"Pleasant enough."

"Good. I'd like to meet with you tomorrow, Mr. Mann. What time would be convenient?"

"Any time. If you have something interesting to say."

"I believe I do. Did you bring the package I requested?"

"I have nothing here in this hotel room," Mann said in a very hostile voice. Ryan figured Mann was constantly on guard against robbery. He had heard that Strasser had killed more than one man who had tried to hijack his boss.

"I understand that," Ryan answered

quickly. "I know that you want to see what you're buying before making any commitment."

"I'm not here to buy anything," Mann said casually. "I came to New York mainly to see a few shows. They are having a Shakespeare festival in New York this summer, you know."

"No, I didn't."

"Oh yes. I am particularly fond of *Othello.* Though I always wonder why Othello did not take greater precautions against his so-called friends. I certainly take very great care in choosing my associates." This was said very pointedly.

"Noted," Ryan replied.

Mann allowed himself a small laugh. "Good. Then perhaps we will have a successful meeting at that. When shall I see you? And where?"

"Tomorrow morning at nine," Ryan suggested. "I'll call you then."

"And the place?" Man inquired. "Is it close or far?"

Ryan felt like allowing himself a small laugh. "Close enough. I'll call you in the morning."

He put down the phone and looked at Hazlitt. "Will that give you enough time?"

Hazlitt nodded. "Sure. If I can't find guns in New York City I'd better get myself over to the old folks' home."

They had not brought guns because the airlines check too closely on what their passengers carry these days. Ryan didn't want to walk into a meeting with Mann unarmed, so it was Hazlitt's job to put his hands on some guns between now and nine A.M. tomorrow. Hazlitt claimed he could find a handgun in a monastery and Ryan didn't doubt him. Hazlitt had been born to guns. When he was a boy, the only food the Hazlitt family had had some weeks was what he brought home with a Sears-Roebuck .22. He had learned not to miss. Later, in the army, it came as a complete surprise to Hazlitt to discover that shooting at people sickened him. He could kill rabbits, deer, bear, wild hog, anything that provided food. But something in him rebelled against shooting at people.

When Hazlitt left, Ryan and Terrio unpacked and checked the money. Then they went to work on the sitting room adjacent to Mann's room. They worked quietly, moving the long conference table directly under the overhead light in the center of the room. Every other lamp was disconnected. It was still bright outside so they drew the drapes and turned on the overhead lamp. The effect was exactly what Ryan wanted—the center of the sitting room was brightly lit but the balance of the room stayed completely dark.

Satisfied, they called room service for dinner and sat back to wait for Hazlitt.

He returned shortly after nine, assorted bulges showing themselves in his suit. He plucked handguns out of his clothing the way a magician produces pigeons, and tossed them onto the bed.

"Nice going," Terrio said, picking up one of the guns. "What have you got here?"

"All .38s. That way I had to buy ammo just once."

Ryan took a .38 short and examined it. It was old but serviceable.

"Where'd you get them?" Terrio asked.

"Dangedest thing," Hazlitt mused. "I bought the first one off a fifteen-year-old kid down in what they call the Village. Offered me a gun or a girl for fifty dollars, take my pick. Second one I bought off a cab driver. He had three of them under his seat. Said he'd shot at a guy who tried to stick him up last week and might have hit him. Maybe the stickup man kicked off, maybe not. Maybe the cabbie missed. Anyways, he didn't want this gun around anymore. Forty dollars. The third one I bought off a cop. A cop! Walked right up to me down there in the Village and said a kid told him I was buying guns. I was ready to run like hell when he asked how high I'd go. I understood right away that he was selling and I'd better give him a good price. I said two hundred dollars and his eyes bulged. He sold me his own gun *right out of his holster.* I danged near passed out. I'm getting out of this city as soon as I can. Any place where the cops are selling their guns ain't too safe."

"You aren't through yet," Terrio reminded him.

Hazlitt bridled. "I know it, Terrio. Just hold on a danged minute." From his pockets he produced some more hardware. Not guns this time. Three short lengths of copper pipe, a handful of small aluminum strips, and a package of steel wool. Ryan had decided that if they had to use guns, they shouldn't make any noise. He had asked Hazlitt if he could fit the pistols with silencers and that's what the materials was for.

"This should do the job," Hazlitt assured them. He sat down at a desk and went to work. A silencer is simply a tube fitted over a gun barrel. It holds a series of baffles. When a gun is fired, air is pushed out of the barrel at a tremendous velocity. The air rushes back in with a bang. Hazlitt was fitting strips of aluminum and pieces of steel wool into the copper cylinders to act as baffles. He then fitted the cylinders to the pistol barrels with metal screws. It took him about an hour to rig all three guns.

"There you go." Hazlitt passed his handiwork around. The .38s looked awkwardly long and were too heavy at the muzzle for really accurate aiming, but Ryan felt that if they had to use them, there wouldn't be time to sight down the barrels anyway.

"How many times can one of these be fired before the baffling wears out?" Ryan wanted to know.

"Only about three shots," Hazlitt said. "The first shot will make a noise like a belch. The second like a good fart. The third like a cough. After that they'll start making a lot of noise again. Best I could do on short notice."

"That's fine," Ryan said. "I really don't think we'll need them anyway."

"Amen," Hazlitt said. And he meant it.

any more. We have [illegible] of the [illegible] [illegible] with [illegible]

"The sound of the [illegible]," Hewitt [illegible] [illegible]

[illegible] [illegible] [illegible] [illegible]

[illegible] pieces of steel went into the [illegible] [illegible] [illegible]

[illegible] Hewitt passed the [illegible] [illegible]

[illegible]

[illegible]

[illegible]

FRIDAY
JULY 7

The next morning Ryan called Erwin Mann at precisely nine A.M. from the sitting room.

"Yes?"

"This is the man who spoke to you yesterday. Are you ready?"

"I'm ready," Mann answered. "Where shall we meet?"

"That will be simple. Draw the drapes in your room. Turn off all lights. Unlock the door leading to the connecting room to your left as you face your windows. I'm in that room."

Whispering. Mann and his bodyguard were conferring.

"How do I know I will not be attacked?"

"Mr. Mann. I have about six hundred thousand dollars in cash with me. You have assured me that you have no money in your room. I'm the one who should fear an attack."

More whispering.

"Very well."

"One more point," Ryan put in quickly. "Your associate, Mr. Strasser, will stay in your room. He can protect you from there. I'm sure he's armed. I hope you're armed yourself, because I am. I have a backup man in the room behind me. Neither of us will be out of sight of our bodyguards at any time."

"I see." A long pause. "I understand. Your plan looks workable. I'll open the door now, and if everything appears correct we will have our meeting."

A few seconds later Ryan heard the latch turn on the connecting door. He had unlocked his side of the door very quietly ten minutes before. The door opened slowly. Mann's room was dark. The sitting room was also dark. Drapes had been drawn and Ryan was sitting at the long table directly under the light fixture. He and the table were bathed in light but the rest of the room was black. Hazlitt sat behind him in his equally dark bedroom, watching through the open door.

Mann opened his door and came into the room as cautiously as a deer advancing on an alien waterhole. He stepped into the ring of light and looked down at Ryan. He was an older man than Ryan had thought he would be.

Perhaps in his sixties. Ryan didn't think a man in his business would have lived that long. He had a stylishly Prussian appearance. Gray hair combed straight back. Shoulders and spine stiff. Dark Savile Row suit and white shirt. A flinty face unlined by age.

"So," he said. His eyes flicked to the two suitcases on the table. "Very well." He sat down opposite Ryan.

"You say you have six hundred thousand dollars." His eyebrows moved upward. "Taken from a certain military robbery, I assume." He bowed his head slightly. "My compliments on an admirable operation. No one killed." His eyes moved to the money again. "I will have to verify the amount, of course. But let's see if we can reach an agreement first." He took a pack of cigarettes out and offered them to Ryan. They were European. Mann flipped open the cardboard top.

"No, thank you," Ryan said.

To that Erwin Mann answered, "Two hundred thousand dollars."

"Unacceptable," Ryan said just as shortly.

The eyebrows moved again. "That's quite generous. This money is serialized. The bills are new. They will be very difficult to circulate."

"Not for you. I want four hundred thousand dollars. Small bills. Nothing larger than a fifty. And not many of those. Tens and twenties will do."

Mann laughed and lit his cigarette. His eyebrows wigwagged merrily. Ryan had him figured out now. There was no expression in his face, but he used his eyebrows as a bushy semaphore through which he revealed his pleasure or displeasure.

"Let me see the money," Mann said.

"Certainly." Ryan got up and opened the suitcases. The money loomed like green mountains. Erwin Mann's eyebrows undulated.

For the next half hour they talked money.

Mann quoted a figure. Ryan argued that it wasn't enough and mentioned the names of other currency experts who would give him more.

Ryan quoted a figure. Mann launched into a detailed list of his expenses.

Mann quoted a figure. Ryan told him he would burn the whole bundle rather than take that amount.

Ryan quoted a figure. Mann shook his head and told a chilling story of how close he had come to arrest by Dutch authorities on his last currency deal.

Mann quoted a figure. Ryan told him how many years he could get in prison for the robbery and figured out the paltry per-year sum Mann wanted him to take.

During the negotiations Mann's eyebrows moved like the hands of a symphony conductor—contracting here in pain, expanding there with gestures of generosity, falling and twitching as points were made. Finally a figure was agreed upon. Mann would pay Ryan fifty percent of the face value of the payroll up to five hundred thousand dollars, plus forty percent of the value over five hundred thousand dollars.

"You haven't counted it?" Mann asked.

"No. We didn't want to take it apart or put our fingerprints on it."

Mann nodded sagely. "Very wise. You're a professional, sir. And a very fine negotiator. I will count the money now. May Strasser bring in my equipment?"

Ryan said he could.

Strasser emerged from the darkness for the first time. He wasn't as big as Ryan expected, but he had the longest arms he had ever seen on a man. And the coldest eyes. Strasser gave his employer a small leather case, then retreated to his own room. Mann opened the case, which contained an odd assortment of items: a jar of hand cream, several pairs of rubber gloves, a handbook of international currency exchange rates, a compact chemical set for testing paper stock and inks, and a few other things Ryan couldn't see well enough to identify. Mann took off his coat and put it over the back of his chair. He opened the jar and covered his hands with cream to make it easier to slip on the tight rubber gloves. The tips of the gloves' fingers were of extra thickness and sandpaper coarseness. A man who handled so much money couldn't afford to be unprepared.

For the next two hours Mann systematically counted the money. He noted the sum in each package of money on a pad of paper next to him. Mann stopped once to ask permission to have a pot of tea brought up, and Ryan agreed. Strasser called down and tea and coffee were delivered to Mann's room for all of them.

It was almost noon when Mann said, "Very well. The money is genuine. The total is six hundred and twelve thousand, four hundred and twenty dollars. Under our agreement I will pay you two hundred ninety-four thousand, nine hundred sixty-eight dollars. Correct?"

Ryan checked the math. "Correct. When and where?"

Mann drew out a large pocket watch. "The banks in this city stay open until three P.M. You are familiar with the Manufacturers Bank on East Forty-fifth Street?"

"I'll find it."

"Splendid. My money is on safe deposit there. We will meet at one P.M. They have small rooms available for private business transactions. I will reserve one under the name they know me by. John Miller. How many will you be?"

"Three."

"Oh?" Mann could account for Ryan and he knew of Hazlitt's presence, but he was uncomfortable in not knowing the whereabouts of a third member of Ryan's team.

"The third one has been in the lobby and hallways all morning, making sure we weren't interrupted."

Mann smiled. He looked like a family attorney when he smiled, or perhaps a trusted brother-in-law. "Excellent. It is a pleasure to do business with discreet people." He rose and slipped on his coat. "One o'clock then. Manufacturers Bank."

He retreated into his own room and locked the door on his side. Hazlitt come out of the dark, blinking like a bear after hibernation.

"We made it," Ryan said to him.

"That old boy scares me, though," Hazlitt

drawled. "He'd reach down in your pants if he thought you had a stray dollar there."

"He'd do worse than that. His buddy Strasser is a killer if I ever saw one. But I think he knows we're set up to handle him."

Terrio came in. "I saw them leave. They took a cab."

"Did you hear the address they gave the driver?" Hazzlitt asked.

"Manufacturers Bank, wherever the hell that is. How did it go?"

Hazlitt told him what happened.

"Well, that's not bad then. Almost a hundred grand apiece." Terrio relaxed somewhat. Enough, at least, to erase the perpetual lines in his forehead. "And we only put about eight thousand into the job. That's a good return. Even Uncle Tony would approve."

"Who's this uncle of yours, Terrio? You've mentioned him twice this week but I never heard a word about him in four years in Leavenworth."

"He's no one," Terrio snapped. "It's none of your damned business anyway."

Hazlitt laughed delightedly. "Money sure don't change you none, Terrio."

They put on gloves and repacked the money in the suitcases. It wasn't easy now that the neat packages of bills had been broken up for counting. But by one o'clock they presented themselves to an assistant manager at Manufacturers Bank and asked if Mr. John Miller was waiting for them. The assistant manager escorted them to the rear of the bank, showing a mild curiosity about their two suitcases which he abandoned after one fierce scowl from Terrio.

Mann and Strasser were in a small walnut-paneled room, Mann seated at a table and Strasser standing with his back to the wall. The assistant manager left. Ryan opened the suitcases and Mann spent half an hour verifying that this was the same money he had examined in the morning. When he was satisfied, he sent Strasser to the vault. He returned with a large safe-deposit box. It was now Ryan's turn to count money while Hazlitt and Terrio watched his back.

"All here," Ryan said an hour later. "But there are more fifties than I asked for."

Mann shrugged. "I have my problems, too. You must understand."

Ryan nodded. "This will do."

Strasser brought another box, even larger, and put the army payroll into the two containers. Mann bowed curtly and they left, Mann carrying the smaller box and Strasser the big one. Ryan helped Terrio and Hazlitt put their money into the two suitcases. They only needed a single suitcase now, but they couldn't leave one behind in the room. As they left, Mann and Strasser were putting the payroll into the bank vault. They took a cab to a second hotel where Hazlitt had reserved a single room. There they split the money evenly into three overnight cases and ditched the guns in the hotel trash bin. They each had a plane to catch by six P.M.

"I guess we won't be seeing each other again," Ryan said.

"Wouldn't be safe," Terrio agreed.

"Might be fun though," Hazlitt ventured.

"Fun is staying out of prison," Ryan reminded him. They shook hands and took separate cabs to different airports.

Moody was waiting for General Hanson in a bar in Manhattan, Kansas, a small town twenty miles east of Fort Riley. The bar was called The Final Exam, alluding to its intimate relationship with students from the University of Kansas two blocks away. The Final Exam had all the earmarks of an off-campus bar; it served a lot of draft beer, pizza, and very bad Chianti wine. Moody had chosen it as a meeting place because neither he nor General Hanson would be likely to be seen there by anyone he knew.

The meeting was scheduled for five P.M. Because of the hour and the few students attending summer session the bar was almost deserted, which suited Moody. He was nursing a draft beer and staring at the red and white checks on the tablecloth when the General came in.

Moody had asked Hanson to wear civilian clothes when he phoned him to arrange the meeting. The General had harumphed but agreed, and he arrived now wearing brown slacks cut in a military style, a plain gabardine jacket, a soft beige shirt and solid-colored tie, and black shoes shined to a high gloss. He could not have looked more like an army officer if he had pinned the two stars to each shoulder of his jacket. Moody sighed and rose so that the General could see him at the softly lighted corner table.

Hanson came over and sat down, looking uncomfortable. "I hope you have a good reason for this meeting, Sergeant. My attorney told me to stay away from everyone else involved in those damned hearings."

"So did mine," Moody told him. "Don't worry. No one's going to see us together."

Hanson peered around. "I hope not."

A waitress came up and Moody ordered a beer for the General before he could speak. The damned fool might call attention to himself by ordering a bottle of rare old burgundy.

"I loathe draft beer," Hanson said in his most condescending voice.

"I'll drink it for you," Moody offered. When the beer came he dragged it over to his side of the table. "I didn't invite you here to drink beer with you, sir. Not that it wouldn't be an honor, but I've got other things on my mind."

General Hanson showed his impatience by looking pointedly at his watch. "Get on with it, Moody."

"The way I see it," Moody began, "you and I are in pretty much the same fix. However the House investigation comes out, our military careers are finished."

"That isn't necessarily true," the General argued, but his speech lacked its usual snap. He sounded tired and dispirited and there were sagging gray circles under the usually clear brown eyes.

"Maybe not," Moody said agreeably. "But I don't figure on collecting my thirty-year pension from Uncle Sam. And with all due respect, I wouldn't count on that third star for yourself, General. Matter of fact, sir, I wouldn't be surprised to see Washington find a nice, respectable way to take away your command."

For the first time since Moody had known him the General's square shoulders sagged. "They've already done it," he said in a low voice. "I've been relieved of command of the Seventh Infantry Division and placed on special assignment to the Fifth Army."

"When did this happen?" Moody said quickly.

"This morning. General DeCroix called me personally. He said he wanted to soften the blow, but I think the malicious old bastard just wanted to see how I'd take it." His shoulders straightened. "I didn't give him the satisfaction of whimpering about it."

Moody was glad to hear that. The General might work out for what he had in mind after all.

"When does your special assignment start, sir? And where are you supposed to report?"

"It starts immediately, and I gathered Washington would be happy if I could report to the far side of the moon." His teeth made a grinding noise. "What it amounts to is that I'm on administrative leave."

Hanson abruptly transferred his ill humor to Moody. "Now what the hell do you want, Sergeant? I have better things to do on a Friday than watch the lower ranks drink beer."

Moody thought it might be fun to drop his information on the General like an artillery barrage, so he said, "I know who stole your payroll."

At last he had the General's undivided attention. "You know—what?" Hanson grabbed Moody's arm. "Do you mean that? Why, damn it, man, that's wonderful! How did you find out? No, just tell me who those men are and where they can be found." The General's face glowed. "DeCroix won't be so eager to find himself a new division commander if I can personally apprehend those thieving bastards."

"You're kidding yourself." Moody spoke harshly, deliberately dampening Hanson's enthusiasm. "You could deliver that payroll to the Secretary of the Army himself and you wouldn't get your division back. Your command is finished and so is your career. Get used to the idea."

"By God, I don't have to listen to that from a master sergeant no matter what's happened to my career!" Hanson jumped up, tipping back his chair. It toppled with a clatter. "Report to your quarters immediately, Sergeant. And confine yourself until my charges are brought against you."

Moody sneered at him. "Shut up and sit down, you pompous old crock. The day you can order me around has just about come and gone."

The General's mouth swung open as if on hinges. He stared dumfounded at Moody. No one had ever ignored one of his direct orders before, and he could think of no way to handle Moody without a detachment of MPs to back him up.

"I told you to sit down," Moody repeated in a more reasonable voice. "People are looking at you."

The four other patrons made little shrugs

at each other and turned away when General Hanson slowly put his chair upright and sank into it. He looked ill. He avoided Moody's eyes for a long while. When he did speak, his voice was a whisper. "I don't understand the world anymore. Noncoms swearing at general officers . . . congressmen yipping for my blood . . . payrolls disappearing . . . fellow officers insulting me." He shook himself. "There was a time when I could *command.*" His right hand spread itself out on the table. He turned it over and tapped the face of his VMI ring against a ceramic ash tray. "This is part of it. If I'd been graduated from West Point those bastards in Washington would have closed ranks behind me. But a VMI man can be sacrificed." He looked searchingly into Moody's face. "That's right, isn't it? You never would have called me a—you never would have said that to a West Point man. Would you?"

"What's the difference?" Moody pointed an enormous index finger in General Hanson's face. "You're in trouble and I'm going to hand you a way out."

"A way out?"

"You're absolutely right about recovering that money, General. It's our duty and all. But why should we turn it back to the army when the army's all set to hang our asses in public?"

Hanson shifted his weight as if physically wrestling with the idea Moody had presented. "You mean we should find the money and . . . keep it?"

Moody shook his head in mocking admiration. "You officers! You are sharp. Always a mile ahead of us enlisted men." He laughed and drank some beer. "That's it, General. You're on administrative leave anyway. I put in for three weeks' leave starting tomorrow. We'll leave tomorrow."

"Six hundred thousand dollars split two ways," the General mused.

"Not quite," Moody corrected him. "By this time the three men who did the job have fenced that payroll. It's too hot. The bills are serialized. They probably got somewhere near half the face amount. That means we'd split three hundred thousand. You could use that in your coming retirement, couldn't you, sir?"

Hanson seemed to have fallen back into his mood of suspicion and resentment. "I don't understand you, Sergeant. Why are you inviting *me* into this lucrative affair? If you know who stole the money, why don't you find the men and keep it all for yourself?"

"I'll tell you why, General." Moody had considered and rejected three or four different ways of saying this. In the end he had decided to just plunge ahead without trying to soften his words. "You were part of the Phoenix program in Vietnam. I've learned from absolutely reliable sources that you know a dozen ways to make a man talk. Guaranteed ways. That's what I need, General. I can find those guys and I can kill them when I'm through with them. But I need someone who can make them tell me where the money is. That's your job. They say you're a born torturer."

Moody was watching Hanson closely as he talked. He realized the General was an unstable man, full of half-hidden fears he couldn't control. One of Hanson's fears, Moody suspected, was that people would learn about the extent of his participation in the Phoenix program. Most regular army officers had shunned it like the plague. Hanson might come apart when he learned that his deeds were not a closely held secret. But if he could accept the fact that Moody knew—and if he agreed to use his talents—then he might be of use.

The first reactions were not promising. General Hanson's hands moved in spasms toward his jacket pockets. His eyes roved. "There was nothing illegal about the Phoenix program, Sergeant. You must understand that. It was funded by the Congress. Administered by the CIA. Those of us who were—close to the program—understood its goals better than the press or the public. Murder and torture are all you hear about today. But we saved American lives! We eliminated traitors who were taking American and Vietnamese lives, too." The wandering eyes settled on Moody. "It was an important military program. You must understand."

"I do," Moody said smoothly. "I just want you to put some of that valuable expertise to work again, sir."

Hanson's head jerked. "Yes. I suppose I can."

Moody was pleased. The General's fear of going back to civilian life with empty pockets overpowered his horror at having his Phoenix activities unmasked.

"Who are these men?" Hanson inquired, anxious to change the subject but also genuinely curious.

"Three ex-soldiers," Moody said. "Also ex-cons." He unfolded a piece of yellow legal-sized paper on which he'd written all the information. "Dan Ryan. Paul Terrio. LeRoy Hazlitt. I spotted Ryan on the post Friday night but it wasn't until a few days ago that I connected him with the robbery. Never mind how. He used to be a top soldier. The personnel people in Washington tell me Ryan was convicted of dealing in black-market goods in Vietnam five years ago and sent to Leavenworth. You know that the army detachment at Fort Leavenworth helps run the prison. I called a buddy in the admin office at Fort Leavenworth. He looked up Ryan's record. Ryan shared a cell for about four years with Terrio and Hazlitt. The three of them were real tight. Ryan was RA and ran his cell like an infantry company. They had their own physical-training program to stay in shape, their own work schedule for cleaning their cell, their own system for dealing with trouble. If anybody messed with one of them, the other two came on like Patton's army.

"I know Ryan. He'll be the hardest to find. Terrio sounds pretty tough, too. He's a wop from the North Side of Chicago, and apparently he was tied in with the mob there somehow. Hazlitt's a country boy from Texas. He sounds like the softest of the three so we'll go after him first."

"Where does Hazlitt come from in Texas?" Hanson asked.

"Lubbock. I think he and Terrio are the kind who'll head back to their home territories. That should help. But Ryan was raised in a foster home or something. The army was the only real place he ever had. We'll have to make Terrio and Hazlitt tell us where to find Ryan."

"Don't these men have any close relatives? Surely they had mail and visitors."

Moody turned over the piece of paper. "Not many visitors. Hazlitt has a sister in Lubbock. She came to see him a couple of times. Terrio's old lady lives in Chicago. He wouldn't let her visit him there, apparently. They all got mail, but once a man is discharged they get rid of the record of whom he exchanged letters with."

General Hanson felt relaxed and his mind was running fast again. Logistics were always his strong suit, and this was almost like a military operation. "We'd better move fast."

"We can head right down to Lubbock in my car," Moody agreed.

Hanson shook his head. "No good. Point one: we need to move faster than that. I think your appraisal of these men is accurate. Terrio and Hazlitt have strong ties to their homes. That's where they'll head. They'll want to show off their new wealth a little. But they've each spent several years in prison. Sooner or later they'll want to break out into the world and start throwing some of their money around. They won't be able to do that safely at home. Who knows where they'll go? Europe? Hawaii? We have to get to them before that happens.

"Point two: weapons. We should be equipped for anything. That means both handguns and automatic weapons."

"What's your idea?"

Several plans had been formulating in Hanson's mind. He selected one. "We need a private plane and a dependable pilot who can keep his mouth shut. Preferably a man's who's done some illegal flying before. I know where we can borrow a small private jet that won't draw attention. The owner is highly respectable. We must travel by air in order to get to Texas, Illinois, and wherever Ryan is before they begin to spend that money. Driving all over the country would take too much time, and we can't carry weapons on board commercial airlines."

"You're right," Moody said. He might not have agreed with Hanson so quickly if he hadn't immediatety thought of a good pilot. "You line up the plane. I'll get the pilot."

"Dependable?" Hanson questioned.

"Yes. Only one thing bothers me. I don't want to split three hundred thousand into thirds. For that matter we might not even find all three. One might get away from us with his money."

Again Hanson was prepared. He had a reputation for always being ready for the arguments of lower ranks. "I propose we pay the pilot a flat fee in advance. Fifty thousand dollars. We'll each put up half that sum." He watched Moody frown and decided it was his turn to tighten the screws. "You can come up with that much cash, can't you?"

Moody wasn't amused. He answered "I can" with a low growl, smarting at the implication that he might not be accustomed to handling big money.

"Good. Get the pilot. I'll meet the two of you in Tulsa on Sunday."

"Why Tulsa?" Moody didn't like the feeling he was getting that the General had suddenly assumed command of this venture.

"That's where the plane is. Call me at my quarters tonight and I'll tell you where it's hangared." Hanson had seen Moody's rising resentment and moved quickly to remove any misunderstandings. "There's one more important point to be settled. I am a general officer in the United States Army. I won't take orders from a sergeant. I will command this expeditionary force, if you want to call it that. You'll take my orders. If you won't agree to that I'll turn the information you've given to me over to the provost marshal."

Telling the General that he was through giving orders had been a mistake, Moody realized sourly. But it had been just too tempting. Now he'd have to pay for that pleasure. "All right, sir. I'll go along with that." But only if things went smoothly, Moody decided privately. If not, this "expedition" would get a new commander very suddenly.

"Good," Hanson said briskly, in a tone that announced he had known Moody's answer in advance. "Now about the weapons. Can you handle that, too?"

"I can buy two Russian AK-47s for five hundred dollars."

"Including ammunition?"

Moody nodded. "I've got my own sidearm."

"So do I. Tell the pilot to bring his own handgun as well. The AK-47s will give us plenty of firepower. I doubt that we'll need all of it, but we should be ready."

It was after six P.M. when they left The Final Exam. Hanson drove directly to his quarters and tried to phone his wife in Roanoke, but it was past eight on the eastern seaboard, and she had already left for a party. He told the maid he would be on leave and traveling for at least two weeks, in case Mrs. Hanson tried to reach him. Not that he thought she would. Then he called Bob Brannigan in Tulsa. Brannigan was still in his office. He practically lived there. Hanson told him he wanted the use of his plane for two weeks. Brannigan evaded answering until Hanson said he'd forget about his help with the hunting lodge if he could have the plane. He assured Brannigan a qualified pilot would be flying his Cessna and got the address of the field in Tulsa where the plane was kept.

Moody was just as busy.

He paid a call on the division armorer and bought two AK-47s. They cost slightly more then he had planned to pay—three hundred dollars apiece—because the armorer had to take them out of a shipment of twelve he was selling to a Filipino terrorist group. But the armorer threw in six magazines and four hundred rounds of ammo because Moody was an old friend.

The AK-47s and a random assortment of other weapons the armorer dealt in were kept in a dark corner of the armory. Moody had the weapons and ammo put away in his car trunk within an hour after his meeting with Hanson.

From the division armory he drove up to Custer Hill. The 14th Infantry was finishing an exercise on one of the open ranges to the west of the Hill. Moody parked on a high road where he could watch the action conclude.

The object of the exercise was to assault a rocky knoll jutting up at one end of the range, which was a rolling stretch of land about five miles long and a mile wide. Every tree and blade of grass on the range had been destroyed over the many years the land had been used to train infantry, so that Moody could see most of the exercise from his car.

First the artillery put down a barrage on the pock-marked field directly in front of the knoll. The barrage was supposed to accomplish two tactical goals: to drive an imaginary enemy back and to explode antipersonnel and antitank mines that were theoretically planted through the terrain. Watching the artillery rounds land was like seeing a movie in which the sound and action are out of sync. First Moody saw the bright explosions and sprays of dirt, and a second later the *thump thump thump* of the shells reached him.

Finally the barrage ceased. Most of the range was obscured by drifting smoke. As the smoke dissolved or was carried away by the perennial Custer Hill winds, a ragged line of assault vehicles could be seen moving up the valley toward the knoll. The vehicles represented the usual mixed force of heavy weapons: half a dozen tanks, perhaps twenty armored personnel carriers, and a sprinkling of jeeps equipped with recoilless rifles. When the assault vehicles reached a predetermined point, they opened up their guns on the knoll. The tanks' big guns belched thunder and the recoilless rifles made their flat, cracking sounds, and the machine guns mounted in the APCs chattered and stopped and chattered some more.

The knoll seemed to shrink under the assault as various-sized rounds chipped pieces off it.

The line of vehicles stopped below the knoll where the rear ends of the APCs opened to disgorge the infantry. A couple of platoons of recruits stumbled out of the APCs and fell into a wavering skirmish line. They were wearing steel pots that jiggled as they ran, and for a moment Moody thought some lunatic had given them live ammunition. He was ready to get the hell off the hill if recruits were running around with live ammo. Too many sergeants are killed every year by recruits training with live ammo.

But Moody saw that the NCOs were not bothering to keep their recruits in an absolutely straight line, as they would have done if the troops carried live ammo. Instead, the platoon sergeants allowed their men to double-time forward at pretty much their own pace with their weapons at port arms. When they reached the knoll, the recruits surrounded it and began popping blank ammo. Moody almost felt sorry for the recruits; blank ammo fouls up a weapon with more dirt and carbon than live rounds. They'd be cleaning their weapons for hours.

When the skinheads ran out of blank ammo, they stayed belly down in a circle around the knoll. A few moments later an L-19 flew through the valley at about two hundred feet. A roll of black telephone wire was fixed under the small aircraft, and it unwound automatically as the plane came down the range, laying wire between the knoll and an imaginary command post a few miles back. A helicopter followed the L-19. The chopper waddled in and sat down on the cone of the knoll. Several officers jumped out—the company headquarters team, followed by enlisted men with communications equipment. With the knoll secure and the battalion commander set up with communications, the exercise was as good as over.

The chopper swirled upward and banked to the south toward Marshall Air Field. Moody was watching it because the pilot of the chopper was the man he hoped to hire. He was about to start his car and follow the aircraft to its pad when the chopper's motor coughed twice and stopped. It hung almost stationary in the air for a moment, then dropped. The motor caught again and lifted the chopper with a snapping motion. The sudden stress on the big machine as it jerked back into a vertical climb caused something to give way. Moody thought he saw a black object spin away from the helicopter, which immediately began plunging again even though the rotors continued to turn. Smoke burst from the rotor housing and the chopper fell in slow motion, rolling first to one side and then the other.

If the helicopter had been higher when the rotors failed, the pilot would have been killed, but the crash was more like a hard emergency landing. The chopper hit down with a terrible rending sound, its rotors whipping like straws in the wind. One rotor snapped and flew away, almost decapitating a grunt who came running up to help the pilot.

Moody breathed a sigh of relief when Captain Bob Price tumbled from the collapsed machine and staggered clear of it. But the copter didn't explode. It just sat there like a toy smashed by some gigantic careless child.

A couple of men supported Price as he walked away from the crash. They led him off a hundred yards and sat him down against the side of an APC. Moody got out of his car and walked down the hill. When he reached Price a medic was bending over him, dabbing iodine at the scratches and bruises that seemed to be the only effects of the crash.

"How are you, Bob?"

Price looked up. "Okay, Joe. What the hell are you doing up here with the grunts? You'll get dirt on your two-hundred-dollar uniform."

"You okay?"

Price winced. He put his hand to the back of his neck and held it there while he rolled his head slowly. "Except for my neck. If I were a civilian I could sue someone for whiplash."

The exercise over, the noncoms and officers were forming up their troops to march them back to quarters. It was almost eight o'clock and the sun was very low. A fire truck came bouncing belatedly across the field toward the copter.

"Can I give you a lift back to quarters?" Moody asked.

"Sure. Thanks. I don't feel like bouncing around in a jeep right now." He let Moody help him up, then shot a suspicious look at him. When Moody had contacted him in the past, it was to hire him for special jobs. Once to fly contraband arms down to Florida for the division armorer and another time to shuttle whores between Kansas City and Fort Riley for one of the General's parties. "I don't feel like doing any jobs for you right now, Joe. So if that's why you're offering me a ride, maybe I'd better take a jeep."

Moody shrugged. "Take the ride anyway. I'm going past the BOQ."

Price was too tired and aching to argue. He fell in beside Moody. From a distance Price looked like a very young man, perhaps still in his teens. He had a very round and pink face, a lithe boyish body, unruly hair. But up close you could see he was at least forty. There were deep lines in his face, etched by scores of combat missions in Asia, and a bald spot was expanding from the crown of his head. He was the absolute minimum height allowed for an officer.

"I'm getting too old for this business, Moody. If I had my twenty in I'd retire."

"You got some leave time coming? Why not take it and have yourself a long rest?"

Price groaned as he slid in beside Moody. "It takes dough to get yourself in a good rest in some nice resort town. I don't have it."

"You would if you took the job I've got for you."

"No thanks. What I need is another overseas tour. Then I can get even again, and this time I won't blow it."

Moody knew what Price was talking about. In Asia Price had flown drugs out of Thailand for one of the big dealers over there. He had come home with a big bundle, some said as much as forty thousand, and lost it when his first assignment in the States turned out to be only a three-hour drive from Reno.

"You could get even on this one job, Price." Moody drove carefully down the winding road. "My partner and I will pay you fifty thousand dollars for a couple weeks' work."

Price forgot the soreness in his muscles. "Fifty thousand!" A hundred calculations crossed his boyish face. "When do I get it?"

"You get it up front, before the job starts."

Price's eyes popped and he asked what kind of stuff he'd be flying, assuming that only narcotics would pay that well.

"Before I tell you anything about it, you have to be in. And once you're into this, Price, you're *in*."

It didn't take Price long to make up his mind. "I've got forty days' leave coming. I won't have any trouble getting half of it after this crash. My CO will expect me to take some leave. I'm in—as long as I get the cash up front like you said."

So Moody told him what he was after. Price's eyes really popped then, and he was sorry he'd settled for fifty thousand. But he knew that a deal with Joe Moody couldn't be changed or broken once it was made. And besides, Moody might not even find all three. If not, he'd still have his fifty grand. It was a good deal at that.

Moody told him all of it, except the name of his partner. They would be seeing the partner soon. All Price asked was, "What kind of plane is it?"

"A small executive jet. I don't know what kind."

"I can fly anything," Price laughed.

Of course Price wanted his money immediately. He wouldn't completely believe his luck until he had it. Moody took Price to the NCO Club and parked the pilot in his office while he removed twenty-five thousand from the green box in the wall. He had a few qualms about parting with all that money on a speculative deal, but he swallowed them because the General was right about moving fast.

Price smiled hugely and snatched the money out of Moody's hand with a weasel's lunge.

"Leave me my fingers!" Moody warned. But Price already had the money spread out on the desk, counting it with his lips moving silently to the numbers on the bills.

While Price counted, Moody called the General. "I've got the pilot."

"Who is he?"

"A helicopter pilot right here at Riley. He can fly anything. He wants his money tonight, by the way. I've already paid over my share. Are you able to pay him this evening?"

"I have it. Bring him over."

Moody said he would, though he was slightly disappointed that the General had not found himself embarrassed on that point. Still it was interesting to know that General Hanson also squirreled his cash away in places he could get to fast. Might be profitable to find out where.

They drove to the General's house in Moody's car. When they pulled up in front of the post commander's official residence, Price stared at Moody. "You're bullshitting me," he scoffed.

"Come in and find out."

Price trailed Moody up the walkway, still dubious. But when the General himself opened the front door to admit them, Price whipped off his fatigue cap and followed Moody inside.

"This is Captain Bob Price," Moody said.

"Sir," Price snapped.

Hanson hardly bothered looking at Price's face. Instead he studied the pilot's decorations and shoulder patches, reading his history in them. He was evidently satisfied with what he saw, because he nodded curtly and said, "Captain Price. I'm pleased to have you with us. Has Sergeant Moody outlined the details of this operation?"

"Yes, sir."

"Very well." He handed a slip of paper to Price. "This is the type of aircraft we'll be using and the location of the airfield."

Price glanced at the note. "Nice aircraft, sir. It should do the job for us."

"Just see that you do." He went to a desk in the corner and removed a bulky envelope. He gave it to Price. The pilot opened the flap to look inside, but Hanson said "Not here!" with an agitated frown that made Price hastily tuck the envelope out of sight.

"I've got the weapons, sir," Moody said. "We'll see you in Tulsa Sunday night then." He tugged at Price's arm.

"Splendid!" General Hanson said heartily. "This should be a very interesting operation, gentlemen."

When they were back on the porch and the heavy oak door had closed behind them, Price whispered, "Have you looked close into that man's eyes, Joe? He's crazy!"

"Sure he is," Moody laughed. "That's what makes the old crock valuable to me."

THURSDAY JULY 13

The morning had gone quickly. The plum orchard needed water once again, and Ryan had been working at that since dawn. Twice he had rearranged the maze of sprinkler pipes, taking the twenty-foot lengths apart, carrying them to new locations, and hooking them together again to form new patterns for watering. Luis was helping. They would do Ryan's acres in the morning and his in the afternoon.

"You know what we both need?" Luis said, bending low to couple two pipes. "Enough sprinkler to do our orchards in one watering."

"Neither of us has a pump that gives

enough pressure for that," Ryan reminded him.

Luis straightened and wiped grease off his hands with a rag. "I know. But we could put in duplexed pumps. I saw a setup like that in Santa Clara last week. If I have a good year I might do just that." Luis was a tall Chicano with curling black hair and a bristling mustache. In the early morning the ends of the mustache curled upward at a jaunty angle. As the workday progressed it began drooping with sweat until, by the day's end, it curled down around the sides of his mouth with an Oriental flourish.

Ryan was mentally totaling the tonnage he expected from his plums and the market price per ton. "I won't make enough to buy any new equipment this year."

"Maybe next year," Luis said cheerfully. It was a phrase he used often, like a ballplayer. He had used it when he lost his first small orchard to beetle blight and when the parole board at Soledad turned him down the first time and when the husk fly decimated half his previous year's walnut crop.

"Sure. Maybe next year," Ryan agreed. It occurred to him that he could put in a new pump and sprinklers whenever he wanted. He had more than ninety thousand dollars in cash.

Maria came out on the front porch of Ryan's house and banged a wooden spoon against the mailbox. "Lunch!"

Luis waved to her. "We'll be there in a minute."

They went to the pump where Ryan turned a cumbersome valve. Huge jets of water fanned out through a large portion of Ryan's plums. The recently turned black earth glistened as it began soaking up the water, and the air hummed with flies escaping the wetness. A rabbit hopped to a dry patch of ground to avoid a soaking and sat down to shake itself.

"Too bad I didn't bring my .22," Luis said. "I'd like to have him for dinner."

"I'll get him for you," Ryan offered. He went quickly to the galvanized metal tool shed and ducked his head as he stepped inside. He felt around and found the hunting slingshot Hazlitt had made for him. Hazlitt had presented it to him on one of the trips they'd made to case Fort Riley.

"What's that thing?" Luis asked.

"Watch." Ryan slipped his left hand through a V-shaped extension of the slingshot's handle. The weapon was specially designed by Hazlitt for small-game hunting. The extension was actually a wrist brace that made it possible to take the entire pressure of the handle on the forearm just above the wrist. When Ryan pulled back the sling, which was made of surgical tubing, there was no wrist wobble. Accurate aiming was made simple.

Hazlitt had recommended .25-caliber ballshot for ammunition, but Ryan had only a few smooth stones collected from around the grounds. He put one in the pocket of the sling, pulled the sling back, aimed, and let the stone go. It flew like a bullet, slamming into the rabbit with terrific velocity and killing it immediately.

Luis whistled. "That's some weapon. I'd like to try it out."

"Sure," Ryan said. "We'll go up in the

hills and bring in some more rabbits and squirrels. But we'll have to dress them ourselves. Julie doesn't believe it's meat unless it comes from a supermarket."

"Maria's gotten like that, too." Luis collected his rabbit and put it in the trunk of his car while Ryan stowed the hunting slingshot back in the tool shed.

The money from the robbery was buried about twenty yards from the shed in an airtight chest he had picked up at a surplus store in Salinas. Funny. For the first time in his life he had lots of money, but he couldn't use it. He just couldn't bring himself to tell Julie how he had acquired all that money.

His foot came down on the spot where the money was buried as he walked toward the house. He felt satisfied that no one could tell that particular area had been dug up and refilled. After burying the money he had transplanted several clumps of oxalis at the spot. They had already enlarged and partially covered the bare earth.

They tramped through the small living room into the kitchen. Maria greeted Luis with, "Hello, Pancho Villa," and pulled his drooping mustache. They kissed and Luis dropped into one of the kitchen chairs.

"What's for lunch?" Ryan asked. He poured himself a tall glass of milk. They never gave you enough milk in prison.

"I don't know," Maria said. "I just got back from town with groceries."

Julie had been rummaging in the refrigerator when they came in. Her head popped out and she said, "Tuna-fish sandwiches."

Luis and Maria looked at each other.

"What's the matter?" Julie said.

Maria laughed. "Luis hates tuna."

"How about ham and cheese?"

"Great," Luis said. "Sorry about the tuna. When I was a kid my pop used to say tuna makes you impotent. I don't know why. But I guess he convinced me."

"You must have been eating tuna last night," Maria teased.

"Woman! You've broken the code of the Rondas!" He leaped for her and Maria, with a shriek, ran out the kitchen door into the orchard with Luis after her.

Ryan watched them with a mixture of fondness and envy. When he and Julie were first married they'd joked around like that. But since his return there had been a tenseness between them that made horseplay impossible. Their lovemaking had been good. Better than before he'd left for Vietnam and then gone to prison. Quieter and more subtle, with climaxes that lasted longer and were infinitely more pleasurable than anything Ryan had ever known. But before and after there were these . . . silences.

They were having one of those silences now. Julie was building an enormous ham and cheese sandwich for Luis, her hair moving to the motions of her body. She glanced at Ryan, started to say something, then smiled instead and continued with her work.

Ryan stood up. "I'd better wash." He felt irritable without knowing why.

"I'll get you a clean towel." She put Luis' sandwich on a plate and went ahead of Ryan to their bedroom. She took two fresh towels off the closet shelf and put out Kleenex, fresh soap, and other items Maria had picked up for her at the store.

After washing and drying himself Ryan reached out and pulled Julie to him. They stood in the bathroom for several minutes, kissing and letting their hands roam. Presently Ryan felt foolish just standing there and brought Julie to the bed.

"Luis and Maria are out there," she objected in whispers.

"The bedroom door is closed," Ryan reminded her. Julie didn't object when Ryan began removing her clothes. When he stymied on a zipper she helped, and in seconds they were under the sheets. They made love silently, knowing Luis and Maria would be coming back into the kitchen any minute. They communicated their love with physical attention since words wouldn't form between them.

Afterwards they lay together, knowing they should be getting up, but not caring. They exchanged a few words, and before they realized it they were having a conversation. A whole conversation! They were both amazed. It was a conversation consisting of whispers and furtive glances at the bedroom door, but their first extended conversation since Ryan's release from prison more than ten months ago.

"I know I haven't been very communicative, Julie. I'm sorry. I've had something on my mind."

"Your trips?"

"Yes. But they're over now, I promise."

"That's good. I wouldn't have let you go

away again. I was losing you through those trips."

"I understand why you'd feel that way. Though I've been aware something else has been bothering you, too."

"Yes," Julie admitted. "I was kind of shocked when you got out of prison. You looked just the same. You *are* just the same. While I look years older." She put one of her hands up to his face. "I had beautiful hands when we met. A pianist's hands. Now look at them! Red and hard. I spend a fortune on skin creams."

Ryan took her hand. "You look better than ever." Julie started to deny that, but he held her hand tighter and said in an insisting voice, "Better than ever! But I know what you mean by being shocked by the differences between us. When we were married you were playing the 'glamorous lady' part. You were hip and beautiful and fun to be with. You still are, but now you're something more besides. You're as much at home on this ranch as you are singing in a chic little lounge." He searched for better words. "When I came home I had the feeling I'd lost my identity while you were finding yours. I'm just not as sure of myself as you are. Sometimes I feel like your backward little brother."

They were silent again, but it was an improved silence. A sharing of thoughts.

"What were those trips all about?"

Ryan looked pained. "I can't tell you right now. Someday I will."

"I see." Julie pulled her hand out of Ryan's grip and got up to dress. "We'd better get out to the kitchen." She was mad about the trips all over again and didn't bother hiding it.

"I'm going over to Luis' place after lunch," Ryan told her, to change the subject.

When they returned to the kitchen, Luis and Maria acted elaborately casual. They obviously had guessed what their friends had been up to. Ryan wolfed down his sandwich and left a few minutes later in the pickup to follow Luis and Maria to their place.

He spent four hours helping Luis work his orchard. The Ronda orchard was identical to Ryan's, but he had learned enough about growing to see that it was a better-tended spread. The trees were all pruned to uniform shapes that promoted a greater growth of fruit. The earth between the trees had been tilled in a way that siphoned the maximum amount of water to the roots. Ryan was sure he could develop his orchard to the same quality. It would only take work and time, something he had plenty of.

By six o'clock he was home for dinner. Their lunchtime conversation had broken down some of the stiffness between them, although Ryan's refusal to tell Julie what he had been doing during his absences had resurrected some of the barriers. Gradually, however, they managed to revive the lunchtime spirit and talked over a whole range of subjects from baseball to current women's fashions to the army. "Do you think you'll ever get over your hatred for the army?" Julie asked.

The question surprised Ryan. "What makes you think I hate the army?"

"Your eyes burn whenever it's mentioned. I know they gave you an awfully bad deal, but you liked the army so much when we first met that I can't get used to your not liking it."

Ryan wasn't sure how to phrase his answer. He stirred his coffee as he thought about it. "I don't hate the army," he said finally. "I'm just disgusted with it. When I first went into the army the system worked. The officers fought for the chance to command a line company, and the noncoms took their work seriously. Now the officer corps is heavy with ass kissers and politicians. Instead of commanding troops, they're looking for staff jobs in Washington or leaves of absence to get graduate degrees at Yale or ways to make a fast buck. The combat outfits have suffered the worst. And guys like me got ground up and thrown out with the garbage."

After dinner Ryan settled down with the San Francisco *Chronicle* while Julie cleared the table. He had never been much of a reader, but since coming out of Leavenworth he read everything he could find. Newspapers, cereal boxes, magazines, billboards, phone books, restaurant menus. Anything to help him soak up the present and find out what the world had become while he was away.

Turning the page, he found a full-page ad placed by a group of prominent Americans announcing their support of a new gun-control bill. Their names were listed at the bottom of the page. To illustrate the need for strong legislation they ran a black-bordered list of all the people killed or injured by guns in the United

States during the past week. There were more than three hundred names. One leaped off the page at Ryan:

LeRoy Hazlitt, Lubbock, Texas

It was maddening. The ad made no distinctions between those killed and those hurt, or between people shot deliberately and those shot accidentally. Ryan thought of Terrio and his eyes skipped to the Ts. Terrio's name wasn't there. That was a relief. But he was still faced with the problem of Hazlitt. Was he dead or alive? Had he shot himself accidentally, perhaps while hunting, or had someone deliberately shot him? Did this have anything to do with the robbery?

He went to the phone and called Lubbock information for the names and numbers of every hospital in the town. There were only four. Hazlitt was in the second hospital he called. They switched Ryan to the floor nurse and he asked, "How is Mr. Hazlitt doing?"

"He's in critical condition," the nurse answered, finding it easier to use standardized jargon than to give out any real information.

"Is there a phone in his room? Can I talk to him?"

"Certainly not."

"What about his doctor?"

"He's not on duty at this hour." She seemed to have second thoughts about the packaged answers the hospital administration provided for her. "Mr. Hazlitt really couldn't speak to you," she said in a softer tone. "He's heavily sedated."

"I see. Thank you."

Ryan was still seated by the phone when

Julie came into the living room. She had changed from the shirt and Levis into one of her favorite dresses, a short-sleeved blue cotton outfit she had made herself with Maria's help. "How about going into Monterey for a movie? Or we could have a drink on the wharf."

"Hazlitt's been shot," Ryan said.

"Hazlitt?" She remembered the name now. A friend of Dan's from prison. "How did you find that out?"

"It was in the paper." Ryan shoved it into her hands. Julie looked at the ad, still somewhat confused, while Ryan dialed the phone again. He was calling the Monterey airport and asking about shuttle flights to San Francisco.

"Dan?" He couldn't be leaving again. Not after he promised. "Dan? What are you doing?" She stared at the newspaper, found Hazlitt's name, and dimly began to perceive that he was going away again. To Texas. To find out what had happened to his friend Hazlitt.

"No, Dan," she said as soon as he put down the phone. "You promised you wouldn't leave again."

"I have to." Ryan looked pained by the decision, but Julie no longer cared about his discomforts. Or even Hazlitt's. "I'm your *wife*. I need you here, Dan." She gestured at the dark orchard. "I can't handle all that by myself anymore." She shook her head to contradict herself. "No. That isn't true. I could run the orchard while you take another of your 'trips.' But I won't."

Ryan had to tell her about the robbery now. He sat down with her at the dining-room table. "When I was inside," he began, "I got pretty bitter about what had happened to me. I wanted to make the army—and General Arthur Hanson—pay for it. I've told you about Terrio and Hazlitt. The three of us put together a plan. Did you read about the payroll robbery at Fort Riley, Kansas? It was a week ago."

"Sure," Julie said. "The TV news carried a story about it . . . Dan! Is that what you went away for?"

He nodded. "General Hanson is the commanding officer at Fort Riley."

"My God!" She tried to comprehend what Dan had done, but it was so bizarre. "You might have been killed, Dan. You could have been caught." Her eyes widened. "You could still be caught! And be sent right back to prison. Aren't you—or weren't you—afraid of that?"

"Afraid? No." Ryan had never fully understood the concept of fear. Tension was familiar to him, of course. In tough situations his mouth might go dry and he would feel a downward tug in his chest and bowels. But he never allowed his tensions to dominate him, or to turn him back from a thing he had to do. That would be unprofessional. He knew his attitude often caused people—even Julie—to consider him somewhat cold and insensitive to others. That's what she was accusing him of now. "Afraid or not, it was something I had to do, Julie. I wanted to make Hanson look ridiculous. And we showed them. Terrio and Hazlitt and me. We showed them just how easily this new army can be taken."

"Them!" Julie shouted. "Them! What

about *me?*" She was pounding her fist against her chest. "What would have happened to me if you'd been caught? Or killed? Did you give one thought about how your cops-and-robbers game might affect me?" She jumped up, pulling back from Ryan, and began to cry. "And you're going away again! Why?"

"Don't you see?" Ryan said patiently. "Hazlitt's shooting may be connected with the robbery. I have to find out. Not only to help Hazlitt, but for our own safety."

"How can I feel safe with you running off to Texas?" Julie countered. She was blazing mad; her rage had temporarily dried up her tears. "I don't think you have to go. You want to. Isn't that the truth? Grubbing around an orchard isn't nearly as exciting as fighting a war or stealing an army payroll. I don't think you want to live with me, Dan. You just want a place to sleep between adventures."

"No," Ryan argued. "I have to go."

"Wait a minute!" Julie cried. Dan's determination frightened her. There had to be a way to keep him from going. "Can you give back the money? Do that, Dan. Give it back. No one will look for you if you give it back."

"That's impossible. We already fenced the payroll for half its face value. My share of that's buried outside."

Ryan went into the bedroom and threw some clothes into a suitcase and changed into his one suit. He had retained a thousand dollars from the strongbox. He took the money from its hiding place in the closet and folded the bills in half and stuck them in his pocket. When he came back to the living room Julie was by the phone, turning through the yellow pages so furiously that pieces ripped in her fingers and fell to the floor.

"What are you doing?"

Looking for real estate brokers!" she yelled. "This place is going on the market tomorrow." She stopped turning the pages. "Here they are." She tore out the page and slammed the book shut. "If I can be gone before you get back, I will."

"You can't sell property that fast," Ryan pointed out. "It takes time to find a buyer and go through escrow and all that. Wait till I come back before you do anything. This could be—"

"Don't tell me about it. Don't make me any promises. Just go." She was crying again, after telling herself she wouldn't. That made her even angrier, and she raised the phone book and threw it. "Damn you!" The phone book toppled a lamp.

"You'll need the pickup," Ryan said. "I'll walk to the highway and hitch a ride to the airport from there. And I'll phone you tomorrow."

She was still crying when he left.

FRIDAY JULY 14

Terrio walked into the furniture store on North Clark Street and asked for the manager. When the manager came out of his cubbyhole and saw Terrio, he shuddered. He had spent twenty years sorting good prospects from bad ones, and this was definitely a bad one.

"How can I help you?" he said in a way that put across his opinion that this over-dressed ethnic was wasting his time.

"My name is Terrio."

The manager's back straightened and his condescending manner lifted with the mechanical bounce of a theater curtain. "*Yes*, Mr. Terrio. A pleasure, sir."

"Paul Terrio."

"I see." The store manager's question appeared on his face.

"Tony Terrio is my uncle."

"Of course."

"My mother came in here yesterday. She picked out some new furniture for her apartment. I'm here to pay for it."

"Certainly. Right this way." He seated Terrio with flourishes at the customer service desk and turned to his new customer accounts. He found no Paul Terrio listed.

"Excuse me, but what is your mother's first name?"

"Barbara. But I told her not to give any names. Just pick out the stuff she wants and give me a list. Here it is."

The store manager took a sheet of paper from Terrio and looked it over. The furniture was listed by brand name and stock number. His stomach went queasy as he recalled the elderly Italian woman who had pestered him about these pieces the day before. A window shopper, he had thought. A looker, not a buyer. He had hustled her out rather abruptly. Barbara Terrio. That meant she was Tony Terrio's sister-in-law. Jesus.

Tony Terrio owned twenty-five percent of the furniture store. The manager had met him only once, but he knew him well by reputation. If Tony Terrio heard that he had treated his sister-in-law with disrespect. . . .

"Yes, sir. I'll have this furniture delivered

immediately. You mother has excellent taste, if I may say so."

"How much?"

"How much," the store manager echoed. Another dilemma. "Yes." He examined the list again and used his catalogues to hastily total a bill. "That comes to twelve hundred and forty dollars. But"—he flashed what he had always believed was a winning smile—"a relative of Tony Terrio naturally receives a twenty percent discount."

"I don't want a discount," Terrio said roughly. "I don't take handouts from my uncle. Tell him I said that." He pulled out a wad of hundred-dollar bills and threw thirteen of them on the desk. "My mother's address is there on the list. Deliver the stuff tomorrow. She's expecting it."

"Certainly, sir." The store manager's hand shook as he wrote a receipt and made change. "Is there anything else I can do for you?"

Terrio looked around the manager's cluttered domain. He sneered and left.

Out on the street Terrio felt very pleased with himself. He went over the events of the past few days as he shouldered his way down the sidewalk. On his first day back in Chicago he had sent his mother to a downtown dress shop for a complete new wardrobe. His second day was spent picking out a new car for himself. Later in the week he had casually dropped a thousand dollars in a poker game in Gary. And today he had paid for his mother's new furniture.

The most important aspect of each of the

four transactions was the fact that Uncle Tony owned pieces of the furniture store, the auto agency, the dress shop, and the clip joint where he found the poker game. Terrio wanted his Uncle Tony to hear about him and to understand three things: that he was back in Chicago, that he had plenty of money, and that he still wasn't taking handouts from his big-shot uncle.

Actually he was looking forward to seeing his uncle again and telling him about the Fort Riley job. Tony would be impressed. Aside from Ryan, his Uncle Tony was the only person Terrio had ever felt the need to impress.

Terrio had parked in an alley because of the heavy street traffic. He turned up the alley and walked toward his new Buick. It was a beautiful blue two-door job, but the air conditioner wasn't working right, and that was bad news on a July morning in Chicago. He was looking forward to busting the salesman's head if it wasn't fixed by five o'clock. Terrio was concentrating on that upcoming pleasure when a kid—no, he was a man with a little boy's face—stepped out of a doorway between him and the Buick and pointed a gun at him.

"Hold it," the man with the gun said. "Lift those hands."

Terrio reacted with his instinctive stubbornness. Instead of stopping, he shouted an obscenity and rushed the gunman with his head down and his hands clenched into clubs. The man with the gun, Captain Bob Price, was under orders from Hanson and Moody not to fire. His job was simply to stop Terrio while Moody and Hanson came up behind him. Price swung the automatic wildly at Terrio's head but missed, allowing Terrio to hit him with a smothering barrage of blows. Price fell to his knees and collapsed against a garbage can, covering his face with his hands.

"Cheap punk!"

Terrio spat on Price and reached down to pick up his gun. He half-turned when he heard Moody, but the big sergeant moved with surprising swiftness. He carried a length of pipe concealed in a rolled-up newspaper, and he hit Terrio with it carefully across the back, just below his neck. Terrio fell across Price's legs, conscious but in terrible pain. He managed a shout before Moody hit him a second time, again avoiding any possible killing points. The blow came across his lower back this time. Terrio shrieked and passed out.

When he came around, Terrio knew where he was. Approximately. The old Chicago stockyards had been shut down for some time, but its aroma was harder to dispose of. A putrid, shifting scent of dried dung enveloped him. A wind going across the old pen area rattled boards.

Terrio blinked his eyes but it did him no good. Two-inch swatches of tape were plastered across each eye. He was sitting on a straight-backed chair with his arms held behind the chair. Something metal encased his wrists, heavy wire or chain or maybe handcuffs. But most annoying was the realization that he was naked.

"Feel all right?" a voice asked.

Terrio didn't answer.

"We're here for the money. And we want to know where to find Dan Ryan. Save yourself a lot of trouble and pain. Tell us."

The words were spoken in rote. The speaker knew Terrio wouldn't talk, so Terrio didn't even bother telling the guy to shove it. A gritty aroma filled Terrio's nostrils. Cigar smoke. That would be the big guy who had caught him from behind.

"It's useless to question him without persuasion," another voice said. A more cultured voice, but with a hint of cracker in it. "We'll have to deal with him just as we did the other one."

The other one? They were still looking for Ryan so Terrio figured they must be talking about Hazlitt. Poor old Hazlitt. He wasn't such a bad guy. Good thing neither of them knew exactly where Ryan's place was; just that it was up in northern California near San Francisco. Terrio's head wrenched to one side as a fist hit him in the face.

"Stop that!" the smoother voice ordered.

"The rotten wop cost me a tooth!"

That was Baby Face talking. Terrio felt a surge of satisfaction.

"Your tooth is unimportant," the same smooth voice said. "You better get out of here, Price. Patrol the neighborhood in this man's car. Make sure we aren't disturbed."

"You won't be," Price promised. He was happy to get out. He had made the mistake of staying to watch Hanson work on that hick Hazlitt when they were down in Texas. What a butcher! After ten minutes he'd lurched outside to throw up. Hanson was nuts, General or not.

"Just a minute," General Hanson said. He was dressed as he had been at The Final Exam, but his usually immaculate appearance was marred by flecks of dark matter that spotted the front of his gabardine jacket. "Is that an ice-cream truck?"

Moody and Price cocked their heads and heard the cheerful music of an ice-cream vendor coming from one of the streets in the rundown neighborhood. "That's what it is," Moody agreed. "So what?"

"Find that truck," General Hanson ordered the pilot. "Bring me a big hunk of dry ice."

Price shrugged and slipped out the door. The place they were using was the kitchen of a shut-down café on the fringe of the old stockyard. When the yard closed down, it took a lot of small businesses with it, leaving the old café pretty much isolated in a block of vacant lots and empty industrial buildings.

Hanson slipped on a pair of leather gloves and walked up to Terrio. "Listen to me," he began. "I'm going to hurt you pretty badly. Scream all you want. No one will hear you. The moment you tell us what we want to know, you'll be all right again. Remember that as you're suffering. Understand that your pain is your own fault. You can stop it any time."

"Fuck you," Terrio said. He didn't fear what was going to happen, but he wanted to get it over with. A flaming pain shot from his groin in several directions, and he drew in his breath with a groan.

"Easy, General," the cigar smoker said. "Don't let him needle you into finishing him off."

"General?" Terrio laughed. "I get it now. Major General Arthur Hanson; right? And you want the money. Not to give back to the army, either. And you puffing on the El Ropo. I've got you pegged, too. Ryan's buddy. The one he ran into at Riley. Some buddy. I'm not surprised, though, General. Ryan said you were nothing but a prick with ears . . . Ahhh!"

Hanson had started to work. Moody watched, sitting up on one of the kitchen's ancient stoves. The General had done an inspired job on Hazlitt and Moody was sure he could make this wop talk, too. But ever since Texas the General had been a little flaky. In the plane he'd talked to himself. At first Moody thought he was going over his testimony for the hearings, but finally he caught a few snatches of what Hanson was saying. Something about cups . . . mixing . . . chives. A recipe. The General had been reciting recipes to himself. Chinese food. French cuisine. Italian stuff. Once Moody caught on, he could follow it. The General was supposed to be some kind of gourmet, but he was talking like something else. The last thing Moody needed on his hands was a freaked-out two-star general.

Terrio finally cried out. Moody was beginning to wonder when he would. A real tough one. Hanson was working him over the way he had Hazlitt. Pain followed by a quiet question. More pain and a question. Double pain and a question. New pain and a question. Worse pain and a question. But it wasn't working yet. Terrio had balls. But they wouldn't last through the day at this rate.

A few minutes later Price returned carrying a lump of dry ice wrapped in a rag in his right hand. His left hand held an Eskimo pie which he was nibbling at. When he saw Terrio he paled and tossed the Eskimo pie in a corner. "Here's your ice. I'll go back outside and look around."

Moody observed what Hanson did with the dry ice. After a while his cigar began to taste bad. He threw it in the corner with the melting Eskimo pie.

"How about it, Hanson?"

The General whirled on him. "*General* Hanson, Sergeant. Or *sir*. But never just Hanson."

"Yes sir." A lifetime of military service made it impossible for Moody to say anything else. Though he dearly wanted to kill Major General Arthur Hanson.

General Hanson motioned to Moody and they stepped out of the kitchen into the front of the old café. They weren't worried about Terrio making a break for it. He was slumped sideways. The only reason he didn't fall was that his hands were wired to the back of the chair.

"This is an unusual man," Hanson said.

"You mean you can't make him talk?"

The General shook his head. "I didn't say that. He'll talk, but physical torture isn't the complete answer. He has a very high threshold of pain. I've seen this before in communists who were highly motivated. Apparently Terrio has a great loyalty to Ryan. I think that's one thing keeping him from talking. If it were just the money he might not be so tough."

Moody thought that over. "Hazlitt didn't know just where Ryan lives. Maybe Terrio doesn't either. Just northern California." He tapped the dusty Formica counter top. "We have to find out more about Ryan."

"We might have learned a lot more from Hazlitt if you hadn't shot him," Hanson said severely.

"I had to! Price let Hazlitt get loose and grab his gun. Another two jumps and he'd have been out to the highway."

They both fell silent. Finally the General said, "Terrio might tell us where he's hidden his share of the cash if we promise to leave Ryan alone."

"He'd never believe us," Moody scoffed.

"Hand me Terrio's clothes," Hanson said abruptly. He took the clothes and put them on the table in one of the booths. He went through each piece of clothing carefully. One of the lessons of the CIA adviser in the Phoenix program came back to him: "You can break a weak man through his body, but a strong man must be attacked through his mind."

He showed Moody a snapshot from Terrio's wallet. It was of a plump, kindly-looking lady in a flowered print dress. "You and Price were following Terrio yesterday. Is this his mother?"

"Yeah. So what?"

"He has three pictures of her in his wallet."

"So?"

Price pulled up at the side door of the café. They could see him through the alley window. The General got out of the booth. "You stay with Terrio. Price is going to drive me on an errand."

"Whatever you say." Moody went back into the kitchen and returned to his seat on the stove. It was easy duty. Terrio was conscious but immobile, his naked body covered with raw wounds. Some of them were in unusual places. Places Moody never would have thought of. Cutting in Hanson had been a smart move, everything considered. They had Hazlitt's ninety thousand, so the trip had already showed a profit for both of them. Terrio couldn't have spent much of his split yet. He'd be good for at least eighty-five thousand. Not a bad week's work.

Price and Hanson returned. The General carried a package wrapped in butcher paper and his mouth was twisted into a queer little smile. He came up to Moody and whispered, "Watch this, Sergeant. It should be fun," and giggled like a schoolgirl.

Flakier and flakier, Moody thought. But he was interested in what the General was going to do. To his surprise Hanson unwrapped the package and produced . . . a chicken. A plain ninety-cent supermarket fryer. Moody looked at Price, who rolled his eyes.

Hanson proceeded to tear both wings and

legs off the chicken and toss them into one of the sinks. "Bring me some water," he ordered, though he was standing next to the sink.

Price, grumbling, found a cracked and dirty glass and filled it. The General had been issuing orders ever since the trip started, just to remind them he was in command. Moody let Price carry out the orders. The little pilot provided a convenient dumping ground for the hostility between him and Hanson.

Now Hanson poured some of the water over Terrio's head. He wanted the man concious but slow in his mental processes. "Are you awake?"

Terrio coughed.

"You were unconscious for quite a while, Sergeant Terrio."

"I'm not a sergeant. I'm a civilian and I don't want any part of your goddam army."

Hanson ignored that. He didn't like it, but he ignored it. There was no profit right now in side issues. "Since we couldn't talk to you, we decided to look at your apartment. Your mother made us feel right at home."

Terrio straightened up with some effort. "She doesn't know anything about this," he said evenly.

"I believe that's true. I questioned her at some length and she gave me no useful information."

"If you hurt her . . ."

"I'm afraid I did."

"You can kill me but I've got an uncle . . ."

"And I'll hurt your mother more if you

don't tell me exactly where your share of the money is. Forget Ryan. We'll let him go. Just tell me where to find the money."

Terrio lunged forward but was dragged back by the wire around his wrists. His breath started coming in enormous gasps. "You're a dead man if you've touched her, Hanson. Dead!"

Hanson gave Terrio one of the queer little smiles Moody didn't care for and turned away. He picked up the wingless and legless chicken and carried it over to Terrio. Holding it with both hands, he put it against Terrio's face. Terrio cringed from contact with the cold lump of flesh.

"Don't you recognize that?" Hanson said in a taunting voice. "Feel it again." Once more he thrust the flesh of the chicken right into Terrio's face, rubbing it around in an almost sensual way. "Don't you recognize your own mother's breast?"

Suggestion is a powerful force. Moody and Price stared at the oblong hunk of poultry and for just a split second they believed they saw a woman's breast. But Terrio really believed. The suggestion had him. His mind, drugged with pain, took Hanson's statement at face value. Because he was afraid for his mother, and because he knew what Hanson was capable of, he *believed.* With a wild moan he threw himself in Hanson's direction, toppling the chair and crashing to the cement floor.

Hanson went down on his knees, talking in a soothing tone an octave below Terrio's howls. "She's alive . . . hurt . . . we'll take her to a hospital . . . she'll be all right . . . she'll live . . . if you talk now."

"The car!" Terrio screamed. "Rip out the overhead liner. The money's up there."

Moody raced out into the alley. He slid inside the car and ran his fingers along the stitching where the liner was attached to the frame. He yanked at the overhead liner and it ripped. Thin packets of money cascaded out and fell over Moody's shoulders. Lots of packets of money. He laughed, recalling that he had noticed the extra-heavy locks on the car doors and security devices on the steering wheel. He had assumed that Terrio, being a thief himself, was naturally nervous about the possibility of having an expensive new car stolen. But it was more than that. He'd put the money here. Sure. Where else would a loner like Terrio hide it? He'd want it near him all the time.

Hanson and Price came out to the car, too. Moody wished Hanson would drop that shit-eating grin of his.

"Looks like all of it, except for what Terrio already spent." He scooped up the packets and pushed them into one large pile on the seat.

"Count it," Hanson said.

Another order, but one that Moody was delighted to follow. He flipped the bills with his thumb. Estimating. Five thousand to a packet. "Something over eighty thousand."

"Only eighty thousand?" Hanson frowned, displeased. "How could he have spent ten thousand dollars in a single week?"

Moody tapped the steering wheel of Terrio's car. "Buying stuff like this."

"What about Ryan?" Price asked. "Does it look like Terrio doesn't have his address either?" Price was tired of the chase and scared of Hanson. He hoped they'd be satisfied with what they had, almost a hundred and seventy thousand, and go back to Fort Riley. Price had his fifty thousand, and these two wouldn't put out a cent more no matter how much they recovered.

"All they say is that he lives in northern California," Hanson replied. "We also know that he's married and that his place is out in the country somewhere. That's not much to know. Northern California is a big place."

"Married," Moody repeated. He scooped up Terrio's share and pushed the money into Price's arms. "I want to ask that wop one question myself. If I had any brains I might have gotten the answer from my buddy in the admin office at Leavenworth."

They went back inside and sat Terrio upright in his chair. Moody slapped his face twice.

"What's the name of Ryan's wife?"

Terrio's jaw moved loosely. "My mother. You didn't . . ."

"She'll be all right if you answer me. Ryan's wife. What's her first name?"

"Julie."

Moody smiled widely. "Thanks." He pulled a large automatic from under his arm, thumbed the safety forward, cocked the hammer, and fired once.

Even in the age of jet travel it isn't easy to get to Lubbock, Texas. Ryan found that out. He caught the last air shuttle from Monterey to San Francisco on Thursday evening, but arrived at San Francisco International too late to connect with a night flight to Dallas or Houston. So the next morning he caught a seven A.M. American flight to Dallas, connecting with a three P.M. Braniff into Lubbock.

That's why it was after four P.M. on Friday before Ryan arrived at the Lubbock airport. He rented a car but felt reluctant to go straight to the hospital. Whoever shot Hazlitt might still be around hoping for Hazlitt's friends to show up. By now Ryan was convinced that Hazlitt's shooting was connected with the robbery. He'd gone over all the other possibilities. Hazlitt just wasn't a troublemaker. Not the kind who'd be shot in a barroom fight. Nor was he a man who'd make a mistake with a gun on a hunting trip.

Instead of going straight to the hospital, Ryan bought a copy of the Lubbock *Avalanche Journal* and turned to the classified ad section. He found a whole column of guns for sale, from .22 rifles to shotguns to tiny Beretta automatics and .357 Magnums. In Texas you can buy guns as easily as toothpaste. The map in the glove compartment of his rental car directed him to the nearest advertiser.

He found the place, a small frame house sitting on about an acre of property off one of the county roads. A two-trailer diesel truck sat in the driveway. When Ryan got out of his car, a couple of small boys in jeans and bare feet ran to the house calling, "Pa! Pa! Company comin'."

A burly man in work clothes came to the door, wiping his mouth with a paper napkin. He had gray curls and the wide-open friendliness of a long-haul freight driver, which is what his rig indicated he was.

"Howdy!"

Ryan came right back with a "Howdy!" of his own. "Saw your ad for a .38 Smith and Wesson in the paper."

"Sure. Come on it."

Ryan was ushered into a tiny front room containing four chairs arranged around a color TV.

"Meg!" the burly man bawled. "Another cawfee here. And warm mine, y'hear!" He winked at Ryan. "Come t'the den and setcherself down." He led the way down a dark hallway to a paneled room at the back of the house. Guns and trophy heads lined the walls, and an oak gun cabinet with a shatterproof glass front held the most prized weapons.

Ryan took a chair at his host's insistence. A pregnant young woman just verging on slatternliness brought two steaming cups of black coffee and went away again. "She's the reason I'm sellin' some of my guns," the man explained. "Got another kid comin' next month and those doctors don't take iron for payment. Not like when I was a kid. My old man paid off our family doc in hogs when I was born. There's them that say it was payment in kind." He grinned slowly. "My name's Billy Jo Brewster, by the way."

"Dan Ryan."

They shook hands rather formally. Ryan was in a hurry but he knew the quickest way to offend or raise suspicions in a man like Billy Jo would be to decline his hospitality. So he sat for about ten minutes talking over the weather and the holes in the Texas roads and the advantages of an open sight over a peep sight. When the coffee and conversation ran out, Billy Jo rose from his chair and took a pistol off the wall. He handed it to Ryan as if it were an heirloom.

"Right nice weapon," was all he said in the way of salesmanship.

Ryan checked it. He was sure it would be in perfect condition, cleaned and oiled at all times. Billy Jo would be that kind of man. It was, and he asked, "How much?"

This was clearly painful to Billy Jo. He didn't want to sell it in the first place, but if he had to, he wanted a decent price. "Paid a hundred and ten for it," he offered. "Gun prices have gone up since then, of course."

"I'll give you a hundred and twenty-five if you throw in a box of shells."

Billy Jo broke into a grin. "That's just what I was gonna ask if you made me do the askin'." He unlocked the bottom of the gun cabinet and took out a box of Peters center-fire .38 cartridges. Ryan paid him cash, putting the shells in his coat pocket and sticking the pistol inside his coat.

"So long, Ryan. Thanks." Billy Jo added in a joking voice, "Don't shoot no white folks with that .38."

"I can't promise anything," Ryan answered. When Billy Jo looked surprised, Ryan grinned to show he was joking, too.

The hospital was on 13th Street. Ryan circled it twice in his car but saw nothing out of the ordinary. He parked and loaded the .38 and tucked it out of sight again under his coat. It felt as cold and alien as a sleeping rodent.

It was six P.M. by that time. Visiting hours wouldn't begin until seven-thirty, but Ryan explained insistently that he had come all the way from California to see his cousin, LeRoy Hazlitt, and they finally let him go upstairs to talk to the floor nurse just to get him out of the lobby. At last Ryan had some luck. The floor nurse turned out to be the motherly type, more concerned with her patient than with the maze of procedures she had to work with. Her name was Mrs. Moffett. She took Ryan aside and opened the chart on Hazlitt and told him everything she knew about the case.

"A construction crew found your cousin out on Route 14. He came staggering out of a cotton field. Someone had apparently shot him and left him for dead." She shuddered and tucked a wisp of gray hair under her cap. "Poor man. He had been shot twice. And before that..."

When she hesitated Ryan prodded her. "Before that what?"

"Before that he'd been tortured. I know it seems bizarre in this day and age, but his body was horribly mutilated."

"Will he live?"

"No," Mrs. Moffett answered candidly. Death was no stranger to her and she saw no purpose in deceiving people. "The doctors are amazed that he's still alive. The shock to his system was enormous. And then the pain and loss of blood . . ."

"Can I talk to him?"

She sighed doubtfully. But her eyebrows knitted with an idea. "Let me look around." She patted Ryan's arm and padded off down the hallway, returning a scant five minutes later. "It's all right. The doctor isn't here. He's across the street in his office. He's allowed no visitors except for your cousin's sister, but I can't see what difference it makes to let you in. You're kin, too."

"Thank you."

The door to Hazlitt's room was closed. He followed Mrs. Moffett inside. It was a private room, especially equipped for critical cases. Hazlitt lay in the bed with tubes and wire leads running from various parts of his body to a computer-like console next to the bed. Ryan supposed the information on Hazlitt's condition was being monitored at the nursing station.

He hardly recognized Hazlitt. The false teeth Hazlitt had been issued in Leavenworth had been taken out of his mouth, shrinking the lower half of his face to the shape and size of a monkey's. The carroty hair had been shaved. His skin was a parchment gray. He looked like a very old man.

"Is he awake?"

Hazlitt's eyes fluttered at the sound of Ryan's voice, but didn't open. His mouth did move, though. "Hey . . . that you?"

"I'm here."

Mrs. Moffett studied the charts and graphs oscillating on the various instruments. "I'll be at the desk," she said and slipped out the door.

It took several seconds for Hazlitt to open his eyes. He stared at the ceiling awhile, then moved his head with care. "Ryan . . . what . . . brings you to God's country?"

"You do, you big hick. What the hell happened?"

Hazlitt tried to smile but gave it up. "I got myself . . . creamed . . . old buddy. Three of them. Big . . . guy. Good cigar. Little guy. Kid's face. Third one was . . . give you a laugh . . . your buddy, General Hanson."

"Hanson." So the stories about him were true. The big one would be Moody, of course. And the third man would be another GI as crooked as themselves.

"They got my share . . . coming for yours, too . . . and Terrio . . . recognized Hanson from . . . seeing him that once . . . staff car . . . remember?"

"I remember."

"I told them . . . where to find my . . . share. Couldn't help it . . . hurt me . . . I surprised them, though . . . got loose . . . grabbed a gun."

"Did you get one of them?"

Hazlitt laughed feebly. "You . . . know me . . . had the drop on . . . the big guy . . .

couldn't pull the trigger." His eyes closed and he lay silent for perhaps ten minutes. Ryan thought he'd gone back to sleep. When he opened his eyes he continued the conversation as if he had never broken it off. "Terrio's next. . . . You got to stop . . . them." Again his eyes closed. Hazlitt's eyelids were so translucent Ryan could almost see through them. They reopened more quickly this time. "Think I'll . . . take a transfer . . . out of . . . Leavenworth Irregulars . . . casualty rate . . . too high."

He began coughing and the graphs and needles started moving erratically. Ryan put his hand on Hazlitt's arm to let him know he was still there. When he finished coughing, Hazlitt responded with another of the awful smiles. Seeing the concern in Ryan's face, he searched for an optimistic side to his situation and somehow found one. "They only shot me twice," he said haltingly.

Ryan stayed with him another half hour. About seven-thirty Hazlitt took a series of deep, rattling breaths and died. The instruments attached to him were apparently working properly, because before the last breath had left him Mrs. Moffett rushed in with an intern. They were too late. There was nothing they could have done anyway. The intern went through the motions of examining Hazlitt, then folded the sheet over his face. The death of the patient seemed relatively unimportant to the intern, though he was clearly pleased that his instruments had functioned efficiently to the end. Before turning them off, he gave them a "well done" tap with his knuckles.

They were good enough to leave Ryan alone with Hazlitt for a few minutes. Ryan went up to the bed and lifted the sheet. He wanted to know exactly what to expect from Hanson and Moody. What he saw shocked him, though he thought he'd lost the ability to be shocked years ago. He understood now why Hazlitt's blanket had been raised several inches above his body by wire cradles attached to the bed. Even the pressure of a sheet and blanket would have created unbearable pain.

Ryan put the sheet back in place carefully and left the hospital room. He received a sympathetic good-bye from Mrs. Moffett and found the nearest phone booth to call Julie. She came on the line sounding tired and immediately added a layer of coldness to that.

"I put the orchard on the market today. The realtor says we might make a quick sale if we throw in this year's crop. That will wipe out any profit we might make, but I don't care."

"I'm in Lubbock," Ryan said. "Hazlitt just died."

"I'm sorry," Julie replied with genuine feeling.

"I want you to listen to me," Ryan continued. "Some people are after Terrio and me. I want you to leave the ranch right now. Go to Luis and Maria's, or better yet stay at a motel in Monterey."

"Are you coming home now?"

It was a cat-and-mouse question. "No. I'm going to Chicago to try to stop them from getting Terrio the way they got Hazlitt. I've tried to reach him by phone but there's no answer."

Julie's voice became cold again. "I thought so."

"You'll be okay. Just get out of there."

She was not going to be put off. "When will you be home?"

"In two or three days at the most. Let Luis and Maria know where you are. Or let's just pick a spot right now where I can find you. Go to the Holiday Inn at Monterey. The one on the beach near Fort Ord. I'll call you there tomorrow."

"All right."

"Good. I'll talk to you then. And Julie . . ." Ryan struggled with words, as he always did. "I love you too much to lose you because of this."

"Good-bye, Dan."

It was two hours earlier in California, not yet six o'clock, and Julie still had work to do. Luis had helped her rearrange the watering pattern earlier in the day and now she went out to the pump and turned off the water. The section she had been watering smelled sugary. The fruit was ripening fast. Branches drooped under the weight of the plums.

The phone rang again in the house, and Julie turned and ran back. She lifted the receiver just as the caller was about to hang up.

"Mrs. Ryan?"

"Yes."

"Bob Raymond here."

"Yes, Mr. Raymond. I didn't expect to hear from you this soon." Raymond was the realtor she had listed the property with.

"Tell the truth, I didn't think you would either. But I've got a prospect. He's just in the area for a couple of days. He's from down south in El Centro where he has a pretty good-sized operation in dried fruit. Figs and the like. Nice fella. He'd like to take a look at your place tomorrow morning."

Julie had never intended going to a motel. So she said, "Of course. I'll be here all day. Tell him to come along any time."

SATURDAY JULY 15

Price was watching the instrument panel of the Cessna Citation with a relaxed alertness. They were moving through the early morning light at five hundred miles per hour, twenty thousand feet in the air. "Jesus but this is a great plane. I'd give a whole bunch to own one."

"You'd have to give about half a million," Moody remarked, looking at the pockets of light in the blackness below. He didn't like flying. He preferred to walk or drive. Or even crawl.

They had left Chicago at ten P.M. and were flying west toward the San Francisco Bay area. Moody sat in the passenger seat next to Price. Behind them were two more passenger seats, and behind these a tiny lounge where General Hanson was stretched out drinking scotch and staring out the window.

"What the hell's he doing now?" Price whispered.

Moody glanced over his shoulder. Hanson was talking to himself again, between sips of scotch. He had talked to himself all the way from Chicago to Denver, where they had stopped to refuel because the Citation's range was only thirteen hundred miles. They would have just about enough fuel for the leg from Denver to northern California. At Denver the General had walked around the plane during refueling, talking numbers. Math problems. Simple ones, but the kind that had driven Moody crazy as a kid. "If a man is rowing upstream at ten miles an hour against a current moving downstream at seven miles an hour . . ."

Now it was something else.

"He's still at it," Moody said.

"He's really flipping out," Price grumbled.

The whine of the twin fan-jets partly obscured the General's words. The noise in turn made it difficult for him to hear the conversation between Moody and Price. Price tilted his head and listened. Logging almost three thousand hours in helicopters had made him adept at carrying on conversations over the roar of engines. In a few seconds he picked up the cadence of the General's words and understood what he was saying.

". . . and Mizraim begat Ludim and Anamim and Lehabim and Naphtuhim and Pathrusim and Casluhim, out of whom came Philistim . . ."

"He's back to the Bible again, like he was when we left Chicago."

"I didn't know you were a Bible thumper, Price."

"Southern Baptist since my great-granddad's time."

Moody spread his hands out to the sky around them. "Welcome to the Kingdom of Heaven."

Price cast a sidelong look at Moody. "You're still sore at me for letting Hazlitt get loose."

"It wasn't the smartest thing you ever did, Captain. We'd have lost ninety thousand dollars because of you if Hazlitt hadn't already told us where his money was."

"How was I to know he still had the strength to move like that? Especially after what Hanson did to him." Price checked his heading and looked at the stars for confirmation, then returned to the subject of Hazlitt. "I wonder why he didn't shoot when he snatched the gun out of my belt? He could have blown at least one of us in half. But he just looked at you over the sights, then turned and started running for the highway. I don't get it."

"According to his record Hazlitt just didn't like to kill people. That's what got him sent to Leavenworth."

"The creep!" Price was always angered when he heard of a soldier who refused to kill people. It was like farmers refusing to grow food or doctors declining to treat sick people.

"Sergeant!" Hanson's voice barked from the rear of the small jet. "What's our position?"

Moody let Price answer.

"We're about to pass over Salt Lake City, sir."

"I'll want a shower and a nap and a fresh change of clothes when we reach the coast."

Price saw that Moody wasn't going to answer, so he said, "Yes, sir."

The General began muttering to himself again.

"What are you going to do about that, Joe?" Price asked in a sotto voice.

"I don't know."

Price thought about it. On the seat behind him were two heavy gun cases that held the Russian AK-47s. Under those weapons was a smaller suitcase containing the money they had taken from Hazlitt and Terrio. Price concluded that he'd made a bad deal. Sure, he had fifty thousand dollars up front. But if Moody found Ryan, the total take would be close to three hundred thousand. Fifty grand wasn't a very big cut out of that amount of money.

One of the accessories to the Cessna Citation was a stereo tape deck. Both speakers were located in the small lounge where General Hanson sat talking to himself. Price flipped the stereo switch, and music came on in the rear of the plane. He waited to see if the General objected. Hanson didn't seem to notice the music, which made conversation even more difficult between the lounge and the pilot.

Price leaned toward Moody and said just loud enough for him to hear, "I've got an idea."

Moody raised an eyebrow.

"Why not get rid of him? No one knows you two are connected. You could keep most of the money and I'd take a slightly bigger cut for helping you dump him."

"What did you have in mind for our gallant leader?" Moody inquired.

The pilot let one wing of the plane dip and looked down. "We'll be over the Great Salt Lake in a few minutes. You take care of him and I'll slow the plane enough for you to slide open the door and drop him out. No one will ever see him again. He'll just disappear."

While Moody was considering the idea, Price added, "Listen, I've done it before. Not here, but overseas. A guy I was working with on the heroin run turned out to be chipping into other people's money. One of the slopes put him away, and I took the body out over the Gulf in a Huey and we lost him. No one ever knew what happened to him. It's easy."

Price studied the landscape. "Good moon. I can bring us right over the Salt Lake. The fall will mash him good, and after two days in all that salt he'll be nothing but a lump of brine. Even if he's found, no one will identify him. Just strip off his ID before you dump him."

The suggestion appealed to Moody. He wanted the money, and he was sick of Hanson. People would naturally think that General Hanson wasn't able to face the House hearings and had taken off. Disappeared of his own free will. Only two things stopped Moody from killing him. First, he might need Hanson to make Ryan talk. Hanson was good at that. The chicken gimmick had been a bitch. Second, Moody was afraid to open the door of an airplane in flight. Just looking down with a belt strapped tight around his waist gave him butterflies.

No. Not yet. In the back of his mind he had planned to kill Hanson all along. But not up here. Down there on the ground, Moody decided. No one has ever killed better than me down there.

"Not now," he said to Price. "I still need him. But after we've dealt with Ryan he'll just be overhead. Then we've got a deal."

Price grinned at the lights of Salt Lake City.

An hour and a half later they put down at Oakland International just across the bay from San Francisco.

Price asked if he should get a tie-down for the day.

"Not yet," Moody said. "I want you to make a phone call for me first."

They climbed out of the Citation. Hanson looked around. "I'm going into the terminal for breakfast, Sergeant. Bring my luggage. I'll clean up and change in the rest room."

Moody decided it was time to level with Hanson. "You aren't going anywhere right now. Price and I are going into the terminal. We have to use the phone to find out where Ryan is. You watch the money and the weapons; I don't want any airport people snooping around. We'll bring you back some coffee and doughnuts."

"Is that so?" the General bristled, but without his uniform and aides and driver and staff he somehow felt not quite formidable enough to deal with Moody. The longer they were separated from their military units, wearing civilian clothes and living together as equals, the more difficult it would be to maintain military discipline. "Very well." He turned to Price. "I'll have black coffee and mind that it's hot. Two English muffins crisply done. And a piece of fruit. An apple or orange will do."

"Yes, sir," Price said, trying to copy some of Moody's sarcasm into his voice.

They went into the terminal and found the phones. Moody searched the San Francisco yellow pages for theatrical booking agents. "Here he is. Ernie Bronson. He booked Julie into the Fort Ord NCO Club when I was running it."

He briefed Price on what he wanted him to tell Bronson. Moody would rather have talked to Bronson himself, but Bronson might recognize his voice. Price placed the call.

"Ernie Bronson here."

"Mr. Bronson," Price began, "my name is John Phillips. I'm in the restaurant business. East Coast mainly, but I'm opening a place in Carmel. I need some quality entertainment for my lounge. What I had in mind—"

"Don't say another word," Bronson interrupted. "I've got a real fine deal for you, Mr. Phillips. Lucy Malone just closed twenty weeks at the lounge of the Silver Slipper in Reno. She's a doll. Sounds like Peggy Lee in her prime and looks like a million dollars. And she don't play grab ass with the customers. I can have her down in Carmel for an audition in three hours."

"Sorry. I've got my mind set on someone else. I haven't seen her perform lately, but she has just the kind of class my new place needs, and I understand you handle her."

"Who's that?'" Bronson asked.

"Julie Walters."

"Julie! You're right. She's got a lot of class, that little girl. And a lot of talent, too. I don't know whether I can get her for you, though. She got married and hasn't been working much the last couple of years. She's as good as ever," Bronson added hastily. "Don't worry about that. And she still lives down near Carmel."

"Whereabouts?" Price asked casually.

"Got herself a ranch near Salinas. Raises plums and walnuts."

"I believe I heard that," Price said smoothly. "Near Salinas, you say?"

"Yeah, down there between Salinas and Gilroy. Why don't I give her a call right now and find out if she's interested in the job? How many weeks do you figure on giving her?"

"I'm not sure." Price was anxious to get off the phone now that he had the information Moody wanted. "Why don't you hold that call? I'll talk to the manager I've just hired to run the Carmel spot and we'll get back to you Monday."

"Good," Bronson said happily. "I'd like to see Julie in a class spot again. Talk to you Monday."

As soon as he got off the phone, Price went over the conversation with Moody.

"So she's living on a ranch," Moody repeated. "Between Salinas and Gilroy. That should be easy to find. Let's hope it's way out in the boondocks. Get the plane fueled again, Price. We're flying down the coast to Monterey."

The Ryan place was isolated. The grower from El Centro whom Julie showed it to that morning remarked on its isolation. "Who owns all the grape vineyards around here?" he wanted to know.

"One of the big wineries," she told him.

"They don't have anyone living on those big vineyards, I take it."

"That's right. My nearest neighbor is about three miles away. The vineyard manager lives in town."

The El Centro grower shook his head. "I'm big, too, in my own way. But I wouldn't live in no dirty city."

"I know how you feel."

"Why are you selling this place? Looks like it's doing right nice for you."

"Personal problems."

"Sorry," the grower said. He was a stringy man with an Oklahoma drawl who kept picking up clumps of dirt and rubbing them between his fingers until they broke down into grainy soil. "I'm looking for some plum orchards, but I need two or three adjoining spreads that I can put together into a single operation of maybe three or four hundred acres. I like your place, but there's just no room to expand with all these vineyards around you."

Julie said she understood, and the grower tipped his gray Stetson politely and drove away. She spent the next hour checking the husk-fly traps and recharging them by adding an additional tablespoon of ammonium carbonate to each trap. The number of flies caught in the traps was growing. Soon it would be time to spray. Funny. She'd almost miss the husk flies. Watching them build their numbers and mass for their attack on the walnut trees was exciting in a way. As much as she complained about it, Julie loved to fight the various elements that tried to destroy her orchards every year. She recognized some unarticulated need to prevail over them. The husk fly wasn't just a nuisance; it was Professor Moriarty to her

Sherlock Holmes. Defeating the husk fly in the annual battle gave her the feeling that besides growing crops, she was defeating some of the pestilence of the world.

She realized (the belated insight was embarrassing) that Dan felt that same way about General Hanson, who was as destructive to Dan's precious army as the husk fly is to a walnut orchard. Still, she couldn't forgive Dan for going away again after promising he wouldn't. And as for moving into a motel, that was just plain ridiculous. She could take care of herself.

Julie was not totally unimpressed by Dan's warning, however. The fact of Hazlitt's killing was sobering. She went into the house and took out the .22 target pistol kept in the bureau. One of her biggest problems in the early fall were the flocks of crows that invaded the walnut orchard for food, and the .22 was originally bought to deal with them. The crows had an interesting way of breaking open the green shell of an unripened walnut. Taking the nut in its beak, a crow would fly a hundred or so feet up in the air and drop it. When the walnut hit the ground it would often crack open far enough for the crow to work its beak inside and get at the kernel. Julie usually scared them off early in the season by potting one or two as they dived. Practice had given her a good eye for it. The crows got the idea fast and would usually move on to easier pickings.

Rats that occasionally nested in the trees

and rattlers that came down now and then from the barren hills to the east also made good target practice.

In the back of one of the kitchen cupboards were half a dozen empty wine bottles that Julie had been planning to do something artistic with for a long time. Better they should sacrifice themselves in the name of home security. With the pistol bumping in one pocket of her jeans and a handful of shells in another, she hiked out past the plum trees to an acre or so of vacant land with the wine bottles in her hands and tucked under her arms.

She set them out at various ranges from ten to fifty yards and on various elevations, using rocks and boulders and the branches of trees. For the next fifteen minutes Julie broke wine bottles. Not without missing quite a few times, but with consistently good marksmanship. When all the bottles were shattered, she shot at the larger pieces for a while and was gratified to see that she could hit them most of the time, too. She could take care of herself very nicely without Dan.

Ryan arrived at Chicago's O'Hare Field at about four P.M. Central Standard Time. He went to the phone booths immediately and tried Terrio's number again, as he had from Lubbock. Still no answer. The phone he always reached Terrio at was in his mother's apartment on the North Side. Someone should have answered. He looked in the book and found another Terrio listed. Anthony Terrio. Okay.

He figured to be the Uncle Tony that Terrio had mentioned twice during the job.

He called that number and asked for Mr. Terrio, harboring a hope that whoever answered would ask "Which one?" Instead the voice that did answer, a man who sounded bored and gruff at the same time, called "Tony! For you."

"Yeah?"

"Mr. Terrio?"

"Right."

"I'm looking for Paul Terrio. I think he's your nephew."

"Who are you?"

"Dan Ryan is my name."

"And you want to see Paulie?"

It was difficult to imagine anyone calling Terrio "Paulie." Ryan answered, "Yes. I'm at O'Hare Field right now. I just got into town."

"Well, I've got an appointment with Paulie tonight myself. We can go over there together. Why don't you swing by my office right now?"

Ryan didn't like it. The welcome was too smooth. But he didn't have much choice. "All right. I'll catch a cab."

Tony Terrio gave him an address on Wabash Avenue and Ryan told him he'd be there in half an hour.

It was the rush hour but most of the traffic was headed the other way. The cab pushed downtown on an expressway that had rapid transit cars running down the middle divider. Ryan was let out at a small tavern on Wabash Avenue behind the old Sheraton Blackstone

Hotel. It was an unimposing little bar without even a marquee to announce its name. The only decoration was a sign above the front door that read: "Vote the Straight Democratic Ticket."

Ryan went in, his footsteps hushed by a thick blanket of old-fashioned sawdust that covered the floor. There was a bar to the right, booths to the left, and tables in a partly enclosed room at the back. Half a dozen men lounged at the bar like birds along a telephone wire.

"Mr. Ryan? Come on back."

At one of the tables in the rear a man half-rose and motioned to him. Ryan walked on through to the back room.

"Sit down, Ryan."

The man who invited Ryan into his presence bore a strong resemblance to Terrio. He was squat but well muscled, dark, given to frowns and grimaces, and he had the same belligerent eyes Ryan had spent four years with in a cell.

"So you're looking for Paulie."

"That's right."

"What do you want with him?"

"It's a personal matter." Ryan interpreted a searching silence and added, "It's okay. We're friends."

"From where?"

"The army."

Tony Terrio laughed harshly. "Paulie never had a friend in his life. I know that for a fact."

"You're wrong. He had two friends. Okay,

it wasn't in the army. I knew him in Leavenworth."

A phone rang in a corner. One of the men came from the bar to answer it in tones too guttural to understand. He brought the phone over to Tony Terrio. "Bianco."

Tony grunted and took the receiver. "Bianco. I told you I'd settle things Wednesday. No. Absolutely not. They don't like that kind of thing in New York no more. They got too many politicians there, that's why. Yes. I got something else to do right now." He glanced at Ryan. "No. I don't need no one for this. Goodbye."

As Tony Terrio talked, his man stood at his side holding the phone. When he finished his conversation, Tony handed him the receiver and got up. "You want to see Paulie? Let's go."

They went out through a side door to an alley and climbed into the back seat of a black Lincoln. The half dozen characters in the bar came along, two of them in the front seat of the Lincoln and the others in a second car behind them.

"You like a lot of company," Ryan remarked.

"Sometimes," Tony Terrio agreed.

"Where to?" asked the driver.

"I want to take this guy to Marino's. He wants to say hello to Paulie."

The driver laughed and started the engine.

"Take Division Street. I want to show Mr. Ryan something."

As they wound through a maze of bumpy Chicago side streets, Tony said, "You ever wonder how a guy like Paulie ever got into the army in the first place?"

"Often," Ryan admitted. "But he never volunteered the information and he's not the kind of guy you push for it."

"I'll tell you a fact, Ryan. I'm kind of a big man in this town. Not the biggest, maybe. But I can park this Lincoln wherever I want and not worry about finding a ticket on the windshield." Tony Terrio's hand shot out. "Look there! That's what I wanted to show you." He leaned forward and cuffed the driver on the back of his head. "Slow down, jerk."

The driver hit the brakes and the Lincoln slowed to twenty miles an hour as they cruised past a neighborhood post office that also housed an army enlistment center.

"That's the place where Paulie enlisted. Six years ago, it was." He sighed with an angry rush of wind. "I would have set Paulie up in any kind of business he wanted. A legitimate business. Real estate. Automobiles. Insurance. I'm into all that stuff. But Paulie was always too independent to take anything from me for himself or his mother. He became a burglar. A burglar, for Chrissake! They used to call him the A and P kid, he knocked over so many supermarkets on the South Side. Then one night he opens a safe in a bar on Rush Street. The bar belongs to a friend of mine. A business associate. It's a goddam embarrassment to me, you know? So I paid the business associate back out of my own pocket. But there's one catch, he says. Paulie has to be disciplined. For a minute I had the shakes. I could see myself putting out a contract on my own dead brother's kid. But no. He just says Paulie's either gotta apologize personally or I have to send him out of town for at least two years.

"So I pick up Paulie in my car and we're driving around while I try to talk some sense into him. This is a big man he's fucked with. But if you know Paulie like you say, then you know how he came back at me. He don't apologize to no one. Ever. I'm getting madder and madder and finally I spot that post office and I slam on my brakes in the middle of the street. 'Okay,' I tell him. 'You don't apologize to my friend, then you get out of Chicago and you go straight in the goddam army. Either that or I'll put out a contract on you myself.'

"I was bluffing, of course. But Paulie don't bluff. He laughs at me and gets out of the car and goes in there to join the army." Tony Terrio groaned and let his chin fall to his chest. "You should have heard the noise his old lady gave me about *that.*"

The Lincoln made a sharp turn into an alley and stopped behind a red brick, two-story building. It struck Ryan that Chicagoans must have something against front doors; they seemed to come and go exclusively through alleys.

They got out and Ryan followed Tony again.

"This way," he said. They went through the rear door and down a long hallway. The building had a clinical odor of some kind. Ryan couldn't quite place it. They made an abrupt right turn and went through some heavy red curtains. Ryan found himself in what appeared to be a small chapel. He recognized the aroma then. It was the antiseptic staleness of a funeral parlor.

At one end of the room an oak casket stood open for viewing, draped with flowers. Additional displays of roses, gladioli, and carnations were arranged around the casket. Ryan walked past the rows of neatly spaced folding chairs and looked into the casket.

Terrio looked happy. It was the first time Ryan had ever seen his face in repose. He was surprised to see that Terrio had been a very handsome man. The creases and twists of perpetual anger had disappeared, leaving the straight, powerful lines of his face unobscured.

A small bald man came out from behind the curtains in back of the casket. He was wearing the whitest shirt and the blackest suit Ryan had ever seen. The suit was blacker than the ones train conductors wear. So was the tie.

"Is everything suitable, Mr. Terrio?"

"He looks fine, Marino. Is the other thing ready?"

The little man—Marino—glanced at Ryan. "Yes."

"Why didn't you tell me he was dead?" Ryan demanded.

Tony Terrio didn't answer the question. Instead he pointed to the curtains the undertaker, Marino, had come through. "Go in there," he ordered.

The six men who had accompanied them arranged themselves around Ryan so that he had no other choice. One of them patted him down.

"You don't use guns?" Tony inquired.

"I had one yesterday but I ditched it. You can't carry them on planes anymore."

"Go on in there."

Ryan went, pushed from behind, into a larger room where a variety of caskets were on display. There were large oak caskets like Terrio's, silvery aluminum coffins with tassled handles, tiny caskets for children, and even a few very simple ones, little more than wood boxes, for those without cash or credit ratings.

"Pick one out," Tony Terrio said. "Never mind the price tag. If you have to go, you might as well do it right." He patted one of the caskets the way a used car salesman shows his fondness for a late-model heap with no dents.

Answering would have been playing his game, so Ryan stepped away from them and stood in the center of the room. "You're making a stupid mistake, mister," was all he said.

At that moment Tony Terrio looked exactly like the other Terrio Ryan knew so well. His face was illuminated with a ruthless energy. "I don't know who the hell you are, Ryan, but it's no coincidence that you turned up here the day after my nephew gets himself killed over by the stockyard." He turned to his men and said, "Pick one out for him!"

Ryan was grabbed by six pairs of hands and lifted up to shoulder height. He hit one of the hoods squarely over the eye before both his arms were pinned. It didn't do much good. He found himself thrust inside one of the caskets. The bottom half of the casket cover shut with a bang and he lay on his back looking up at the ceiling.

"Where's Marino?" he heard Tony say.

Someone went and found the undertaker.

"Start it up," Tony ordered.

A moment later Ryan heard a muffled sound, like a heater coming on in a cold house. His brain was racing for a way out of this mess. All he wanted now was to get out of Chicago and get back to Julie. Sooner or later Moody and Hanson would turn up there.

Tony Terrio's face appeared above him.

"Comfortable, Ryan? That's real silk."

"I didn't have anything to do with killing Terrio—Paulie. He was a buddy. We were cellmates in Leavenworth."

"Marino's a good businessman," Tony continued, ignoring Ryan's remarks. "He has all the latest equipment. I insist on that, see, because I own a piece of this establishment. You hear that noise? That's the crematorium. The oven. You shove a casket and a body in there and it's nothing but ashes five minutes later. That's where you're going, Ryan, if you don't convince me right now that you didn't have anything to do with what happened to Paulie. And don't give me that crap about being a buddy of Paulie's. He was a genuine loner."

The silk pillow under Ryan's head began to dampen with his sweat. He swallowed hard and started talking. He told Tony Terrio how he and Hazlitt and his nephew planned and carried out the Fort Riley payroll robbery. He told them that Terrio was his friend and related a few of their adventures together. Hazlitt's death was something they could check out, so he told them how Hazlitt died even though it made him sick to talk about it. Finally Ryan said he knew who killed Hazlitt and Terrio, but that was his business. He'd settle it with them. "I got them into this. The robbery was my idea. I'll take care of the men who got Terrio. If you'll just stop playing Al Capone and let me out of this goddam box."

When he finished talking he expected the top half of the casket to close and to feel himself lifted up and dropped onto a conveyor belt that would carry him into the oven.

Tony's face disappeared. "Get him out," Ryan heard him say.

The bottom half of the casket cover was opened and Ryan was dragged out and put on his feet.

"Take off," Tony told his friends. "I'll see you later at the tavern." They left and he explained, "We're having the wake tonight. Paulie's mother will be there. She'd like to meet you, I think. She'd like to hear that Paulie made a couple of friends in his life. She always wished he was more social, like my brother." He looked Ryan over and reached out to straighten his tie. "You're a little rumpled. Sorry about the coffin, but I had to make sure you were who you said you were. Let's have a drink."

They went to Marino's office and settled down with a bottle of good bourbon. Tony told Ryan about the strings he pulled to have Terrio's body released so quickly. It had been found only last night. "They did the same things to him that they did to your other buddy," Tony said. "And you're next, Ryan."

"That's why I have to get back to California. They'll go there next, though I think it will take them some time to find my place. I never exactly advertised where I live."

"I don't like this business of you not telling me who killed Paulie." Tony swallowed his bourbon sourly. "I got a right to know."

"No," Ryan said firmly. "I told you. It's my problem and I'll handle it. If you don't like that, then you'd better light the oven again."

"I could send some of my people with you."

"No."

"Goddam it!" He almost broke the bottle of bourbon setting it down with a crash. "You can't deal me out of this altogether."

"I could use a gun," Ryan said. "But not here. I need one when I get to San Francisco."

Tony consulted the ceiling. When he lowered his eyes he said, "When you get into San Francisco go to the Curtis Hotel on Van Ness. Ask the man at the desk for a package for Mr. Johnson. Got it?"

"A package for Mr. Johnson," Ryan repeated.

"Don't worry about the gun. It'll be clean." He leaned forward in his chair and put a strong hand around Ryan's arm. "Those bastards . . . if you don't take care of them, I will. You don't have to tell me their names. I'm good at finding people, Ryan."

"I have to get them," Ryan reminded him. "It's them or me."

"That's what I'm saying," Tony barked with an exasperated look. "What if it's you?"

"It won't be."

Tony peered into Ryan's face for a long time before he seemed satisfied on that point. "I believe you. I got an idea why you were Paulie's friend. You have eyes like us Terrios." He pushed the bottle away and got to his feet reluctantly. "Come on. I want you to meet Paulie's mother now."

They went back to the chapel. Dozens of people were milling around in the foyer by now, going into the chapel where Terrio was laid out and coming out again. Talking. Taking nips from flasks in the corner.

"I thought you said Terrio didn't have any friends."

"These are *my* friends," Tony bragged.

The crowd parted for them, Tony patting backs and shaking hands and putting his cheek out for the women to peck at. Inside, a plump woman with broad features sat in the front row of folding chairs directly across from the casket. She had pools of tears in her eyes but she had stopped crying. Meeting her was difficult for Ryan. Tony made a big thing out of what a good friend Ryan and "Paulie" had been and told her that Ryan came all the way from California to pay his respects.

Tony also whispered in her ear, "He knows who did this terrible thing. He's taking the responsibility for avenging Paulie."

Mrs. Terrio grabbed Ryan's hand. "Kill them!" she said, startling Ryan with her fierceness. For a second she was as wild and hard as Terrio himself. Then she became a grieving mother again.

It was an hour before Tony would let Ryan slip away. There was an eleven P.M. flight to San Francisco but when he arrived at O'Hare he found the field blanketed in fog. Departing flights had been canceled. He would have to wait for a morning flight again.

When he called the Holiday Inn in Monterey, the hotel operator told him that Mrs. Ryan wasn't registered there. Thinking she might have misunderstood, he called the Carmel Holiday Inn a few miles south. But she wasn't there either. He knew then that Julie had not taken his instructions. He called the ranch, and when she answered he said, "What the hell are you doing at home? I told you to get out of there and I meant it." For the first time in their marriage he was really mad at Julie. Without waiting for her explanation, he told her, "Pack a bag right now. Go to the Holiday Inn. I don't want any arguments about this, Julie, because it's not something you're doing for me. It's not nothing to do with whether or not we stay together. There are some people looking for me and for your own sake it would be safer to move out of the house for a while."

Julie waited the space of several seconds

before answering him. "Are you through? Then you might as well know that I'm not going anywhere." She continued in a very even voice. "I'm perfectly fine here. I've had two prospects for the place today and I don't intend to miss any others who come by." Her voice softened. "Terrio—your other friend. What happened to him?"

"Never mind." He wanted her safe, but not too scared to function. Besides, he felt certain that he hadn't left as wide a trail as Hazlitt and Terrio. It would take them a few days, at least, to track him to his ranch. "Look. I'm at O'Hare Field in Chicago. The city is socked in but I've got a flight out of here for San Francisco in the morning. I'll be home tomorrow by mid-afternoon."

"That won't change anything."

"We'll talk about us when I'm sure you're safe."

"We won't talk about it. I've decided. You went off once too often." She hung up.

Ryan cursed the fog and airlines and women in general. It was ten o'clock and he had nine hours to wait for his plane. As he was leaving the terminal to find a motel, a story just above the front-page fold on the Chicago *Sun-Times* caught his eye. He bought a paper and scanned the column of type.

ARMY PAYROLL RECOVERED IN CANADA; GUNMAN KILLED BY CUSTOMS AGENT

The $600,000 army payroll stolen in a daring robbery from Fort Riley, Kansas, more than a week ago was recovered today when two men described as German nationals tried unsuccessfully to smuggle the money out of Canada.
One of the Germans, identified as Heinrich Strasser of

Munich, was killed by a Canadian customs agent, William Whyte.
According to Whyte, Strasser and the second German, identified as Erwin Mann, also of Munich, were boarding a private aircraft at a small field near Toronto when Whyte and two other customs agents stopped them to search their aircraft. When the money was discovered, Strasser and Mann attempted to escape custody. "Strasser pulled a Luger and he and the other guy started running for the car they'd driven to the air field," Whyte stated. "I didn't want to shoot, but he opened fire and I had no choice."
Mann had been recognized by customs agents when he crossed the U.S.-Canada border at Niagara Falls two days earlier. Whyte said that Mann was alone at the time and offered a theory that Strasser brought the money across the border at another spot. Customs agents were watching Mann when he met Strasser the following day in Toronto.
Federal authorities in Kansas City say they doubt that Mann and Strasser actually took part in the robbery. Mann is known to InterPol as a dealer in various foreign currencies. He surrendered quietly after his partner was gunned down.

Ryan shivered. That bundle of money had turned out to be poison to everyone who touched it. He found himself wiping his palms on his pants as if to rid himself of the taint of the money.

Julie felt better after talking to Dan. It was always therapeutic, she believed, to hang up a phone on a man. It ranked right up there with painting fingernails in the car and wearing rollers to bed as a way to annoy a man.

However, now that Dan was definitely on the way home Julie found herself beginning to have second thoughts about selling the ranch.

But what if he left again? she asked herself.

Why should he? she answered.

An emergency like this one didn't come up every day. The time had come to admit to herself that she didn't really want to leave him. She realized that she'd been punishing him by threatening to sell the ranch. Would she even want a man who could be manipulated into abandoning his friends? One of the qualities that had attracted her to Dan in the first place —a quality that made him stand out from other men—was his tough-minded determination to do what had to be done whatever the cost. That's what got him sent to Leavenworth, of course. He didn't have to run medical supplies to that orphanage. It wasn't a strictly legal thing to do, even though it was the right thing. Damn!

She paced the small living room for fifteen minutes, then called the realtor again. "Mr. Raymond. This is Julie Ryan. I'm sorry to call so late."

"It's only seven, Mrs. Ryan. I'm usually here in the evenings unless I'm out showing property. Any luck with those prospects I sent over?"

"No. And frankly I'm just as glad I haven't found a buyer. I think I've changed my mind about selling."

"I see. Well, I don't blame you. You've put so much work into that place."

"Thank you."

"But—if you change your mind again, remember your friendly Salinas realtor."

Julie promised she would and was saying good-bye when Mr. Raymond stopped her. "Just happened to think. A party called about your place a couple of hours ago. Man name of Fred Jones, he said. I wanted to bring him out myself but he said he didn't know when he could get away. Said he'd drop by alone in the next day or so. I'm afraid you'll have to tell him about taking the place off the market. Hope he doesn't get sore about driving all the way out there for nothing."

"I'll handle it, Mr. Raymond. And thank you very much for everything."

At seven P.M. in July the sun is still above the range of coastal mountains to the west, so Julie went out to the front porch with a glass of wine to enjoy the last light.

She was sitting on the steps when the green Ford came up the driveway. It was a rented car. She could tell that from the Valcar sticker on the front grill. "Oh, God! I hope they didn't rent a car just to come out here." She dashed inside to put on fresh lipstick and get rid of the wine glass. When she came back outside, two people were standing in front of the Ford, one a small man with the grin and movements of a large child and the other a tall, handsome man with iron-gray hair who held himself very straight. The way Dan does, she noticed.

"Hi." She spoke with unnatural brightness, thinking that if she were cheerful enough they might not be too disappointed that the ranch was off the market. "I'm Julie Ryan."

"Good evening, Mrs. Ryan," the taller of the two said. The small man had started around the house already. There was another man in the back seat of the car. He was big—not just tall, but big all over—but his face remained far enough back in the shadows so that Julie couldn't see what he looked like. There was something familiar....

"I understand from your realtor that Mr. Ryan is out of town," the one who stood like Dan said.

"Yes. I'm sorry you've come all the way out here. The ranch has just been . . . taken off the market." She had turned to call to the small man, who was disappearing around the side of the house.

"He didn't hear me."

"When will your husband return?"

"Tomorrow afternoon. But, as I said, the ranch isn't for sale anymore."

"Is anyone else here?"

"No. I don't think you understand..."

"There aren't any other houses around here, are there? We didn't see anything but vineyards as we drove in."

"No. Our place is sort of isolated . . ." Julie grasped that this man did understand the place wasn't for sale. He wanted something else. The third man—the one in the back seat of the Ford—opened his door and squeezed out. He stood grinning at her with his huge arms resting on the top of the car.

"Hello, Julie. It's been a long time."

Julie whirled and ran for the house. She heard no footsteps behind her, but that didn't slow her down any. She had to reach the .22 target pistol.

Bob Price opened the front door just as she hit the steps. They collided. Price was stronger than his size indicated. Julie rebounded off his wiry body like a basketball, bouncing backward and sprawling at the foot of the front steps. Price stood at the door, unmoved, holding the target pistol.

"I found this in a bureau. I don't think there are any more guns in the house."

Moody came around the car. He stood over her with the others, watching her silently without moving to help her up, his hands on his hips. Huge in a red-and-black-checkered hunting shirt, he was even more imposing than Julie remembered.

"Julie, Julie!" He smiled. "You're as beautiful as ever, girl. Tell me, can you still sing?"

"I can sing," Julie snapped back. "And I can scream."

"Go ahead," Moody laughed. "We're away the hell out in the boondocks, like you said. I'm obliged to you for living in such an isolated place. Couldn't have picked a better spot myself."

"Help the girl up, Sergeant," Hanson ordered. "Captain Price, get back in the car and recon the area more thoroughly. Make sure no one's around. And see if you can find a secondary headquarters; we might not want to meet Ryan on his own terrain."

The last thing Moody wanted was to take another order from General Hanson, but his directions were sound, so Moody nodded his agreement to Price. The pilot climbed into the car and drove away, and Moody reached down to pull Julie to her feet.

"Yeah. You're still some woman, Julie."

Moody continued to hold her as he spoke, stroking the underside of her arm with a thumb like a large sausage.

Her skin crawling, Julie struggled to get free.

"Don't worry, Julie. No one's going to hurt you. We just want the money Dan stole. Do you know where it is?"

"No!" She was suddenly very glad that Dan hadn't told her. If she knew, they'd find a way to get the information out of her. And once they had the money, she'd be dead. Julie knew that for a certainty. "He buried it, and he didn't tell me where."

Moody studied her and believed what she said.

"Bring her inside," Hanson ordered.

"Yes, General." Moody's reply was thick with sarcasm.

"General!" Julie took a closer look at the erect figure and knew why he reminded her of Dan. The military bearing was no coincidence. "You're General Hanson!" She was so shocked that she let Moody lead her docilely into her own house.

"Where's the telephone?" Hanson inquired.

"You want the money, too? What kind of General are you?"

Hanson ignored her and found the phone himself, half out of sight on a low end table next to the living-room couch. "The living room is off limits to you, Mrs. Ryan. Stay in the kitchen and dining room and never move out of sight of one of the three of us. If you do,

I'll discipline you myself. And you won't like my methods one bit."

Moody laughed. "Lays it right out, don't he?" Seeing Julie again was a tonic. Despite the way her auburn hair was piled on top of her head and the work jeans and man's shirt, she was still one hell of a woman. Her waist was as narrow as ever and the eyes bolder than police sirens. He reached out and pulled off the elastic headband holding back her hair. It fell to her shoulders before she could raise her hand. "Yeah. That's how you wore it at the club in the old days. 'Try a Little Tenderness.' Remember that one, Julie?" He spotted the small piano in the corner. "Come on. Give us a chorus for old times' sake."

"Go to hell, Joe."

He laughed and drew a fresh cigar out. "You always were a sassy one. Couldn't see me for batting your eyes at Danny boy."

"I wasn't about to become one of your whores, if that's what you mean."

"Real sassy," he repeated. His voice dropped. "We're gonna take some of that sass out of you, Julie. You and Dan both." He stripped the cellophane wrapper off the cigar and let it drop to the floor. "Has he phoned you today?"

"No." But her mouth twitched involuntarily and Moody read the truth in that movement.

"Where was he? Chicago? Texas?"

Julie didn't answer.

"How did he discover we were after him, Mrs. Ryan?"

Hanson's voice was so pleasant and reasonable that Julie found it hard to believe he was the man who had sent Dan to prison.

"Was it the newspaper ad?"

Moody blew an expanding cloud of blue cigar smoke and chuckled. "We saw Hazlitt's name in that ad, too. In the *Chicago Tribune*. Damn near choked on my panatella. I knew that if Ryan saw it he'd be on our trail, but we're just a couple of steps ahead of him."

Hanson went to the front window and peered out into the fading light. "The money's in the back of the car. What if Price doesn't come back?"

"Don't worry none, sir. He'll be back. He wouldn't want us on his trail. He saw you work on Hazlitt and Terrio, remember."

Hanson jerked around, shocking Julie by the change in his features. The General's stern good looks had been transformed into a glowering ugliness. His fears swept over his face like waves across a beach. It was hideous to watch. Julie turned away.

"He'll be back," Moody said in a soothing voice. Hanson needed something to do, a job that would take his mind off himself and the things he'd done in the past few days.

Moody went to the service porch and found a coil of washline rope. He cut four lengths from it and went back to the dining room. "Sit down there, Julie."

She moved reluctantly to one of the dining-room chairs. Moody set her down in it and tied her wrists to the arms of the chair and her ankles to its legs.

A car could be heard churning gravel as it came up the driveway. Moody took a pistol out and moved to the front window.

"It's Price," he said to no one in particular. He went out to the front porch and waved the pistol at the side of the house. "Put the car in back with their pickup," he called.

Price drove around back and parked. Moody followed him. They came in through the back door, Moody lugging an oversize suitcase which he dropped on the dining-room table.

"What did you find?" he asked Price.

"No one around for miles," Price said with his infant's grin. "The vineyards all seem to be owned by some big wine outfit. No houses on them at all. I found a side road and took it about three miles up into those hills to the east. There's an abandoned quicksilver mine up there. Little office building and everything. Might be a good place to take Ryan and her when we've got them both."

Moody opened the suitcase and took out some long cylinders. It wasn't until he had one of the AK-47s partly assembled that Julie realized what they were. Two automatic weapons. Moody assembled them quickly and expertly. He inserted long, banana-shaped magazines into the weapons and let the bolts slam home.

"There. Price, you'll have to spend part of the night out in the orchard." Price groaned but Moody ignored him. "Ryan might show up any time." He looked at his watch. "It'll be dark in half an hour, so you get out there and find a spot with a good field of fire. You'll be out there until one A.M. I'll relieve you then so you can come in and sleep. General Hanson can pull interior guard duty while I grab some sleep right now. That way we'll always have two men awake and covering the situation from both the house and orchard."

"Christ, I was up all last night flying the plane," Price complained. But he picked up one of the AK-47s and followed Moody to the front window.

"That looks like the best spot." Moody pointed to the pump housing fifty yards from the house. "Good cover, and you can put a field of fire on the whole front of the house. Not that I want any shooting. Remember that we need Ryan alive."

"What if he's armed and spots us?"

"We've got his wife. I don't think he'll use his gun when he sees that."

"But what if he does?" Price persisted.

"Then cut his legs out from under him. But if you kill him, Price, you're a dead man yourself. The General needs a live body to work on."

Julie could hardly believe what she was hearing. A major general in the United States Army was listening to the conversation and adding his agreement to what Moody said. This man Price, apparently an army captain, was eager to take Dan and her up in the mountains and do whatever he had to do to put his hands on that money. She expected callousness from Moody, but she had thought he was an exception. A one-in-a-million case of corruption. Apparently Dan was right. There were more men like these, hiding behind army uniforms for their own dirty reasons, than anyone cared to admit. She no longer blamed Dan at all for leaving her. If she'd known . . . understood . . . she would have sent him after them.

"I'm hungry," Price complained, managing to sound like a child as well as look like one.

"I'm sure Julie runs a good mess." Moody winked at her. "Take what you want from the refrigerator."

Price went into the kitchen and came out a minute later with the automatic weapon slung over his shoulder and a triangular cut of cheese and a carton of milk in his hands. "This'll do me."

The valley darkened. Moody did not turn on any of the living-room lamps. Instead he placed one floor lamp in a position in the dining room where it would throw some light to both the kitchen and living room, but not enough for anyone to see into either of those rooms from outside the house.

"I'm gonna take a few z's, General," Moody said. He gave his weapon to Hanson and stretched out on the couch. Before long Julie could hear him snoring with mild, sonorous wheezes.

Her arms and back were aching before midnight. Every new position she wriggled into gave her fewer minutes of relief from the pain.

General Hanson heard her moving around. He came in and put his heavy gun down on the table. "I'll loosen the ropes on your wrists for a moment," he offered. "Can't let the circulation stop."

"Thank you." Julie had no feeling of gratitude, but there was a slack hunger on the General's face that she didn't like. Perhaps she could hold him off with politeness.

At first he did nothing except loosen the ropes, one set at a time, and gently massage some feeling back into her wrists. But when both hands had been loosened, massaged, and retied, he let his hands fall to her legs.

"Sergeant Moody is a clod, but he's right about one thing. You are very beautiful. I can see why he dislikes your husband so much."

"Please, General." She used his rank to try to remind him of his position. His hands were moving over her body, exploring and caressing with a roughness she would have expected more readily from Moody. "No! Please!" She thought of crying out, but feared that Moody or Price would only decide to join the General and make an old-fashioned gang-bang out of this. "Stop, please!" His hands were like lobster claws on her breasts.

She expected him to pull off her clothes. But instead he sank to his knees and pressed the lower half of his body against her legs. She could feel the shape of his genitals through his pants, rubbing circularly against her legs.

"Yes! Yes!" he said urgently, but still quietly enough so that he didn't waken Moody. "Yes! Ah! Ahhh!"

Julie, her eyes closed so tight they hurt,

felt the release and a sodden wetness on her legs. Her stomach churned. She was shaking so hard that the chair rattled on the floor.

When her eyes opened, General Hanson was standing with his back to her, wiping at the stained crotch of his slacks with a brilliantly white handkerchief. He carefully folded the handkerchief when he was done, put it into his hip pocket, and took the submachine gun back to his chair in the living room.

SUNDAY
JULY 16

In the morning Julie came awake trembling. The back of her neck seemed to be gripped by a strong hand. She had fallen asleep with her head hanging to one side. Now, with small movements, she managed to lift her head. Blinking at the sun, she pulled herself upright. Her hands were numb and looked unnaturally pale. The flesh had swollen to a puffy blue color around the ropes.

Moody came in the front door. "Wake up, General. Your turn to work outside."

Hanson sat up on the couch. "Very well, Sergeant." He looked through Julie as if she didn't exist. As if nothing had happened between them during the night. "Loosen Mrs. Ryan's ropes, Sergeant. We'll need to be fed. I'll have hot tea and toast. You can send it outside." He got up and took one of the AK-47s from Moody. "Carry on." He went outside and walked toward the pump.

"Ain't he something?" Moody laughed.

Price was sitting in the living-room chair with the other automatic weapon, yawning and scratching his beard. He watched listlessly as Moody untied Julie and helped her to her feet.

At first she couldn't stand by herself. Her feet were too numb to work and her hands couldn't grip the dining-room table for support. It was galling to have Moody supporting her, but she had no choice. Anything was better than another hour in that chair.

"Are you gonna be a good girl, Julie? If you are, I'll let you make us some breakfast."

"All right." She'd agree to anything just to be able to *move*.

In a rare gesture of gallantry Moody helped her to the bathroom and left her alone. She sat on the side of the bathtub, waiting for the circulation to improve in her hands and feet. She heard Moody tell Price to keep the AK-47 slung over his shoulder so she couldn't get her hands on it and to stow his handgun out of sight as well. Good advice. If Julie had a chance to grab a gun, she would. And the first shot would go straight into Major General Arthur Hanson. When she felt well enough to stand, she washed her face and brushed her teeth.

As Julie came out of the bathroom, Moody motioned her into the kitchen. It seemed almost natural to begin assembling the elements of a big breakfast. Eggs on the stove. Bacon simmering in the pan. Bread in the toaster. Coffee boiling. The sounds of breakfast cheered her. *Something* would happen to stop these people. She had confidence in Dan. If only she'd taken his advice and gotten away from the ranch. Pride goeth. . . .

"You and the General have a good time last night?" Moody asked.

"Me and the General?" She turned on him. "You were awake? You heard what was going on?"

"Sure. I figured something like that would happen."

"I don't understand. You seem to have wanted it to happen."

Moody poured himself a cup of coffee. "I did. The General doesn't have all his smarts, as you must have guessed by now. What I mean is he's crazy. Freaked out. He needed something to calm him down awhile longer, and you were it."

The mingled aromas of breakfast were usually like perfume to Julie, but now they turned her stomach. Moody's calculated use of her as therapy for the General was almost as bad as what Hanson had done. She went through the motions of fixing breakfast, and when it was ready she was sent outside with toast and eggs and coffee for General Hanson.

As she carried the tray across the fifty yards of open space between the house and pump, she had to fight her nerves to keep from dropping the food and running. That would be useless, of course. They'd catch her immediately. Or shoot her. Price had the keys to the pickup anyway.

Hanson glowered when she set his tray down by him. "This isn't what I ordered for breakfast."

"We don't have any tea," Julie snapped. "And Joe said you might want some eggs and coffee with your toast. I don't care whether you eat or not."

He yawned and put the automatic weapon aside. Julie grabbed for it, but Hanson pushed her away almost absently. "Don't do that again," he said calmly, picking up his coffee. "We've lived with guns all our lives. You can't take them away from us that easily."

Julie returned to the house with her eyes down.

"You had to try it, didn't you?" Moody said. "Okay. Back in the chair."

"What if someone shows up here today?" Price said. "Someone besides Ryan, I mean." He was at the dining-room table gulping down his breakfast. "She'll have to get rid of them for us."

"I know that," Moody barked. "We won't have to tie her up so tight now that everyone's awake."

Julie looked at the clock on the living room mantel. Eight A.M. And Dan had said he would be home by mid-afternoon. *Please God, don't let him be caught.*

"He'll be here," Moody promised, watching her and knowing what she was thinking. "Don't worry about him. Flying is safer than driving these days."

It was eleven A.M. before Ryan stepped off a United Airlines flight at San Francisco International. He rented a car but hesitated taking it on the freeway while he pondered whether to take the time to go north to San Francisco before doubling back to the south toward his ranch. Monterey County is a hundred miles south of the airport and San Francisco is fifteen miles north.

He finally decided to use an hour to pick up the gun Tony Terrio had promised, not that he expected Hanson and Moody to reach the ranch ahead of him. It would take them perhaps two or three days to discover where he lived. Maybe longer. But there was no guarantee of that, of course. So he took the Bayshore Freeway into the city and crawled up Van Ness Avenue past all the auto showrooms to the Curtis Hotel.

The man on the desk seemed an unlikely person to be holding a hot gun for Tony Terrio. He was past sixty, gray in both hair and skin, and his demeanor advertised a desire to remain offensive to everyone.

But when Ryan asked, "Do you have a package for Mr. Johnson?" the desk clerk brought out a flat parcel wrapped in multicolored Happy Birthday paper. It was even decorated with a garish pink ribbon. Thinking there had been a mistake, Ryan accepted the package anyway.

"And best wishes, sir," the clerk said as he left the lobby. Ryan unwrapped the package in his car. He was elated to find that it did contain a gun, a heavy .38 belly gun with the maker's name and serial number burnt out with acid and the indentation refilled with spot welds of steel. The combination of being only two hours from home and having a good weapon and feeling that he was ahead of Moody and Hanson raised his spirits higher than they'd been since he learned of Hazlitt's shooting. He stowed the pistol and extra rounds in the glove compartment and turned back to the Bayshore Freeway to head south for the Salinas Valley.

Nothing had happened all day. No visitors and no phone calls. By one o'clock everyone was jumpy. The previous night's precautions had just been ordinary security. Now they were ready. Moody was out behind the pump with his AK-47. Price had a spot at the front window with the other automatic weapon. Hanson roamed the house nervously, watching Julie as Moody had ordered him to do. She was back in the chair again, tied by wrists and ankles.

Taking the order from Moody seemed to have upset Hanson. He walked ceaselessly from one room to another reciting a strange litany in a subdued voice. Julie caught a few words as he passed by her. It sounded like lines from Shakespeare. At least she thought she heard the words, ". . . I think my wife be honest, and think that she is not. I think thou art just, and think thou art not."

Hanson's mutterings were obviously annoying Price. The captain went out on the porch and called to Moody, who left the shelter of the pump and joined him.

"What's wrong?"

"He's at it again," Price complained.

Before Moody could answer, they both heard a car approaching the house. Moody pushed the pilot inside and they took up positions on either side of the front window.

Julie had planned to yell as soon as Dan came within earshot. Now was the time, but before she could make a sound Hanson clapped his hand over her mouth.

"It's not him," Price said. He had seen their wedding picture on the bedroom dresser.

"Who is it then?" Hanson asked.

"I don't know. A man and a woman."

Julie made a noise behind Hanson's hand and he got the idea that she wanted to tell them something. He took his hand gingerly from her mouth and Julie quickly said, "Please don't hurt them. They're friends of mine."

"How do you know who's out there?" Moody demanded.

"I know the sound of the car. It belongs to Luis and Maria Ronda. Don't hurt them," she begged again.

Moody peeped through the curtains. "It's a couple of Mexican shit-kickers, all right." He untied Julie. "Get rid of them. You know what'll happen to them if you try to warn them about us."

She rubbed her wrists. "Why don't you just put zippers on those ropes?"

"Get out there!"

Julie hurried down the steps before Luis and Maria could leave their car. "Hi! I heard you coming. Hey, I'd like to ask you in, but Dan's on the phone long distance from Chicago. He's coming home."

Luis and Maria both leaned toward the driver's window. "He's coming home?" Maria smiled. "That's great. We heard in town that your place is off the market. I hope that means you two aren't splitting up after all."

The laugh Julie answered with sounded false to her own ears, but Luis and Maria seemed to accept it. "That's right. I guess I just let my temper get the best of me again."

"You all right?" Luis asked.

"What do you mean?" God, make them go. Don't drag them into this.

"You just look awfully tired," Luis said, studying her carefully.

"I am. Look"—she glanced over her shoulder—"I don't want to leave Dan hanging on the phone. I'll come over tomorrow." To cut off further conversation Julie turned and went back up the steps. She stopped at the door to wave good-bye, then went inside and closed the door with her back. Shaking, she continued to lean against the door until Luis started up his car and drove away. "Thank God."

"Very good, Julie." Moody was in a complimentary humor. He set his weapon butt down in the corner and pulled out another cigar.

"This isn't good, Sergeant," Hanson said, pacing the dining-room floor. "We can't have too many people paying social calls on Mrs. Ryan."

Price agreed. "Who's gonna show up next? The dry cleaner?"

"Okay," Moody said. "I agree that it's liable to get too busy around here. You'd better take the girl, General, and fall back to our next perimeter, that mine shaft." As he talked, he planned. He would have to get rid of Hanson soon . . . and Price. I'm not being greedy, he told himself. It's just that three hundred grand isn't enough for three people. They all have to disappear if I'm going to have the money I need when the army busts me. And if I'm going to be safe afterwards. "That's the best plan, General. You dig in there with Julie until Price and I grab her husband."

That was exactly what Hanson had been about to suggest himself. He tried not to appear too pleased.

"Yes. Price says it's a good spot. Plenty of privacy and shelter. Even an old Coleman lantern left in the building. We'll be fine there until you've got Ryan." Let Price and Moody wait for Ryan, he thought. If Ryan somehow turned the tables and finished off Moody and Price, so much the better. He could kill the girl and have all the money to himself, excepting Ryan's share.

A few minutes later Hanson took Julie

away in the Ford with her wrists again tied, this time to the hand grip over the glove compartment. Price complained, "I don't like it, Joe. He's sitting up there in the hills holding all the money while we face Ryan down here."

"He's just in the way anyhow," Moody explained. "The only thing he's good for is making people talk. Now get out there behind the pump and keep your head down."

Luis and Maria were driving north on Highway 101 toward Gilroy to do a little shopping and to talk with a labor contractor who wanted to provide them with workers for the harvest. The reason for their trip was almost forgotten as they discussed their fears about Julie.

"Did you see her wrists?" Maria said. "They were red, as if her hands had been tied for a long time. And I've never seen her so nervous."

"I know. I know." Luis had taken note of both those factors, as well as something Maria did not see. He wasn't positive he saw it either, which made him reluctant to mention it to Maria. She would demand some action and Luis didn't know what to do. In the end he told her.

"I think someone was in the house. I caught a movement behind the front curtains. Maybe I'm wrong, though." He shrugged. "But the curtains did move a little, and I felt we were being watched."

"So did I!" Maria exclaimed. "I didn't

want to say so, but I felt we were being watched, too."

Luis groaned. "Come on, Maria. You're just taking what I said and imagining you had the same reaction. You do that all the time."

"I do not!"

"Sure you do. Remember when I thought I was getting arthritis in my hands? *Your* hands ached for three weeks, until the doctor told me I only had some uremic acid in the joints of my fingers."

She dismissed the similiarity of experiences with a toss of her head. "That was different. I did feel someone's eyes on me today." She was silent for a moment, watching cattle grazing on the brown hills around them. "I think we should go to the police."

"No," Luis said quickly. "No police."

"I know you don't trust them because you've been in trouble with them yourself. But you have to put your own feelings aside. You have to think of Julie."

"It's not my own feelings that stop me," Luis said. "It's Dan. I don't think he'd want us going to the cops."

"Why not?"

"Dan's been making some mysterious trips since he came home, hasn't he? Well I don't believe he's been doing relief work for the Red Cross. I'm afraid he's in the kind of trouble he wouldn't want the police to know about."

"What should we do then?"

"I don't know," Luis said, agonized.

"Dan!" Maria said suddenly.

"What about him?"

Maria turned in her seat and was up on her knees looking out the back window. "He just passed us going south. I could swear that was Dan. He's heading home."

"Julie said she was just on the phone to him in Chicago."

They looked at each other. Luis said, "Hold tight. I'm going to hang a U-turn."

He gave a darting glance in the rear-view mirror and wrenched the wheel hard to the left. His old car spun across the divider into the southbound lanes. Sparks flew up as his muffler scraped the concrete. It tore loose and bounced across the highway into a drainage ditch.

The car straightened and he was highballing south, trying to overtake the gray sedan Maria claimed Dan Ryan was driving. "I hope you're right," Luis said, pushing his foot to the floorboard.

They hit the long grade approaching the San Juan Bautista turnoff, and for a few minutes Luis thought he was going to lose Dan. His old car, making a tremendous racket with the muffler gone, labored so hard on the grade that he couldn't push the speedometer past forty-five. The gray car ahead became smaller. But once he reached the top of the grade, Luis pounded the gas pedal until he was finally gaining on Dan. If it was Dan.

Soon he was only a dozen car lengths behind the gray Plymouth, hitting his horn while Maria leaned out the window on her side to wave and call Dan's name. Their noise finally had its effect. The Plymouth slowed and pulled over on the shoulder of the road. Luis stopped behind it.

Dan was the driver. He climbed out and came back as Luis and Maria got out of their car.

"Luis . . . Maria . . . what's wrong?" He read their expressions accurately.

"I'm not sure, Dan. But something's wrong at your place." Luis explained what they had seen there—the burns on Julie's wrists, the possibility that someone was standing behind the curtain, and her lie about being on the phone to Dan in Chicago.

When Luis finished talking Maria said, "What can we do, Dan?"

"Nothing," he said shortly. "I'll have to take care of this myself."

There seemed little else to say as Dan's face darkened and the veins in his neck bulged like ropes. Luis read murder in Dan's eyes. It took no gift to do so. Luis had seen the look before.

"There is one thing," he said. "If you don't hear from me by . . . tomorrow morning, call the police. Don't give your names. Just say there's trouble at the Ryan place and hang up." He started back to his own car, turned, and said "Thanks." He drove away.

"Luis." Maria had watched Dan change from the quiet but affable neighbor to an entirely different and much less likable man. "I think we should call the police right now instead of tomorrow."

"No," Luis told her with authority. "Dan's made his choice. If it was the wrong one, he'll have to live with it."

Instead of pushing his car faster toward the Salinas Valley, Ryan eased up and approached the Monterey peninsula cautiously. His desire to get in there and take Julie out was almost overpowering, but counteracting it was his military training. They were waiting for him—Moody and Hanson and the third man Hazlitt had told him about in the hospital. They had Julie. She didn't know where he'd planted the money and that was her margin of safety. Moody was too smart to hurt her, Ryan decided. He knows I'd die before telling them anything if they hurt her. Moody probably plans to make me talk by turning General Hanson loose on Julie with me watching. Julie's only hope is my staying free.

Suddenly Ryan felt as if he had a hand at his throat. His breath came in gasps and he began to gag. He pulled the Plymouth off the highway a few miles from the county road leading to his orchards and threw up under a tree. He emptied his stomach twice in as many minutes. When that was over he sank to his knees and slumped against the tree, feeling paralyzed and confused. He knew what was wrong with him. Fear. The kind of fear he'd seen in other men often enough but never felt before in himself. There was a fire behind his eyes.

He forced himself back to the car and put his head down on the steering wheel. Eight hours until dark. I have to pull myself together and wait, he told himself. Going in there in daylight would be suicide. It will be the longest eight hours of my life, but I have to wait it out.

Sleep wouldn't come, of course. But Ryan did manage to get the kind of rest that would prepare him for a showdown with Moody. The despair and self-recriminations were forced from his mind, the doubts churning inside him repressed. He reached a state of cold calm, as concentrated as the edge of a knife. Soon the slow passage of time no longer irritated him. His appointment with Moody and Hanson was assured and that was what mattered.

I'll be there, Julie....

By eight o'clock Moody and Price were nervous and jumping at any sound. No one else had dropped by the Ryan place, and that was good. But Ryan himself hadn't shown when he was expected, and that was bad.

"Joe," Price called from behind the pump. "Where the hell is he?"

"I don't know," Moody yelled back from inside the house.

"How long are we going to sit here?"

"As long as it takes! We can't move now. We've frozen in these positions until Ryan comes in."

"I'm ass-deep in bugs out here."

"Shut up and sit tight. He'll be here to-night. He has to be."

Rule number one for an NCO: issue orders firmly even when you doubt their wisdom. Moody couldn't understand what had happened to Ryan. Ryan had learned about Terrio's death yesterday and told Julie he'd be back this afternoon. So where the hell was the bastard? He left the window and went to the phone. A breathlessly polite girl at United Airlines told him Chicago had been socked in with fog last night but that all weather fronts were clear today. Ryan had already had plenty of time to get here.

He returned to his post at the window and wondered gloomily how Hanson's nerves were holding up at the mine.

"What was that?" Hanson asked. He was outside the tiny building that once housed the administrative office of the now abandoned quicksilver mine. The girl didn't answer, so he went to the door and said, "Did you hear a funny noise?"

Julie snickered. "That's a woodpecker, General."

"I don't believe you." He slipped his Walther out of his jacket pocket and held it close against his side in case the girl tried to grab it.

He heard the sound again.

"A woodpecker," Julie insisted. "He's out there pecking a hole in a tree. Then he'll go find an acorn or a walnut and bring it back and stuff it in the hole. That's how he builds up his food supplies. You see whole trees up here honeycombed with holes stuffed with nuts. They don't make all those holes for fun. They have a logical, useful reason for what they do. Which is more than you have."

General Hanson squinted into the darkness. Where was Moody? Ryan should have turned up by now. Could they have abandoned me? No. That was ridiculous. I have the money. They wouldn't leave that behind, though they'd certainly feel no compunction about dumping me. But I have other plans. Perhaps they'll find themselves dumped instead. Dumped and dead. Right here in this mine. That would be a perfect solution.

The old quicksilver mine burrowed into the side of the steeply rising face of a tall hill. Higher hills surrounded this one, stretching back to a range of mountains perhaps three thousand feet high.

Two huge open pits had been hollowed out at the base of the hill. The small administration office stood on a flat spit of land between the two pits, and a narrow road ran up between the pits to the office. A shaft had been punched into the face of the hill behind the office, probably to test for additional quicksilver deposits in the hill. Evidently there had not been enough to warrant further excavations, and the mine had been closed down and the shaft and small office building boarded up.

"See if you can get that lantern going," Hanson ordered.

Julie was squatting by the door. She got up and complied with the General's order. She would have tried to start the Coleman lantern soon anyway, rather than be alone in the dark with Hanson. And there were the snakes to worry about, too. The light would keep them away from the front of the building, she hoped.

Earlier in the afternoon, when Hanson had pushed her through the door with a warning to be quiet, she had explored the little building looking for possible escape routes. Besides the main office there was a storage room and a tiny bathroom. All the windows were boarded over from the outside, and any attempt at knocking them loose from inside would have been heard by Hanson.

While making her survey, Julie almost stepped on a nest of rattlesnakes in the storage room. They apparently used a jagged little hole in the wall of the storeroom about six inches above the floor as their route in and out of the building. The light filtering through the hole had reflected the gray-and-green diamond patterns of their coils just before Julie put her foot down on them.

As she knelt to light the lantern, Julie felt somewhat optimistic again. If Moody didn't take Dan during the daylight hours, he'd have a hell of a time catching him at night. Dan moved quietly even when he wasn't looking for trouble. Dozens of times Julie had been startled to look up and find Dan in the house when she thought he was out in the orchards. He had the gift of silent movement, or maybe it was a talent acquired in the army. Either way, the darkness would help Dan.

She shook the lantern, drawing a faint sloshing sound. "Not much fuel."

Hanson threw some matches on the floor beside her. "Light it."

After a few false tries Julie managed to coax on a flickering yellow light. She slid the glass sleeve over the flame and put the lantern on the floor.

"Moody and Price should be along soon," Hanson said from the doorway. He was watching the road.

"Unless my husband was too much for them."

Hanson snorted and threw Julie a contemptuous scowl. But she noticed that he clutched his automatic a little tighter.

"They'll get him," he promised her, but without full conviction.

Before darkness completely enveloped the valley, Ryan left his car and began walking through the vineyards on a curving tangent that would bring him up behind his own house after about a half hour's walk.

There were no people working the vineyards at this time of year and no cars on the county road. The isolation of his ranch had never bothered him before, but now he could see that any noise made here would attract no attention.

The earth was soft under his feet. Soon he broke into a jog through the waist-high rows of vines. After about ten minutes his stomach reminded him that it was empty, so he began plucking grapes from the vines and popping them into his mouth as he jogged. They were tart but juicy, their heavy sugar content providing a quick energy lift.

It was completely dark by the time Ryan had circled his property and come up on his walnut groves from the east. He could see at least one light in the house. A three-quarter moon illuminated the countryside more than Ryan liked, creating between the trees pockets of light that resembled the white circles under street lamps.

The closer Ryan drew to the house, the more often he would stop to study the house and orchard. The pistol provided by Tony Terrio was still in his belt; he didn't want moonlight glittering off the metal. He paused longest when he reached the place where the orchards stopped and a bare expanse of earth was all that lay between himself and the house. There were no movements that he could see, inside or outside. A light was on in the dining room.

He covered the open space between the orchards and his home in a dozen steps, neither running nor trying to steal up on the house. The kitchen door was on his left, the dining-room windows to the right. Standing back from the light, he could see into the house easily. The dining room was empty. A shadow moved in the living room and he flattened himself to the wall. One man was waiting inside. Perhaps two. There would be at least one man outside somewhere.

Ryan took a few cautious steps to the corner of the house and examined the orchard again. A faint sound near the pump attracted his attention. Someone shifting his weight? There was plenty of room behind there for a man to stay out of sight. An elbow protruded for just a second as Price moved and settled himself in a new position.

It took Ryan another ten minutes to work his way back around the house and into the groves. When he was within thirty feet of the pump, he could make out the figure of a man crouched down, one arm extended in a peculiar fashion. He was probably holding a rifle. Ryan went down on his hands and toes and covered the space between them like a cat coming up on a bird. He could have moved more quietly on his feet, but he was afraid the man in the living room would see him. He had to use the cover of the pump to shield him from the house. Ryan wondered who this man was. He was too small to be either Moody or Hanson. When he was less than six feet from the crouching figure, he quietly drew out his gun and scrambled forward without worrying about the man's hearing him. Price turned at the noise, but Ryan was on him with a smothering grasp that choked Price into silence.

Price felt a gun barrel at his throat as Ryan whispered, "Quiet! No noise from you at all."

Price froze, one of his arms locked behind him in a grip that made any kind of movement impossible. Out of the corner of his eye he could see that the revolver stuck against his throat was cocked.

"Where's my wife?" Ryan whispered.

"She's up on the hill," Price answered.

"Up on the hill? What do you mean?"

"The old quicksilver mine."

Ryan knew the place. He'd hiked up there one day out of curiosity. "Who's with her?"

"General Hanson." Ryan's grip tightened. "She's okay," Price whispered quickly. The tension eased.

"How many of you are down here?"

"Just me and Moody."

"Moody's in the living room?"

"Yeah."

"How is he armed?"

"Like me. He's got an AK-47."

"How long—"

There was a crunching sound and Ryan's grip on Price loosened. He became dead weight on Price's back. His pistol fell in the dirt without discharging. Price shrugged off Ryan's weight and looked up. In the moonlight Moody's teeth flashed at him. He was holding the butt of the AK-47 like a club.

"Get up, Price. Help me drag Ryan out to the driveway." He picked up Ryan's revolver, put the hammer on safety, and threw it into the darkness under the trees.

Price got to his feet and retrieved his own weapon, then took one of Ryan's arms. Moody grabbed the other. They dragged him out to the driveway and let him lie there.

"He got behind me," Price explained, wincing as he moved his left arm.

"He did it without much trouble, too," Moody said scornfully. "Good thing I saw the shape of your shadow change in time to go out a side window and get behind *him*."

"Thanks, Joe."

Ryan was coming around. When he tried to sit up, Moody put a foot on his chest and pushed him back down.

"Hello, Danny."

"Hello, Joe. They always said you were good in the dark."

"I didn't get all those medals for nothing, Danny boy."

"Can I sit up now?"

"No." Moody lowered the submachine gun so that it was aimed point-blank at Ryan's middle. "Don't move at all. Just tell me where the money is."

Ryan shook his head.

"Okay," Moody said agreeably. "Price, you go on along to where we're keeping Julie and tell Hanson to go to work on her. Do whatever he wants. Tell him to make it hurt."

"Suppose I tell you where the money is," Ryan offered. "What does it buy me?"

"I won't bullshit you, Dan. We have to kill you anyway. Julie, too. But it'll be clean and fast if we get the money right now. I don't want to hurt Julie none, but General Hanson purely loves his work. You must have seen what he did to Hazlitt and Terrio."

Ryan closed his eyes. Opened them again. And took a chance. "Okay. I'll show you where the money is."

They let him stand up. His head throbbed but his mind was racing. One chance left. He led them to the spot where the money was buried, actually just a few yards from where they laid him out on the ground. "Right here," he said, pointing at the clump of oxalis.

"No tricks," Moody warned.

"It's there."

Price giggled and kicked the dirt with his toe.

"You dig it up," Moody ordered Ryan. "Where do you keep your tools?"

"In the shed." Ryan pointed at the nearby hut and prayed Moody would let him go in there.

"Get it."

Ryan walked toward the shed, half-expecting a bullet in the back. If Moody was sure he was telling the truth, that's what the big sergeant would do. Finish off the last member of the Leavenworth Irregulars right now. But Moody wasn't sure, and that's what made Ryan hope for one last break.

"Hold it," Moody ordered after Ryan slid the shed door back on its runners. "I don't think I want you digging up that money after all. You just might throw a shovelful of dirt in someone's face and try to run. Give the shovel to Price. Nice and easy. Then you stay there in the shed."

"Whatever you say." Ryan ducked his head and went inside. He felt around for the shovel and found it among the other tools and handed it out to Price.

"Check the back of that thing," Moody told Price. "Make sure there aren't any other openings."

Price walked clear around the shed. "Just that one door," he reported.

"Okay. You dig while I cover the door. We don't want Ryan wandering off into the trees. He might get lost and hurt himself."

Price set to work with the shovel.

Inside the shed, Ryan found the hunting slingshot Hazlitt had made for him. He slipped his left hand into the wrist brace and reached up to the shelf where he kept a collection of stones for small-game hunting. He put all but two in his pocket. One of them he slipped into the pouch.

"I hit something," he heard Price say excitedly.

Moody shifted his eyes to the deepening hole and then back to the shed. "Get it out."

Ryan drew back the sling with his right hand. The padded wrist brace pulled against his left forearm. He aimed the rock for the middle of Moody's face and let the sling go. The two-ounce hunk of stone flew like an arrow. Moody's head snapped as the rock hit him on the right cheek, just under his eye. He staggered back two steps and fell to a sitting position.

Before Price realized Moody was down, Ryan slipped the second stone in the sling. He aimed as Price took in the sight of Moody spraddled on the ground and began reaching for the automatic weapon he had set aside. The second shot wasn't as true as the first, but it tore a piece off Price's left ear and made the little pilot howl with pain and grab his ear instead of picking up the gun.

"Goddam!" Price cried. "What the hell?"

Ryan bolted out the door, made a sharp turn and ran like hell for the orchard.

"Ryan's heading for the trees!" Moody

roared. He was still in a sitting position when he got the AK-47 in the crook of his arm and fired a long burst at Ryan's back.

The shots ripped through the trees but Ryan was gone.

Moody got up. The right side of his face burned like fire but he took no notice of it. "The son of a bitch!" He reached into the hole Price had been digging and grasped the handle of the partly uncovered metal box. It came loose of the ground with one great heave. Moody kicked it open and saw the green stacks of currency. "We've got the money. Now we have to get Ryan." He glowered at Price, who was crying loudly in his little boy's voice and holding his bleeding ear. "Shut up, Price." He closed the box and lifted it. Price found it thrust into his arms.

"Where did Ryan go?" Price whined. "And what the hell is he shooting at us with?"

"I don't know. But you can be damned sure he's going for his wife. How do you get up to that mine?"

Price gave him quick, explicit directions, using his aviator's talent for picking out landmarks.

Moody listened, nodding, and said, "You've got the keys to Ryan's pickup. Take the money and get up there. You and Hanson can cover Ryan coming in. I'll follow him on foot and cover his back. If he makes it to the mine we'll have him in a cross fire. He can't have anything heavier than a pellet gun or we'd both be dead. Get going."

Price stood there for a moment watching

Moody disappear into the trees, then threw the metal box into the back of Ryan's pickup. He drove it away from the house and turned east toward the hills at the county road. The orchards fell away and Price was driving through vineyard country again. Suddenly, out of the corner of his eye, he saw Ryan come up out of a drainage ditch on his left with one arm extended, aiming something. Price ducked instinctively as an object whizzed over his head through the open car window and hit the glass behind him. He stepped on the gas, and the pickup roared away.

He was half a mile down the dark road before he raised his head. The thing Ryan shot at him had fallen to the seat beside him. Price felt around for it, keeping an eye on the road so he wouldn't miss the turnoff to the quicksilver mine. His hand closed over something small and smooth. He raised it in front of his eyes and stared. "Jesus Christ! The crazy bastard's throwing rocks at us!"

Ryan couldn't help missing Price. The little pilot was so short that his head was hardly higher than the steering wheel. He jumped into the drainage ditch and began running again. The ditch was good cover and at this time of year the bottom was hard enough so that he could move fast. But Moody was somewhere close behind. Not in the ditch. Probably up on the road where he might catch a glimpse of Ryan in the moonlight. Twice Ryan stopped to listen. Each time he thought he heard Moody stop, too. Moody was too smart to overrun his quarry and let it get behind him with a weapon. Ryan figured Moody was at least a hundred yards away and planning to stay there. He didn't know what kind of weapon Ryan had. What its range was. How accurate it might be. So he had sent Price ahead to catch him in a cross fire at the mine.

Okay.

He'd rather go straight into Price and Hanson than into Moody. If he could only keep Moody far enough behind him. . . .

Ryan stopped.

Moody stopped.

Ryan crept back down the ditch about fifty yards. He worked the largest of the remaining stones out of his pocket and put it into the pouch of the sling. Boldly, he stepped up the side of the ditch so that his head and shoulders were above the road bed. They were out of the vineyards now and into open country. Moody stood silhouetted against the sky on the other side of the road, his head cocked as he listened for Ryan. Ryan aimed and let the stone fly. Nothing. Moody continued to listen. The stone had missed completely, so far off its target that Moody didn't even hear it go past him. Quickly Ryan pulled out another stone. The range was too great. He aimed anyway and let the rock fly.

He heard a cracking noise when it struck. One of Moody's legs buckled and he fell like a bull elephant. Ryan ducked back into the ditch as Moody fired an angry burst. Two bursts. Ryan grinned and double-timed down the drainage ditch. Moody was wasting ammo. He must have been hit in the shin or knee. That would slow down even Moody. He came to the crossroad leading up to the mine. It was a company-built road. No ditch. Just a slight shoulder. But lots of brush and trees and other vegetation. He ducked into the brush and leaned forward as she jogged uphill at a steady pace.

"At last!" Hanson said. He watched with relief as Price drove up the narrow road between the two pits. Price parked behind the small building and came around to the front carrying a metal box.

"Is that Ryan's share of the money?" Hanson asked.

"This is it." Price opened the trunk of their rental car, using Hanson's keys, and stowed the box inside. He stepped back and looked at the loot they had taken from Ryan, Terrio, and Hazlitt. "Close to three hundred grand," he said with satisfaction.

"Where's Sergeant Moody?" Hanson asked.

Price waved at the road. "Down there. Ryan got away from us. He's headed up here. Moody's tracking him on foot. His plan is to catch Ryan between us in a cross fire. We'd better get set."

While Price went back to the truck for his AK-47, Hanson considered his strategy. It would be better to get rid of Price right now, before Moody arrived. That meant, however, that he would have to face Ryan alone. It was a hard choice but just the kind of tactical decision he was accustomed to making. And he was a good enough tactician to know you should never allow two hostile forces to unite against you.

"I'd say Ryan will be here in about fifteen minutes," Price estimated. He walked a few paces down the road and squinted into the darkness. "We'd better pick our spots."

Hanson shot him twice in the back, the Walther making popping noises that belied the handgun's stopping power. Price threw both arms out from his sides and screamed in his childlike voice. He turned around and fell face forward on the road. One of the holes in his back was bleeding copiously, the other hardly at all. Hanson noted with a professional eye that one of his bullets must have struck a bone instead of going into the heart.

At the sound of Julie's gasp Hanson spun around. She was standing in the doorway with one hand at her throat.

"Come out here!" He brandished the gun. "Hurry." He enjoyed the fear in her eyes. "Get the rope from the front seat of the car. I'm afraid I'll have to tie you up again."

Julie did as she was told, letting Hanson tie her wrists to the rear-view mirror on the outside of the car.

That should slow Ryan down when he comes in here, Hanson concluded. He hoped that Ryan would run straight to her and attempt to untie her hands. The roof of the building—that's the place to wait. He went around to the rear and saw that he could climb to the roof from the hood of the pickup, which was parked snug against the wall.

When he came back around front he found Julie struggling with her bonds. "You won't get loose that easily," he laughed. His buoyant mood evaporated somewhat as he searched around Price's body and failed to find the submachine gun the pilot had been carrying. It simply wasn't there! He could see the ground perfectly in the moonlight and there was no weapon to be found.

The pit! He walked to the edge and peeped over. A hundred feet straight down. When Price's arms flew out, the gun must have gone over the side into the pit. The stupid little man! He couldn't even die without causing trouble. Well. Hanson looked around him. Price couldn't be left out on the road. Moody would see the body and realize what was in store for himself. Hanson put Price's handgun into his own hip pocket before dragging the body inside the building. Price had carried a hugely awkward .45 Colt army automatic. Why were small men always attracted to large guns? Hanson mused about that as he dragged Price inside. The storeroom in back would be a good place to dump Price. Later he could be put in the mine shaft.

The storeroom was pitch black. Hanson grasped Price under the arms and let his body fall into the void. The body made a peculiar rattling noise when it hit the floor. Almost simultaneously Hanson felt a sharp sting on his left leg.

"Ow! Dammit!" He'd bumped into something. The pain increased and spread up his leg. Hanson stepped back. Another sting jolted him lower down on the same leg.

He moved out into the yellow light of the lantern and examined the leg, which was throbbing clear up to the thigh by now. The elaborate mechanism of the mind had begun subconsciously to assemble the various inputs of information (rattling sound . . . strike of pain . . . second strike . . . dark mountain country) into a tangible idea. "Snake!" He clawed up his pants leg and saw two sets of double indentations in his leg. If there was any doubt, it was erased by the five feet of slithering reptile that moved out of the storeroom and across the floor searching for a safer place to sleep. "Rattlesnake!" Hanson pulled the huge .45 from his back pocket and emptied it at the rattler. A series of explosions ripped the snake into several pieces. When the gun was empty and the clip automatically dropped from the butt, Hanson threw the pistol at the rattler's dismembered remains.

"I've been bitten!" He pulled his pants leg higher and examined the double-prong indentations more closely. The pain had subsided in his leg, but was replaced by a numbness spreading outward from the wounds. Turning, he fled outside where Julie stood in paralytic confusion from the sound of the shooting. "I've been bitten!" Hanson cried again. "By a rattlesnake." His fairly solid grasp of first-aid techniques seemed to have departed his mind.

Julie took in Hanson's panic and automatically looked for a way to use it to free herself. "You have to get the venom out right now," she said urgently. "If you don't you'll die very quickly."

"How?" Hanson begged. "Tell me *how!*" He rubbed at the wounds as if that might make them disappear. "Shall I cut the venom out?"

Julie shook her head vigorously and adopted the attitude of an experienced nurse. "No. It has to be pumped out or sucked out, and the bites should be cauterized immediately afterward." She had no idea whether that would help but it sounded plausible. "Untie me and I'll do that for you." She spread her hands and lowered her head toward her wrists, expecting Hanson to balk at that and marshaling additional arguments for him. But he sprang to the car and began untying the ropes.

"Have I got a chance?" His hands shook so violently that he had difficulty with the knots. "It bit me *twice.*"

"You'll live, as long as the venom doesn't reach your heart." Privately Julie doubted the existence of General Hanson's heart.

As soon as her hands were untied, she dropped them and reached for the gun in Hanson's belt. It came loose and she fumbled for the safety catch, knowing only that automatics have them and that they are usually located where a thumb will reach them. Her thumb caught on a tiny lever and she pushed it forward. As soon as it clicked she aimed the Walther at Hanson's chest and pulled the trigger three times. Again the sounds were so slight that it was hard to believe the gun was doing any damage. But Hanson was shoved one step backward with each pop. With his pants leg rolled high above his knee, he seemed about to go into a burlesque of a can-can dance. Then he collapsed and lay by the car on his side with rivulets of blood flowing from him. His eyes were open and he was still breathing. But very soon he closed his eyes and appeared to go to sleep.

The gun dropped from Julie's hand and she sagged against the car. She knew she should be doing something . . . running or hiding . . . but she was unable to coordinate her mind and body. She could only feel grateful that Hanson had closed his eyes before he died.

Footsteps coming up the road dissolved some of her inertia. She picked up the Walther again and had the presence of mind to move around the car to make a shield of it. She pointed the pistol down the road, not knowing how many bullets were left in it or how to examine it to find that out, and prepared herself to shoot Moody. "Dan," she said aloud, her arm waving as she realized the person coming up the road might be Dan. Price had said Dan was free and coming up here. "Let it be Dan."

The sound of the three shots from the Walther had carried down the road to Ryan. He was no more than three hundred yards from where the road began to run between the pits when he heard them and his first thought was: *They've killed Julie. Now that they have the money, they've killed her.*

Reason gave way to his emotions. He threw away the hunting slingshot and charged up the hill without caring who was waiting for him or how they were deployed. Every lesson he had learned as a soldier was forgotten in his panic.

When he saw Julie behind the car, her arm waving as she tried to steady her grip on a pistol, the joy of his relief almost got him killed. "Julie!" he called out. She aimed and seemed about to fire. "Don't shoot, Julie. It's me."

"Dan?"

He trotted forward more slowly. When she could see his face, she dropped the Walther on the hood of the car and ran toward him.

They came together in an embrace that almost carried both of them off their feet.

"I thought they'd killed you!" Dan said. "I heard three shots . . ."

"General Hanson . . . I got hold of his gun."

They kissed a dozen times before standing back to look at each other. "Moody's behind me," Ryan said. "We have to get out of here."

"Maybe Price left the keys in our truck."

"Where is he?"

"Inside. He's dead, too."

"Jesus. Hanson killed him?"

"Yes."

"We can't take the pickup. Moody's coming up the road with an AK-47. We'd never get past him. What about Price's weapon?"

"It went down there. In the pit. But I have the General's gun."

Ryan went to the car and picked the Walther up off the hood. He looked inside the office building and found the empty .45 and the dismembered rattler. There were no extra clips in anyone's pockets.

"How can you do that?" Julie said as he searched Hanson's body.

"It's okay. I like him better this way." He stood up and stared down the road. "Moody will be here any minute." The hill in back of the mine office went up steeply for several hundred yards. There was no brush for cover, save for an occasional clump of manzanita. "We'll have to climb. Can you do it?"

"Sure," Julie said, almost convincing herself.

The years of beer and late mornings had finally caught up with Moody. His lungs were red hot as he pounded up the gravel road. Besides that, the wound on his cheek was so badly swollen that his right eye was almost closed and his left leg still hurt from whatever Ryan hit him with.

At last he came up to a level piece of road and saw the mind building and a car ahead. He slowed down and unslung the AK-47. Price and Hanson were nowhere in sight. Why hadn't they opened up on Ryan? Ryan could have slipped off the road into the countryside, but Moody didn't believe he would abandon Julie. As he came closer to the mine, he spotted Hanson's body near their car. "Price!" No one answered his call. Where was the little bastard? Did he kill Hanson? He looked in the car. The keys were gone.

Some rocks and dirt came sliding down the hillside in back of the mine office, and Moody ducked behind the car. He searched the face of the hill and saw the two of them sliding downward with the fall of dirt. They had tried to get above him but failed to make it; the face of the hill was too loosely packed.

He raised the AK-47 and fired. The shots hit above Ryan and Julie, loosening more earth and causing them to slide faster down the hill on a slant toward one of the open pits. Moody didn't fire a second time because he expected them to keep right on sliding off the hill and down into that big hole. That would have ended it right there. The fall would have killed them both.

Instead he saw Ryan grab Julie's arm and pull both of them out of the cascading jumble of earth and into a cul-de-sac of rocks perched on the very edge of the pit. The falling dirt made a huge noise at the bottom of the pit, and dust rose and swirled for minutes.

Moody squatted behind the car. "Price!" he called again. That was enough. Price was dead, too, somewhere. And probably with the car keys in his pocket. He had to get rid of Ryan and Julie so he could find Price and the car keys. Ryan probably had a gun, Moody decided. Not the automatic weapon or he would have been carrying it up the hill, but certainly one of the handguns Hanson and Price had carried.

Meanwhile, Ryan was pinned down. To get out from behind those rocks he and Julie would have to edge their way along the lip of the pit for about twenty yards. They couldn't do that without getting shot. Moody's own position wasn't that good, though. He had the car for cover but it was a ten-yard jump from there to the office. If Ryan was armed, he just might get lucky.

It's stupid to sit here wondering, Moody thought. I have to find out.

With great care, Moody leaned around the front fender and fired a short burst at the rocks where Ryan and Julie were hiding. It was less than forty yards and every slug hit its target. But before Moody could duck back, he saw the flash of a gunshot and felt a bullet tear through the fleshy part of his shoulder.

He twisted back into a safe position and looked at his arm. It was nothing. A mosquito bite. The swelling under his eye hurt worse. More painful was the confirmation that Ryan was indeed armed. It would be a waiting game now. Sooner or later one of them would make a mistake. And it would be Ryan. He had a woman to worry about, and no man with a woman on his mind ever made the right moves. I just have to wait him out, Moody told himself.

Ryan was thinking exactly the same thing; that if he hadn't been worried about Moody getting his hands on Julie, he never would have tried to climb that hill with her. Now look at us, he told himself bitterly.

Trapped out here with a mountain at our backs and a sheer drop in front of us and no chance to move to the right or left.

"Goddam!" he swore.

Julie, huddled into the rocks, was giving thanks that they had avoided the plunge into the pit. "What's the matter?"

"What do you think's the matter? We're pinned here."

"Moody can't move either, can he?"

"But he's got time and firepower on his side," Ryan pointed out, never taking his eyes off the car. "How many shots have been fired from this gun?"

"I don't know."

"*Think* about it. This is important."

Julie counted to herself, then said, "Five shots."

Ryan groaned. "And I just used one more to let Moody know I have something to shoot with." He took his eyes off Moody's position long enough to push the button that released the clip. The thin metal container fell into his left hand. He held the clip up and studied it in the moonlight. There were holes along the side of the clip that made it possible to see how many cartridges it held. All the holes were empty except one, where a copper-colored bullet gleamed. He reinserted the clip into the butt of the Walther. There would also be one shell in the chamber. He felt for the small pin that was supposed to stick out above the hammer when the chamber was loaded. It was there. He had two rounds left.

"What can we do?" Julie asked. She

needed to do something . . . be of some help . . . while she was still physically capable of helping.

Ryan gauged Julie's exhaustion and saw that she was apt to slip into a bone-weary sleep if he didn't keep her occupied. It was important that she stay alert in case the chance came for them to get off this ledge.

"Take these," he said, thrusting a handful of small stones into her hand. He slipped off his watch. The luminous hands gleamed faintly. "I want you to toss a stone over toward Moody every thirty seconds. You can see the minute hand, but you'll have to estimate the thirty-second intervals."

"I don't understand," Julie whispered.

"I want a steady drumbeat of noise out there. We have to psych Moody into making a mistake. It's all I can think of and it's Moody's own game, so I don't know whether it will work on him. After exactly one hour, stop throwing the stones. If the sound of the stones doesn't psych him, maybe the absence of the sound will."

The first stone Julie threw fell short and went into the pit.

"Try to hit the car," Ryan suggested. "But keep your head down."

The third stone bounced off Moody's car with a clanging sound, causing Moody to fire another burst at the rocks, knocking some chips off the boulders but doing them no harm.

"Good," Ryan said. "You've got the range and there are plenty of stones around. Keep him nervous." He stretched out on his stomach and covered Moody's position through a small opening in the cluster of boulders that formed their protection. If Moody could be spooked into moving to the mine office, there might be a chance to get a clear shot at him.

Grateful for something to do, Julie kept a steady stream of stones tossed toward Moody. Some of them bounced off the car with an impressive noise and others just clattered on the road. Her timing was at first erratic. But after a few minutes she could sit with her back against the rocks and pitch a stone overhead toward Moody's car with reasonable accuracy and timing. The only problem was that she didn't believe this would do any good. Moody was too smart and tough to let himself be scared by a few pebbles. She was afraid Dan was making a time-consuming mistake.

The first few stones that fell rattled Moody's composure and he replied by firing back. He realized his error immediately. Ryan's trying to needle me into a mistake, he decided.

He busied himself by checking his ammunition. The magazine in his weapon was almost empty, so he removed it and inserted the spare magazine he had been carrying inside his shirt.

The stones continued to fall. They were annoying, but nothing more. Moody pulled out a handkerchief and used it to bandage the flesh wound on his shoulder. The bleeding had almost stopped. The wound ached but it wasn't dirty. His face was giving him greater trouble. His right eye was completely closed now from the swelling. He considered trying to bring the swelling down by lancing it with his pocket knife, but he had seen too many minor wounds develop into major ones from infection. He feared infection more than he feared anything in the world.

For a while he amused himself by observing how unmilitary the corpse of Major General Arthur Hanson looked. But the sound of the stones made it impossible to concentrate on anything for too long. He peeked around the car to see if Ryan exposed himself when he threw the stones, but they continued to fall without his being able to tell when they were tossed. They might have been falling from the sky.

His shoulder began to itch and he fought a battle with himself to avoid scratching it. He won the battle and that made him feel better. And still the damned stones fell. He looked at his watch. It had stopped. Four hundred dollars for a Swiss movement and a dozen diamonds and the damned thing had stopped.

He closed his eyes for just a moment and put his head back against the car. The old touch of the metal revived him and he sat bolt upright. Jesus! If I went to sleep that would be it, he scolded himself.

The stones kept falling.

Moody scratched his shoulder and looked under the makeshift bandage. The wound really needed to be cleaned. He had to finish this up fast and get back to civilization for some iodine and antibiotics.

"Ryan!" he called. "I'll make a deal. Tell

me where the car keys are and I'll drive away. We'll end it right here. I get the money and you get your lives. How about it?"

The stones continued to fall.

How long could they keep that up? You'd think they'd run out of stones. Moody smiled. Maybe they'll use so many stones that they'll undermind the ledge and fall down into the pit. Wouldn't that be a laugh?

The stones seemed to be falling faster. Giant raindrops. Bam. Bam. Bam. How long have they been at that dumb routine? Two hours, perhaps. Maybe three.

He looked under the bandage again and became alarmed. The edges of the deep red crease looked awfully black. He remembered a guy in Korea who was nicked in the hand during a fire fight. It was nothing, the guy said. He didn't even turn himself in to the medics, just wrapped one of the bandages from his first-aid pack around his hand. Twelve hours later the hand was black and purple and he did go to the medics. He was evacuated to a field hospital immediately, and two days later the company heard he was dead.

The sweat was pouring off Moody in waves, washing his closed eye in salt and making it burn as badly as his shoulder.

I'd better start thinking about making a move, he decided.

The noise of the stones stopped then, as abruptly as it had started. Moody scrambled to the rear of the car and looked around toward the rocks. What had happened? Where were they? They couldn't have gotten out from behind those boulders without making some noise. Unless they had climbed up the hill again. His eyes swept the hillside. Maybe they went up there, throwing stones down while they climbed so I wouldn't know they were getting away. Damn! Where are they?

The silence was worse than the sound of the stones. Moody grabbed the barrel of his AK-47 tightly. *Stop it!* he ordered himself sternly. *They haven't moved. They're still behind those rocks. They're trying to psych me just like I thought they would. But they won't succeed. Not with Joe Moody. I invented this game.*

"Ryan!" he roared. "My deal still stands."

He waited. How long, he couldn't tell. Hours. He tried to get his watch going again, but couldn't. In disgust he ripped it off his wrist and tossed it aside. He sat and listened for a sound for what seemed an eternity. Again he crept to the rear of the car and looked at the rocks, seeing and hearing nothing. With his right eye and right arm useless, he was forced to use the left side of his body for everything. That made him feel awkward and exposed. Where were they? He looked down the road. Could they be circling around me? Could they possibly have stayed behind those rocks this long without making a sound?

Behind the rocks Julie put her hand on Ryan's arm and whispered, "It's not working."

"It is," he whispered back.

"We've been on this ledge four hours." She thrust his watch toward him as proof.

"I know. Just be quiet. Moody's coming apart out there. I can feel it."

Moody made a decision. *I'll move to the mine office,* he told himself. Price's body must be in there. He would have put Ryan's money in the trunk with the rest of the cash. And he would have kept the keys because he knew I planned to kill Hanson. When I'm positive Ryan and Julie are gone, I'll take the car into town and patch myself up. Then I'll find those two and finish them off for good.

He got to his knees and crept to the back of the car once more. The mine office was ten big steps away. He crooked the submachine gun in his right arm and slipped off the safety. *If Ryan does show his head, I'll take it right off*. It cost him some pain, but he raised his right arm and gripped the balance of the AK-47 with his left hand. Then he stood and rushed for the mine office.

He squeezed off a quick burst as he ran. The pattern carpeted the area around the rocks, and when he was only two jumps from the cover of the mine office, Moody knew he had it made. Two shots struck him in those two last steps. The first hit him in the hip and twisted him around to make his broad body a perfect target. The second went through his left lung and spine, slamming him against the corner of the mine office.

Ryan stood and took Julie's arm. "Let's go." They edged along the rim of the pit, leaning back into the slope for balance. A minute later they were safe on the flat spit of earth behind the mine office.

"Stay here." Ryan left Julie and went around the building to check on Moody. He half-expected to find the huge soldier sitting up, smoking a cigar. But Moody was dead.

When he came back to Julie he checked their pickup truck. The keys were in the ignition. "I want you to go home," he told Julie. "I'll take care of this mess." He put her behind the wheel. "Can you drive?"

"I'm all right," she assured him. "Watch out for those snakes. They must be all over poor Price's body." She was surprised that she could find pity in herself for any of those three.

"I will. When you get home call Luis and Maria. Tell them everything's all right and that I said they don't have to make that phone call to the police. They'll understand."

Julie started the pickup and drove off down the dirt road.

When she was gone, Ryan put the bodies of Moody, Price, and General Hanson in their car. He found the car keys on Price and looked in the trunk.

"All that money." Stealing it had seemed so important a year ago when they had begun planning the job. But with Terrio and Hazlitt dead—and Hanson rewarded for his greed with several ounces of lead—the act had become meaningless. The money was nothing to him now but an ugly reminder of a world he should have put behind him a long time ago.

Ryan closed the trunk and got into the car.

It took a little maneuvering to back the car out of the narrow drive between the pits and run it forward to the mine entrance. He climbed out and found a large rock to put on the gas pedal. The engine's rpms stepped up. Ryan used a long stick to push the gearshift into drive. The car jumped forward and went straight into the mine shaft, then veered and caromed along, hitting first the right wall of the tunnel and then the left. It bounced from wall to wall a couple of times, sparks flying each time it hit. Ryan watched the car disappear deeper into the darkness like a metallic drunk lurching down an alley.

Then one of the sparks ignited a pocket of gas and Ryan hit the ground as a blue flame flashed out at him. A muffled explosion made the ground heave and the walls of the shaft buckle. Ryan rolled for safety as tons of rock and earth collapsed into the shaft. Beams broke with sharp snapping sounds and dust flew in all directions.

When Ryan got to his feet, the tunnel was completely sealed by the fall of rock and dirt. Only a few broken timbers were left to indicate that a shaft had ever existed. Ryan kicked the timbers into the pit and headed for home.

ABOUT THE AUTHOR

WILLIAM D. BLANKENSHIP is a former newspaper reporter, soldier and advertising copywriter. He once served in the First Infantry Division at Fort Riley, Kansas, the military post where much of this novel is set. He lives in San José, California.

THE PIRAEUS PLOT by HARRY ARVAY

THE PIRAEUS PLOT is based on dramatic, real-life encounters between the Israeli Security Branch (SB) and the Arab terrorist organisation, Black September and is the third book in a continuing series.

Four extremist Arab leaders, and their followers, had joined forces in a common cause: to kill the moderate head of the Palestine Liberation Organisation, Yassir Arafat, SB Commander Max Roth knew that Arafat's safety must be ensured, and the true identity of his would-be assassins must be made known – to Arafat, to the rest of the Arab world, and to the many other interested parties. Accordingly, Itzhak, Heidi, Luke and Baruch, four skilled SB commandos, were despatched to Athens, where representatives of the four terrorist groups, and the hired killers, were foregathering. . . .

0 552 10055 2 – 40p

THE MEIROVITZ PLAN by HARRY ARVAY

When Boris Meirovitz, an immigrant Russian Jew, volunteered his services to the Israeli Security Branch (SB) it looked like the chance they had been waiting for – the chance to infiltrate the liaison between the Russian KGB and the Palestine Liberation Organisation.

But who was this man? Where did his true affinities lie? Was he, in fact, a double agent? It was up to Max Roth and his elite team of commandos to find out – and fast. So they put

THE MEIROVITZ PLAN

into operation – a game of check and double-check in which the entire security of the Israeli SB was at risk in a high-tension race against time . . .

The Meirovitz Plan is the fourth in an exciting and dramatic series by Harry Arvay.

0 552 09895 7 – 40p